Praise for Niall Leonard's

M, KING'S BODYGUARD

"Authentic, rich, and completely absorbing, Niall Leonard's new novel is historical but feels like its own magnificently built world, an Edwardian London as morally murky and lovingly detailed as Philip Kerr's Berlin. We can only hope there are further Melville books to come."   —Charles Finch, author of *An Extravagant Death*

Niall Leonard

M, KING'S BODYGUARD

———··◦∞◦··———

Niall Leonard is a screenwriter for film and television and the author of the Crusher trilogy. Born in Northern Ireland, he lives in West London with his wife, E L James. *M, King's Bodyguard* is his first historical novel.

niallleonard.com

M,
KING'S
BODYGUARD

Niall Leonard

VINTAGE BOOKS
A DIVISION OF PENGUIN RANDOM HOUSE LLC
NEW YORK

FIRST VINTAGE BOOKS EDITION 2022

Copyright © 2021 by Niall Leonard

All rights reserved. Published in the United States by Vintage Books, a division
of Penguin Random House LLC, New York, and distributed in Canada by Penguin Random
House Canada Limited, Toronto. Originally published in hardcover in Great Britain by Little,
Brown, an imprint of Little, Brown Book Group, a Hachette U.K. company, London,
and subsequently in hardcover in the United States by Pantheon Books,
a division of Penguin Random House LLC, New York, in 2021.

Vintage and colophon are registered
trademarks of Penguin Random House LLC.

The Library of Congress has cataloged the Pantheon edition as follows:
Name: Leonard, Niall, author.
Title: M, King's bodyguard : a novel / Niall Leonard.
Description: First American edition. | New York : Pantheon Books, 2021.
Identifiers: LCCN 2020026356 (print) | LCCN 2020026357 (ebook)
Subjects: GSAFD: Mystery fiction.
Classification: LCC PR6112.E646 M25 2021 (print) |
LCC PR6112.E646 (ebook) | DDC 823/.92—dc23
LC record available at https://lccn.loc.gov/2020026356
LC ebook record available at https://lccn.loc.gov/2020026357

Vintage Books Trade Paperback ISBN: 978-0-593-08169-3
eBook ISBN: 978-1-5247-4906-4

Book design by Anna B. Knighton

vintagebooks.com

Printed in the United States of America

To my good friend Hugh O'Donnell
Culture buff and History nerd
See you in the park someday

M, KING'S BODYGUARD

I

IT WAS A MISERABLE DAY in Walham Green, gloomy and wind-lashed and rain-soaked, and it seemed every pedestrian for miles had taken shelter in this Lyons Tea Room. The windows streamed with condensation, and the air was thick with hot breath and the smell of damp wool and camphor and boiled mutton. I'd been lucky to get a table to myself, and I was keeping it to myself, spreading out my legs and seeing off with a cold stare any customer who dared to approach. Selfish of me, perhaps, but I was on the Queen's business and expecting a guest. The waitress, a thin, nervous woman in her thirties, looked worn-out and listless, much like the paper garlands that still festooned the place three weeks after Christmas. She could barely move between the tables, the place was so packed with customers and their sodden overcoats and dripping umbrellas. Stopping by my table she topped up my cup hastily, slopping tea into the saucer, but I made no remark. There are times when it serves to make a scene and times to bite your tongue.

Jakob was late. He was always late. I was used to it, and I understood his reasons: he hated me, and everything I stood for, and himself for associating with me. I found it amusing all the same that he always contrived to be exactly fifteen minutes late. Even his contempt was precisely measured.

And on the dot he appeared, wrestling with the door handle while rain poured off the brim of his grubby slouch hat and a gust of wind tried to snatch the portfolio from under his arm. When at last he wrenched the door open it forced a loud brassy jangle from the bell, causing the young Latvian to freeze momentarily in the doorway. His eyes darted right and left, as if waiting for everyone to stop talking and turn and stare. He was worried about being seen in my company, of course, but I was just as concerned about that as he was. That was why I'd been seated here facing the door for over an hour, discreetly watching the customers come and go, checking for familiar faces.

But the hubbub continued unbroken; no one noticed Jakob or cared. He quickly relaxed and stepped in, pulling the door shut behind him and shaking the rain off his hat. His face was as pale and pinched as ever, and when his coal-black eyes met mine, he nodded, almost imperceptibly. I smiled, and it wasn't just to put him at his ease. I was genuinely pleased to see the lad; I liked Jakob, for all his wrong-headed ideas. I liked his intelligence, and his passion, and his sincerity. All the things that made him dangerous, in fact.

He started making his way over. Barely in his twenties, he was so painfully thin he hardly needed to turn sideways to squeeze through the rows of seated customers, but all the same he jostled a few elbows and knocked a few hats askew with his portfolio. He ignored the angry stares; Jakob often mocked the English for their reluctance to complain even when they were perfectly entitled to, and he had a point. When at last he arrived at my table he did not greet me or offer to shake hands, but merely leaned his portfolio up against the table legs, hooked his hat on the nearest rack and unbuttoned his shabby overcoat. The rain had soaked through its thin material and into the worn jacket beneath. He'll catch his death, I thought. I caught the waitress's eye and summoned her over with a lift of my chin.

"Jakob, what will you have?"

"I am not hungry," he said, shrugging. His words were addressed to the air rather than either of us.

"Away out of that," I said. "You look half-starved, and you're soaked through. Is that mutton stew I can smell?" This to the waitress.

"Not sure if we have any left, sir."

"A bowl of that, if you do. Otherwise some of the oxtail soup."

She nodded, and with a sharp glance at Jakob—his accent had clearly piqued her curiosity—she waded through the throng towards the kitchen.

"So, Jakob, how have you been?"

"The same. Coughing my lungs out." His eyes flickered round the room again, checking for surveillance; old habits die hard. "This city stinks. I don't know how you people can breathe the air."

"It was bad the other day, right enough. Fog mixed with smoke. A proper London Particular. All the same, I dare say you can breathe more easily over here than back home."

He didn't smile, but he did meet my gaze at last.

"And how have you been, Mr. Melville? Cracked many heads this week?"

"I have not. Sure I employ people to do that for me."

"Yes, I have seen them. Hanging around in the street outside our meetings. Sitting in the back of the hall."

"Don't worry. If they need to crack any heads, they'll be sure to crack yours too." Brushing tea from my moustache, I went on, "So, were you at the club last night?"

My lack of subtlety seemed to amuse him, and he smiled at last.

"You have to ask? Were your agents taking the night off? You know, I thought the hall was not so full as usual."

"And who was the speaker?" I already knew the answer, but I wanted to put Jakob at ease. He wouldn't feel any reluctance telling me information I could easily have picked up from a handbill in Soho.

"The speaker? Some German fool," sneered Jakob. "Rocker. Calls himself a 'progressive anarchist.'"

"And what do you call him?"

"A cretin. A liberal democrat in revolutionary clothing." Jakob's smile must have been handsome once, before the Tsar's policemen broke his teeth with their boots. "He claims the principles of anarchy are not fixed but must be revised in response to what he calls historical circumstance."

"A pragmatist, then."

"A bourgeois reactionary. Making his excuses in advance for betraying the workers. There is only one historical circumstance, the oppression of the proletariat, and that has not changed for a thousand years—"

Just as he was working himself up into a fine passion, Jakob fell silent, his face reddening, and looked away. He felt foolish, I suppose, for lecturing me on revolutionary theory. Detective Chief Superintendent William Melville, head of Scotland Yard's Special Branch and occasional bodyguard to the British Royal Family, was hardly the type to be swayed by Marxist rhetoric. I raised an eyebrow, as if he'd made a valid point I needed to consider. I wasn't about to argue with him, but I didn't want to patronise him either, and it was a relief when the waitress banged down a plate of bread on the table between the two of us and a steaming bowl of mutton stew in front of Jakob. Forgetting his embarrassment, the young Latvian snatched up his spoon and dug in, wolfing down the meat and potatoes though they were so hot they must have scalded his mouth. The lad was famished. While he worked away, I stirred another spoonful of sugar into my tea and watched him from the corner of my eye. Presently he stopped for breath and wiped his chin on the sleeve of his jacket.

"I did see one new face," he volunteered, his mouth half-full. I let him read surprise and curiosity on my face, and he hurried on, gratified. "An American, I think, though German or Dutch by birth, judging by his accent. I heard him asking Rocker for a copy of that so-called newspaper of his, *Germinal*."

"And what did he look like, this American?" I was curious to hear if Jakob's description matched the one I'd already heard; Sergeant Dawes hadn't mentioned any accent.

"Thirty-one, thirty-two perhaps? Not so tall as you, or so big. Brown hair, like that man"—Jakob nodded at a slight, balding customer seated at the next table—"brown eyes, full moustache, no beard. His clothes were interesting."

"Interesting how?"

"They were old and worn, like this"—he held out the sleeve of his jacket—"but he was no pauper. He was too well fed. His hair was too well cut."

"Military?"

"He looked too intelligent to be a soldier."

"A reporter, perhaps?"

"He took no notes. Not that informers do."

"Interesting. I'll make some enquiries."

I felt Jakob peering at me as I sipped my tea. He was trying to make out if I was lying—perhaps I knew very well who this stranger was, and I was testing him. Then he seemed to decide that he could not tell, and that it did not matter. It was merely a crumb of information, worthless to his own cause, but something that I might value.

"Any old friends?" I enquired, as if I was worried about him being lonely. There was an instant of hesitation before he shrugged, his eyes flicking away. I didn't press him: the details he was omitting carried their own significance.

"That smells good," I said, nodding at the bowl. Jakob grunted and resumed eating, and I watched him until he'd cleaned the dish and was wiping the last of the gravy up with a heel of bread.

"Another?"

The anarchist shook his head. "I am full," he said. "Thank you." No sooner had he spoken than he blinked self-consciously, and almost bit his tongue. I stifled a sigh of pity. For a moment there he had lapsed into good manners, manners that had no doubt been beaten into him as a child. But now he felt ashamed of his petit-bourgeois upbringing, and of being so polite to me, an agent of the State. Mother of God, but these idealists make it so hard on themselves. They may sneer at those of us who have faith, but at least we Catholics can get absolution for our mistakes; they flog themselves daily with scourges of their own making.

"So, was there any other business?" I asked. Jakob frowned. "At your meeting."

"No. Yes. We held a collection. For the family of Gaetano Bresci."

"The assassin? The one who shot the King of Italy?"

Jakob snorted. "Assassin! The man who acted when others merely talked. For that he gets life in prison, in a cage too small for a dog."

I wasn't about to let that pass. "He's lucky they didn't hang him. He murdered King Humbert in front of two thousand people."

"And why do you suppose he committed this outrage?" Jakob seethed with sudden indignation. "King Umberto's troops opened fire on workers in Milan, protesting about the price of bread. Six hundred people died—men, women, children. Who was arrested for that? Who went to prison? Not the General who gave the order—noble King Umberto gave him a medal. But of course, for Mr. Policeman Melville, the life of one noble parasite is worth more than the lives of a thousand workers."

"That was a shocking business, right enough," I conceded.

"No, for the bourgeoisie, that was business as usual."

Touché, I thought, and I nearly smiled, until I saw Jakob's deadly serious face. He was driven by rage at brutality and injustice, and that was understandable—so was I, at his age. Indeed, I still was, but he could never grasp that, and I wasn't going to try and persuade him. If he ever felt I was patronising him, or trying to manipulate him, or even acting directly on his information, disgust at himself would make him turn on me—perhaps drive him to prove his devotion to the Cause. Right now Jakob believed he was selling worthless gossip in return for a hot meal. His task was to make a fool of me, the infamous Melville, scourge of European anarchists; my task was to let him think he'd succeeded.

"How's the painting going?" I peered over the edge of the tabletop at his portfolio, still propped against the table leg. It was meant to look like leather, thanks to the embossed oilskin glued to the cardboard, but the thin veneer was coming unstuck with damp and peeling away at the corners. "Has the Muse been good to you?"

Jakob shrugged in an attempt at modesty. "I have been working with charcoal. It has that essence of line."

And it's a damn' sight cheaper than oils, I thought, but what I said was, "Show me."

I cleared away the crockery, perching it on an empty table nearby, while Jakob picked up his portfolio, undid the loop of string that held it shut and opened it out across the table. The topmost sketch was of a horse in harness, rearing in fear or pain, the looming bulk of a pantechnicon behind it, the driver a shadowy figure raising his whip. I fell silent a moment, in sincere admiration. Jakob had real talent; this image was simple but powerful, and the way he evoked movement with a single swish of charcoal was masterful. For once I didn't have to dissemble.

"I see what you mean about essence. This is excellent. The driver there—he's just a notion, but you can see the power in his arm, the cruelty . . ."

The next sketch was of the same scene, but a few minutes later: the horse, still trapped between the shafts, had fallen to its front knees, its neck and head twisted back in agony. Its teeth were clenched on the bit as the driver laid into it with his whip.

"Is this taken from life?"

"I saw it happen, in Haymarket, last week. The driver, he flogged and flogged the horse until it was nearly dead, and no one even tried to stop him."

"There's a scene like that in Dostoyevsky, isn't there? Flogging a half-dead horse."

"There are scenes like this everywhere," said Jakob. His look said the rest: that the workers of the world were the horse being flogged, and men like me wielded the whip.

"I'll give you a guinea for the two of them," I said. Jakob gasped in disbelief, God help him.

"You like them?"

"'Like' is not the word. But they're very striking." I fished inside my coat for my pocketbook. Jakob, recovering from his surprise, affected an air of mocking cynicism.

"Where will you hang them? In your office in Scotland Yard?"

"I'll hang them at home. Sure it's my own money." I leafed through the notes in my pocketbook, and Jakob tried not to stare at them hungrily. It was my own money, in the sense that I didn't have to account for it. All the same, I kept a careful record of my payments to informants; many an honest copper has come to grief, accused of having his fingers in the till. And a few dishonest ones too, admittedly.

"Tell you what," I said, "a pound and ten shillings, and you can pick up the bill."

I laid a banknote and two crowns on top of the sketches and tucked my pocketbook back inside my jacket. Jakob picked up the money and stuffed it into a pocket, and I got the strong impression he was fighting the urge to whoop with joy. "And mind you leave a tip," I added.

He looked insulted. "You think I would cheat a worker out of her earnings?"

"You might decide to make a contribution to the Cause on her behalf." I tugged my watch from my waistcoat pocket and checked it. "I'd best be on my way. You're a damned fine artist, Jakob. I think I prefer your work in oils, but that's just me."

"I heard a rumour," said Jakob suddenly. His tone of indifference rang so false I immediately raised my guard.

"What rumour would that be?"

"That your Queen is sick."

I shrugged. "She has a cold, is all I heard."

"Please pass on to her my very best wishes for a full recovery." He smiled. That needled me; I knew the old lady, and I liked her, and I didn't take kindly to his sarcasm. I responded with some of my own.

"Very touching. Coming from an anarchist."

It was Jakob's turn to shrug, and my turn to be surprised: I saw now he'd meant it. "I am a revolutionary socialist. And we are grateful to her, my friends and I. Like you say, we can breathe here. Meet, talk, exchange ideas. England is not Russia, where such things—or being related to someone who does such things—can get you jailed, tortured, shot, buried in lime. No trial, no appeal. Here we do not fear these things. The wise bird does not foul such a nest."

Nice of you to say so, I thought. *But if you and your friends ever did win power over here, you'd be shooting and burying men like me, and you'd be extra generous with the lime.*

"Hm. If I'm up at the Palace anytime soon I'll pass on the message," I said.

I pushed my chair back and rose, glancing over my shoulder first to be sure I didn't squash anyone seated behind me. I've always been big-boned and heavy, as deep as I'm wide, and in my fifties I wasn't getting any lighter. As I shrugged on my overcoat and retrieved my bowler, Jakob rolled the sketches up.

"The next meeting is in March," he said casually. "The eleventh."

"Then let's meet on the twelfth."

"Here?"

"Not here, no. There's a new ABC up the road in Hammersmith, top of King Street. Same time, all right?" I tipped my hat to him. No handshakes. "So long, now, Jakob. Take care."

"I hope Mrs. Melville likes the sketches." Jakob grinned, with his broken teeth.

"Oh, she will, I'm sure."

THE LAST SQUALL had died away and the rain was easing off as I headed up Fulham Broadway. On the corner a piano-organ, cranked by an ancient grinder bent nearly in two, clattered into life with a tinny rendering of a Strauss polka. Urchins in threadbare jerseys crowded round, bare feet splashing in the puddles, to stare and laugh at the broken-tailed monkey that was clambering back and forth on top of the instrument. The wretched creature was fastened to the piano-organ's lid with a thin chain, and it rattled a dented tin mug at the children and me. I fished in my pocket for a threepenny bit and tossed it to the monkey, who caught the coin deftly in the mug and bared its teeth in what I supposed was meant to be a smile of thanks. The old man cranking the handle tugged the brim of his cap as I passed.

So Jakob and his friends had been speculating about the Queen's health? That unsettled me. The general public had no idea how poorly she was, but my own sources at her country residence, Osborne House, told me she was still in a wheelchair and had little appetite. She was nearly eighty-two now, and for a woman of her age there was no such thing as a simple cold; then again, she was a tough old bird who had seen off worse.

Farther up Fulham Broadway a street-sweeper was shovelling horse-dung into his barrow. I paused by his cart and pulled the rolled-up sketches from under my arm. The money would keep Jakob and his friends in bread and beer for a week or two, and maybe help to pay for a few seditious Russian pamphlets; more to the point, it would keep the Latvian on my hook for when I needed to reel him in. As it happened, I did like Jakob's drawings, very much; but I'd lied to the lad. Mrs. Melville would hate them. I looked around to ensure no one was watching, twisted the sketches up into a tight wad and tossed them into the street-sweeper's barrow.

Met at Walham Green with Jakob Piotr, sometimes known as Piotr the Painter. For the usual inducements he briefed me on the meeting the night before at the Anarchist Club in Soho, which was addressed by Rudolf Rocker (see separate file, R/M/00/00331). Confirmed Sgt Dawes's report of a previously unknown attendant, possibly American. Piotr claimed not to know him either. Insp Quinn is cross-checking physical description with port records.

Notably Piotr did not mention the presence of Alexandrovich (see separate file, R/M/94) at the same meeting, though he and Piotr conversed at length. This suggests Alexandrovich's current visit may indeed be connected to the planned shipment of weapons to Latvian rebels via Hartlepool.

Will assign Sgts Dawes and Willerton to covertly monitor Alexandrovich's movements.

There was a sharp rap at the door, and I quickly covered up my notebook, though I knew from the knock it was Constable Jenkins. He'd been with Special Branch twenty years, but the fewer people I needed to trust the simpler my life was.

"Come in."

"Sorry to interrupt, sir." Jenkins, once a cavalry officer, still fought the urge to stand to attention and salute. "The AC has asked to see you, urgent."

ASSISTANT COMMISSIONER Robert Anderson was my direct boss; ten years my senior, he was an Irishman like me, but there the resemblance ended. Short and wiry, he was a staunch Presbyterian, with a white beard that made him look like an Old Testament prophet, which was no doubt the intent. He had been a moderately famous barrister in Dublin when he was recruited by the British government to advise on the Fenian threat. I had joined the new Special Branch around the same time, and my colleagues and I quickly put paid to that particular Fenian threat, without any help from Anderson. But by then he had got his feet under the government table and found the life to his liking. With flattery and flummery he had inveigled his way onto various other official committees and boards, and over decades had slithered up the greasy pole to his present position. He had no direct experience of police work, whereas I had been a copper for nearly thirty years, most of it on the street. That fact seemed to irk him, judging by his constant need to assert his authority.

"William. Take a seat. I left word for you to attend immediately upon your return."

"And so I have, sir."

"Might I ask what business was so vital it took you away from your desk?"

"I was meeting a source. Routine, but necessary."

"You're head of Special Branch. It's past time you learned to delegate."

Our meetings seemed to be moulded on this pattern—a minor scolding, followed by instructions on how to do my job, concluding with orders to do what I was already doing. Talking to informers is one task that can't easily be delegated, but Anderson didn't know that, and he wouldn't have accepted it if I'd told him.

"You're right, of course," I said.

"Hm." He picked up a telegram from his desk, but did not show it to me. "Your presence is required at Osborne House, by His Royal Highness the Prince of Wales."

Osborne House was Queen Victoria's country retreat; I had often worked as bodyguard to the Queen and Prince Albert, but why was I needed at Osborne House? Unless young Jakob's guess had been right, after all?

"Her Majesty?"

"Is gravely ill, according to her doctor."

"That is sad news indeed, sir."

"From his account, I fear the good Lord will gather Her Majesty to His bosom within the week." Anderson, who had published thoughtful tracts on God's Purpose for Mankind, was fond of such pious utterances. I was religious myself, but I tried not to let it interfere with my work; indeed, I suspected one reason Anderson invoked the Lord so often was to remind me of my place—a Catholic peasant promoted far above his station.

"It would appear," Anderson went on, "that Dr. Reid saw fit to send a telegram directly to His Imperial Majesty Kaiser Wilhelm. The Kaiser has cancelled all his plans and is making his way direct to the Isle of Wight. He is expected to arrive tomorrow afternoon."

It was common knowledge that the German Kaiser worshipped his grandmother Victoria, who returned his affection with more warmth than she had ever shown her son Albert. It was also common knowledge that the Kaiser and his uncle Prince Albert despised each other. But not so much, surely, that Albert would need a bodyguard?

"I'll finish my business here and catch the first train down in the morning," I said.

"Be back as soon as you can. Arrangements must be made for the funeral."

"Arrangements are in hand, sir. We have contingency plans. Detective Inspector Quinn has all the details."

"This matter is not one I expect you to delegate, DCS Melville. It's not merely the security arrangements—full consideration must be given to precedence and protocol."

Precedence, of course. The Assistant Commissioner attached the utmost importance to the hierarchy of aristocrats and dignitaries, their ranks and titles and formal salutations.

"Anyway, the sooner you leave . . ."

The sooner you'll be back, he almost said, before realising it was nonsense. To spare his blushes, I stood. "Sir."

2

"OSBORNE HOUSE?" said Amelia.

"I'm catching the first train in the morning."

We were seated at dinner, the children conversing in hushed tones about some American dancer called Isadora Duncan my elder boy William had seen perform at a friend's house. Daring, William had called her, which I presumed meant indecent. Before I could ask exactly which friend it was whose parents laid on such exotic entertainment, Amelia seized on my remark.

"May the good Lord preserve her," said Amelia.

"Who?" I said.

"Her Majesty. The paper said the Kaiser's yacht was to call at Cowes. Is she really so unwell?"

"The message didn't say." I don't know why I was being evasive; Amelia and I had been married ten years, and her powers of inference and deduction often excelled those of my colleagues.

"Have you packed a mourning band? Just in case."

"Amelia, sure let's not get ahead of ourselves."

"I'll see to it now." She rose from the table and bustled off, while the children—hardly children, Kate, the eldest, was eighteen—chatted on, oblivious to the possibility that the world as they knew it might soon be ending. Which was, I reflected, how things should be.

· · ·

ON THE 6:24 out of Waterloo I had a compartment all to myself, but although I'd brought a Gladstone bag full of papers, I found it impossible to focus on work. Instead I watched the lamplit soot-black suburbs of London give way to shadow, and before long could see nothing but my own reflection: a big bullock of an Irishman in a bowler hat staring pensively into the dark, squaring his shoulders against the enormity of the task ahead.

It was hard to imagine Britain, still less the British Empire, without Victoria. She ascended the throne long before I was born and had reigned for twenty-five years when I had abandoned Sneem, County Kerry, as a lad of fourteen. Rather than explain to my father and his clumping fists that I was fed up kneading dough and had no desire to become a baker like him, I took his horse and cart and left them hitched to a post outside Kenmare railway station. In London I ended up kneading dough again to make a living, but only for a few years before I joined the police force. Over the decades I had, through tenacity, low cunning and my own clumping fists, risen from beat constable to Detective Chief Superintendent Melville of Scotland Yard, champion of British justice—or notorious thug, depending on which papers you read—and bodyguard to emperors, foreign and domestic.

In the course of the latter job I had come to know Her Majesty the Queen and grown fond of her. She was tiny, and shrewd, and vigorous, and cared more for her servants than for the smug boobies of her Court. Prince Albert would find it a challenge to succeed her—but of course, that's how monarchies work: Bertie would take the throne whether he was up to the challenge or not. Primogeniture might be an old-fashioned way of choosing a head of state, but it suited most civilised nations. The Americans, after all, had explored the alternatives and still occasionally lumbered themselves with venal idiots.

Anyway, Prince Albert's qualifications, or lack of them, were not my problem; I had enough of my own. Victoria had decreed a full state funeral for herself and had been planning the details for a decade, fussing over colour schemes and flower arrangements. I had been making plans too, but not about the decor—they could drape her coffin in tinsel and feathers for all I cared. My job was to ensure the safety of the people and the realm. And if Jakob Piotr had guessed the Queen was on her deathbed, every anarchist on the Continent would be packing a suitcase by now.

Victoria was aunt, great-aunt or grandmother to more than half the kings and queens of Europe, and every relative that could attend her funeral would, along with ambassadors and ministers and satraps and liveried flunkeys from the farthest corners of every continent. The procession would stretch through London for a mile or more, and for terrorists it would be one long shooting gallery, with every prize a jackpot.

Terrorists. We Irishmen practically invented the concept, when Irish republicans had managed to get hold of Nobel's great invention, dynamite. I understood well enough the Fenian passion for independence—if we Irish were to rule ourselves, we could hardly make a worse job of it than the English—but I had always been repelled by their means, especially when they involved lobbing dynamite at civilians. Violence against the innocent and the powerless infuriated me, and always had, even as a child facing my father's fists and the schoolmaster's tawse; that was why I had volunteered for Special Branch. The Republican Brotherhood's campaign of terror soon collapsed, crippled by informers and turncoats—a good few of which I had helped to turn.

But by then the Fenians had inspired a new generation of radicals who sought nothing so simple as independence or self-rule. Their goal was to smash society and forge it anew, and to hell with democracy or the rule of law. They'd convinced themselves that if only enough emperors, kings and ministers could be slaughtered the common people would rise up and throw off their chains of bondage. And if one or two or a thousand of those common people died in the process, why, they would be honoured martyrs, sacrificed to a greater good. They would have died anyway, under the yoke of oppression! Rejoice!

Lord, how I despised these fanatics, who desecrated the very causes they claimed to support and allowed tyrants the world over to commit atrocities in the name of protecting the innocent.

No anarchist had ever struck in Britain, though London accommodated more than its share; perhaps *because* we did. In the last decade half the radicals in Europe seemed to have sought refuge in our capital. As Jakob had acknowledged, here there were no secret policemen or secret trials, and that was how the British people liked it. Dissidents and revolutionaries exiled from their home countries could meet and talk and publish and make speeches, and we let them, as long as that was all they did. It was not a policy that made us popular with our counterparts abroad, but we were not accountable to them, and it had worked out well for us so far. Russia, Germany and Spain all possessed fearsome secret police forces who cracked down brutally on dissent, but they had suffered all the same—King Humbert of Italy had merely been the latest victim.

In the last two decades Alexander II of Russia had been blown to pieces by an anarchist bomb, the Empress of Austria had been run through the heart with a stiletto as she boarded a ferry, and the Prime Minister of Spain shot to death relaxing at a spa. Only a few months back the Belgian anarchist Sipido had shot at our own Prince Albert and missed him by a hand's breadth.

And it wasn't just the nobility who suffered: twenty theatregoers in Barcelona had died in a welter of blood when two bombs were thrown into the stalls; a device in a cigar box had killed a dozen customers listening to an orchestra in a Parisian café. All in the name of equality and justice and freedom.

These provocations, these atrocities, were specifically intended to terrify the public, to bring down governments, to spark revolution, but they risked far worse. Europe's empires had massive standing armies full of dashing young bucks hungry to prove their valour in war and ravenous for a pretext to start one—the murder of a prince or a king might well drown the continent in blood.

I stared through my reflection into the endless murk of night. I had a team of experienced officers that I had personally trained, and a network of carefully cultivated civilian informants, but nobody can see into the hearts of men, and none of them could tell me when one of our exiled radicals might tire of talking and decide to act. If I summoned every policeman in the Empire to form a cordon along Victoria's funeral route, it would not be enough to stop a single determined assassin. One lucky bullet, one stick of explosive . . .

Somehow, over the clatter of the train's wheels, I heard a sudden burst of birdsong and noticed away in the east the first pale rays of dawn seeping into the clouds. Enough of this brooding, I scolded myself. I had a job to do, and little enough time to do it. I opened my briefcase and pulled out my papers.

FROM THE WINDOW of my carriage I watched the Italianate towers of Osborne House loom up. Evergreen myrtles and cedars lined the western drive, throwing long shadows across the lawn where even now, in the late morning, the grass glittered with hoarfrost. My brougham rocked to a halt outside the Durbar Wing, and as I stepped down I was greeted by the familiar face of Ross, head of staff to the Prince of Wales. I tipped my hat in return to his short solemn bow. Osborne House had never been what you'd call an informal environment, but today it was more solemn than ever. A grim hush hung about the place; everyone there knew an era was ending.

"His Royal Highness is on the lower terrace, Chief Superintendent," said Ross. "If you'd be so good as to follow me . . ."

As we entered the winter drawing-room, the French doors onto the lower terrace opened, and two men entered, engrossed in private conversation. I knew them; I knew all of the Prince's hangers-on. The slight, languid fellow was Lord Peter Eden, and the taller, strutting one was his sycophant, Lord Geoffrey Diamond. Both were dressed in the latest courtly fashions, aping the Prince of Wales: narrow lapels, shirt-collars turned down, waistcoats unbuttoned at the bottom. Diamond was muttering something under his breath to Eden, who burst out in his habitual girlish giggle, only to stifle it when he saw that he and Diamond were not alone. Diamond too tensed, until he took in that we were merely commoners. Instantly we ceased to exist, and the two noblemen moved off without acknowledging either of us.

It was just as well, for if either man had spoken to me, I would have found it hard to assume a proper tone of deference. In the house of the dying a little levity was understandable, even necessary, but I strongly suspected the joke their two Lordships found so amusing had been at Prince Albert's expense. Once a playboy, Albert was a boy no longer, but time had not tempered his appetites for fine food and female company, and that made him a figure of fun to some. I had always found the Prince straightforward, and even charming, but as heir to an empire his social circle was by necessity constrained—a shallow pool, with some right toads in it, like those two Lordships. For one fleeting moment I wished I still carried a truncheon, but it was not my place to teach the Prince's so-called friends some manners, however much I would have relished the task.

Ross opened the door leading onto the terrace and stood back to let me go first.

This part of the gardens faced out across the Solent, where pleasure boats, sailing ships and fishing smacks slid and jostled along the gleaming grey water. A little way offshore a flock of seagulls flickered over a fisherman's rowing boat as he pulled in his lobster pots; the stiff breeze from the sea carried the birds' ragged cries to us, with the sharp tang of salt and seaweed. As ever I was reminded of the shores of Kerry, but I felt no nostalgia; I'd seen enough rocks and seaweed growing up to last me ten lifetimes.

Farther along the terrace the Prince of Wales sat hunched on a bench, swathed in a heavy black woollen overcoat, a grey cashmere scarf wrapped tightly around his neck. As I approached he drew deeply on a cigarette and blew out a stream of smoke that was quickly whipped away by the breeze. I made my bow; Albert looked up, and a smile flickered briefly across his round, bearded face.

"Melville, old man. Good to see you."

He always called me "old man," though at sixty he was nearly ten years my senior. Indeed, it was very late in life to become a king. The Prince nodded at a seat nearby—a bench elaborately carved from jet by his father, years ago—then turned away and stared out to sea. I sat down and waited.

"You'll have heard the news."

"I have, sir."

"Reid says it was a stroke. Won't be long now. Today, perhaps tomorrow. She's hanging on."

"I'd expect no less of Her Majesty. I'm sorry, sir, it must be a painful time."

"Oh, she's being well looked after." For a moment Albert seemed about to say more, but he merely shook his head, as if surprised by the intensity of his own feelings, and, staring down at the glowing end of his cigarette, blinked a few times. Then he flicked the stub into the bushes.

"Alexandra is with her now. She'll be pleased to see you."

"And I her, Your Highness." Alexandra, the Princess of Wales, was vivacious, cheerful, loyal and patient, and she needed to be, married to Albert. Famously approachable, he was famously approached by ladies of every social class and did little to discourage them. Today however there was little sign of the libertine. Perhaps he was seeing clearly for the first time the enormity of the role that would soon be thrust upon him; after a lifetime of playing Falstaff he had found himself cast as Prince Hal.

"You're going to have your work cut out, rather," said the Prince at last.

"It's all in hand, sir."

Albert pulled a silver cigarette case out of his inside pocket, snapped it open and began again his comforting ritual of tapping and lighting and drawing. I'm not one of these cranks who object to smoking, but it has never held any attraction for me; what I really dislike is the smell it leaves on your clothes. In my line of work it sometimes helps to be inconspicuous, and the whiff of stale tobacco can be a liability.

"His Imperial Majesty the Kaiser will be arriving this afternoon," the Prince said at last. "Within the hour, in fact. I'd be obliged if you would remain in attendance." Albert's casual tone, as he fiddled with his cigarette case, failed to conceal the tension in his voice.

"I am at Your Highness's command, as always," I said.

He dug out his pocket watch and squinted at it through a haze of smoke.

"Best get yourself something to eat, old man. While there's still time."

BELOWSTAIRS AT OSBORNE HOUSE was a scene of barely controlled chaos. Not only Albert and Alexandra but almost all the Queen's offspring had taken up residence in the last few days, each with spouse and retinue. Prim battalions of butlers and valets and maids were jostling for space and precedence, and tempers were running short, but thanks to Ross I was quickly served a lunch of game pie and vegetable soup, and just as quickly I demolished it. I'd barely wiped my moustache clean when shouts in the stable yard, the clatter of hooves and the rumble of carriage wheels announced that the Kaiser was arriving.

I made it upstairs just in time to take up my customary position behind Albert, on his left and two steps back, as he and his retinue assembled in the Durbar Room. The high ceiling echoed with the creaking and scuffling of leather boots, the jangling of medals and the frantic muffled whispers of courtiers finding their place. When at last two lines of noblemen had formed, one on each side of the Prince, an imperceptible signal was passed to the valets at the far end of the room, who stepped forwards and threw open the massive gilded doors.

And here in all his pomp strode Kaiser Wilhelm, Emperor of Germany, head held high and back ramrod straight, and in his wake a gaggle of Junkers, princes and generals, all mirroring his strut. The unkind thought struck me, as it often did, that the Emperor's swagger was designed to compensate for his lack of physical stature. His spectacular uniform too, with its medals and buckles and braid, served to distract attention from the withered left arm hanging limply in his sleeve, its gloved hand artfully arranged to look as if it was grasping his belt. Wilhelm was known to blame the doctor that delivered him for that defect—an English doctor, as it happened.

Ten paces from his uncle and aunt, Wilhelm paused, brought his heels together with a sharp crack and made a stiff, deep bow. Albert returned the salute, and the Princess of Wales curtsied, both with a certain lack of conviction. Prince Albert did not always make much effort to hide his opinion of his nephew, and already a slight chill seemed to be seeping into the room, in spite of the logs that blazed in the fireplace. But then Albert strolled forwards and offered his nephew his outstretched hand, and Wilhelm took it, his own right hand still gloved, since he could not remove the glove without using his teeth. When Albert spoke, his tone was formal, but warm.

"Your Imperial Highness, welcome to Osborne House. How was your journey?"

As the two exchanged courtesies, and Wilhelm embraced his aunt, I sensed that I was being watched. I learned long ago never to ignore my instincts, so now I searched among the glittering finery of the German court for my observer. It took me a while to spot him: a slim man in a sombre civilian suit, slight as a shadow, ten feet behind the Kaiser to his left. When I met his gaze, he silently drew his heels together and gave the tiniest nod of salute, as if we were old acquaintances. A head shorter than me, he was in his early thirties and clean-shaven, which among all those bushy beards and handlebar moustaches gave him an incongruously boyish air. He seemed utterly at ease, despite the rigid formality of the occasion. In fact it seemed that while he regarded the ceremony with all the solemnity it deserved, he was observing it as an outsider. I was sure at first that I knew him from somewhere; then I realised the man he reminded me of was myself, twenty years ago.

Interesting, I thought. *Best keep an eye on this one.*

"And how is my beloved grandmother?" the Kaiser was saying. He could speak English as fluently as his uncle, I knew; but here and now he spoke with a clipped German accent as mannered as his military strut.

"I understand she is feeling a little better today," said Albert.

"Indeed, I'm sure your presence will hasten her recovery." A lie, but a courtly one.

"Let us hope so, Uncle. I look forward to paying her my respects."

"I'll take you to see her right away, if you'd like." An almost imperceptible pause.

"That would give me great pleasure. Thank you."

From the twinge of panic that rippled across the household staff in the room I guessed this had not been planned; Albert had changed all the arrangements on a whim. His mother would never have done such a thing, and the way the Prince had dispensed with protocol, as if he were already King, made it clearer than ever how close we all were to the end.

For his part Wilhelm bowed and stepped aside, and his uncle led the way towards the Royal Pavilion, Alexandra in their wake, while ushers and footmen and ladies-in-waiting scrambled discreetly ahead of them. As those doors closed behind the two princes, their courtiers breathed quiet sighs of relief, and the formal ranks dissolved. Old acquaintances mingled and greeted one another, crystallising into groups.

In the normal course of events I would have insinuated myself into one of these knots, to glean some gossip on the Imperial Court; with a little cajoling, old generals can be surprisingly indiscreet. But for now I held back, guessing that curious young German I had spotted would want to make himself known. And sure enough, there he was, weaving like a dancer through the throng, headed straight for me. He bowed again, then stretched out his hand.

"Chief Superintendent Melville, I believe? Honoured to make your acquaintance. My name is Gustav Steinhauer." I waited a moment for him to elaborate on his rank or role, but he did neither.

"Delighted," I said. His handshake was firm and strong and brief.

"The pleasure is all mine," said Steinhauer. "I confess I am a little intimidated, meeting you. Every policeman in Europe knows you by reputation."

"You're in the same line of work, I take it?"

Steinhauer shrugged and smiled. "I am part of His Imperial Majesty's bodyguard." *Not a copper, then,* I thought. His English was so polished it was hard to place; like the Kaiser, his accent had a hint of Prussian, and like the Kaiser's, I suspected, it was not entirely genuine. His smile was warm and his manner open, but I noticed how deftly he'd dodged my question.

"My counterpart, so?" I said. "We should have dinner sometime. Compare notes."

"That would be an honour. But I think I would be the one taking notes."

"You speak excellent English, Herr Steinhauer."

"Why, thank you. I travelled widely before I joined His Imperial Majesty's service. I have even visited Kerry, in the south of Ireland—don't you come from that part of the world?"

"A long time ago."

"Such a wild and beautiful place. No artist could do justice to the landscape. Do you often revisit the old country?"

I've trained many officers to work undercover, and the very first lesson is talk freely and be utterly boring. With a little practice one can chatter all day and say absolutely nothing. Be neither funny nor observant nor original; avoid intrigue and mystery and, if asked a probing question, deflect and ask one in return—every man's favourite subject is himself. Steinhauer, if he had ever taken such a course, must have passed with flying colours.

Thankfully neither of us had to deploy our skills of empty conversation for long; it transpired that the Queen had been so weak she barely recognised her grandson. Wilhelm had insisted she be disturbed no further and had retired to his quarters. On hearing this, the Imperial retinue had followed suit, and Steinhauer, with a respectful bow, had evaporated like a will-o'-the-wisp. The Prince of Wales having no immediate need of me, I returned to my preparations for the funeral, and in the below-stairs cubby-hole that served as my office I worked late into the night, eating dinner at my desk.

It was nearly midnight when I received a summons to the billiard-room, a summons I'd been half expecting. Slipping my papers into a folder, I locked them away in the safe, testing the handle twice. I never took security for granted, even in Her Majesty's official residence—especially there, and especially then, with the household routine gone to pot and the staff quarters teeming with unfamiliar faces.

The Prince was sitting in a winged leather armchair by the fireplace, while the Kaiser had planted himself on the hearthrug, holding court. Both men were red in the face, and I guessed it had little to do with the fire that roared in the massive hearth—the air was thick with cigar smoke and brandy fumes. Princess Alexandra and her attendants had long since retired, leaving the men to their own devices. Ross and several other servants stood in silent attendance all around; Her Majesty's Pomeranian, Turi, dozed under the Prince's chair.

"Chief Superintendent Melville! Join us, please!"

I had heard Wilhelm use that loud, hearty tone before—he'd cribbed it from Albert. The Kaiser fancied he shared his uncle's common touch, and nobody dared to disillusion him. It took me a moment to notice a shape in the shadows behind the Kaiser's armchair—slight and motionless, barely there at all. Steinhauer.

"Your master and I"—the Kaiser stifled a hiccough—"were discussing the qualities of the ideal bodyguard. And we thought, who better to consult than his own man, Herr Melville of Scotland Yard?"

I bowed; from the corner of my eye I could see Albert, who seemed to be finding the exchange less amusing than his nephew. With Victoria on her deathbed it seemed an odd time to be over-indulging in brandy and cigars, but royalty makes its own rules.

"You flatter me, Your Imperial Majesty," I said. "I've often wondered that myself."

"Do not be so modest. You have served in this post for more than ten years."

"Yes, sir, but for all that I'd never claim to be the ideal bodyguard. I'm merely the best available."

Prince Albert chuckled and drew on his cigar. Hearing him, the Kaiser chuckled too, as if enjoying our banter. But I sensed he wasn't. There's a fine line between informality and insolence, and I usually manage to judge it well enough, but Wilhelm was the sort of man to move it on a whim. Then again, what did he expect? That I'd bow and scrape and simper?

"Modesty is certainly desirable, wouldn't you say?" Wilhelm carried on. "Intelligence. And discretion, of course." This with a sly glance sideways to his uncle. "And cunning, as you have, Chief Superintendent."

"Less cunning, sir, than experience."

"Experience, yes, that is certainly valuable. But youth and ingenuity can outweigh experience, don't you think?" I nodded as if I was paying his remarks serious thought. I could see where this was headed; the dog under Albert's chair could. "Speaking of which," Wilhelm continued, "I believe you have met my own bodyguard, Herr Gustav Steinhauer?"

"I have, Your Majesty. Earlier today," I said.

Steinhauer stepped forwards into the firelight and nodded a bow. His expression was studiously neutral, but I could tell he had been happier in the shadows.

"Gustav is very modest about his achievements. He would never be so vain as to boast that he speaks six languages fluently. I daresay he speaks better English than you"—Wilhelm smirked—"since you are Irish."

"Interpreters are two a penny," interjected Albert, without looking up. "And Melville speaks all the languages he needs to." It was as if the two men were discussing our pedigrees; at any moment, I thought, the Kaiser would pull back Steinhauer's lips to show off his teeth. Was that why Steinhauer and I were here? So the Kaiser could compare his prancing young stallion to his uncle's aging warhorse? How condescending and pathetic, I thought, though I kept my demeanour studiously neutral. If Steinhauer, like me, was bristling inwardly, he was doing a damned fine job of hiding it.

"Alas, Uncle," said Wilhelm. "The madmen, the terrorists who wish to murder you and me in our beds, they are not plotting only in English." He waved his brandy glass at the empty air, and a servant stepped forwards to refill it. Wilhelm quite ignored him, as if the glass had refilled itself. "Gustav speaks fluent French, Russian, Italian, English . . ."

"My German, however, is lamentable," Steinhauer interjected quietly. I stifled a grin at that, but the Kaiser, fortunately, missed the quip.

"And he has also a most exceptional insight into human nature. Tell them about Lieutenant Rolf." This to Steinhauer, who smiled but said nothing. The Kaiser did not take the hint but, frowning, insisted, "Gustav. Tell them."

"There is little to tell." Now the young man's smile was becoming strained.

"Rolf?" I prompted, mischievously.

"A wretched spy," spat Wilhelm in disgust. "An officer of the German army who sold our secrets to the French, just to pay off gambling debts. A drunk"—he slung his glass about so the brandy slopped over the brim—"a fornicator, a traitor to his fatherland." He raised his glass to Steinhauer in a toast. "A dozen men tried to bring him back to face justice, and all of them failed. All except Gustav here."

Now Steinhauer's smile was fixed, and I felt a twinge of sympathy. Albert knew better than to boast about my work, what he knew of it. In my business we do not advertise our successes or our failures. Yes, my name was known to coppers and criminals the length and breadth of Europe, but that was a hindrance as much as an advantage; the best sort of reputation is no reputation at all.

"He snared his man the same way the French did," the Kaiser went on, laughing. "By appealing to his base appetites!" Again Steinhauer shrugged and smiled, as if the tale was hardly worth telling. The Emperor drained his glass and turned with a smirk to Albert. "The allure of the fairer sex has been the undoing of many a great man, wouldn't you agree, Uncle?"

The Prince did not rise to the bait, but blew out a long stream of smoke and tossed his still-glowing cigar into the blazing fire. Then he rose, slowly and not very steadily, to his feet. All in attendance immediately stood up straighter. Wilhelm scowled, cut off mid-anecdote, but Steinhauer almost imperceptibly relaxed.

"I am going to retire," Albert announced. Turning to Ross, he added, "If there is any change in Her Majesty's condition, let me and His Imperial Highness know at once."

3

Wednesday 23 January 1901

My dear Amelia,

I plan to return to London tomorrow on the first train, but must go straight to Scotland Yard. Her Late Majesty's funeral will be on a scale no one living has ever seen, and although Patrick Quinn is superbly capable there are a million arrangements to be made. I will not be home until late—very late, I expect—so do not stay up to greet me.

I was in the room when Her Majesty passed away: her children were by her bedside, and she died peacefully in the arms of the Kaiser Wilhelm. Both he, and the King, and all those present—myself included—were in tears at her passing. For England Victoria's decease is the end of an era, but for her family it is a purely human tragedy

I stopped writing.

I have ever been a poor correspondent; I know all too well how the most minor detail in a letter can present an opportunity to a reader with ulterior motives. For that reason my letters home had always been terse, colourless and impersonal, but Amelia was used to that, and understood. Indeed, if I were to carry on in this style, she'd worry that either the letter was a forgery or I was losing my mind.

Yet I had witnessed so much in the last twenty-four hours it was hard to resist the urge to write it all down. The term "historic" has been worn threadbare by lazy journalists, but these past few days had been momentous, and I knew that much of what I had seen would be erased from the official history.

Those last moments by the Queen's bedside were still vivid: how her favourite servant Abdul Karim had been hustled from her presence, his tearful yet dignified protests ignored, and how the Kaiser with his one good arm had held the Queen as she passed away, then given way utterly to his grief; how he had wept over her body like a child, until even Albert had become impatient; how all had been struck dumb until Dr. Reid had taken it upon himself to utter the words "Her Majesty the Queen is dead. Long live the King!" though he nearly choked on them.

And all the while I stood in the corner, motionless and mute, powerless this once to fend off Death.

The next day I had witnessed the two Emperors laying Victoria's body, shrunken and frail, into its coffin, and the heated disagreement—frankly, squabble—among the children over the items that would join her. The late Queen had made her own list; no one objected to the inclusion of the embroidered dressing gown that had once belonged to their father the Prince Consort, but she had also stipulated that a daguerreotype of the Highlander John Brown be included. Her daughter Beatrice loudly insisted that the image should be removed and destroyed and Brown's mother's wedding ring be removed from Victoria's finger—they were tokens of a foolish infatuation, Beatrice had insisted, that would provoke a scandal when mourners viewed the body lying in state. The other princesses were of the same mind, but the new King had stated flatly that their mother's wishes were to be honoured in full. Tempers had become heated, and when I took Dr. Reid aside and murmured a compromise—that the photo and ring be present but concealed by flowers—it was quickly accepted.

The peace did not last long; the acrimony between Albert and Wilhelm intensified at dinner that night. Wilhelm, sneering at the simplicity of colonial natives, had used a vulgar term for blacks, only for the new King to interrupt. He abhorred such language, Albert declared, especially in relation to his own subjects. While not an order, it was as close to one as a polite request could be, but Wilhelm had seen fit to ignore it and had carried on with his sneers and slurs until the glacial chill from the head of the table nearly froze the diners to their gilded seats.

Then came the Court announcement that Albert would not be crowned King Albert, after his German father, but as King Edward VII. The Kaiser took this as a personal slight, with good reason: Albert had neither consulted nor warned him, and in courtly politics such an omission was as good as a gauntlet across the face.

Wilhelm for his part had not tried to hide his anger, but complained loudly to his retinue that Edward's decision was an insult not just to him personally but to all of Germany. Even the Princess Alexandra, warm and patient as she was, made no attempt to intervene or smooth ruffled feathers; she disliked the Kaiser as much as her husband did, if not more. It was as if with Victoria gone the two princes no longer saw any reason to be civil to each other. Royals are as human as the rest of us, of course, and family spats are inevitable, but such rancour between two heads of state did not bode well for future diplomatic relations.

Precisely none of which was suitable for putting down on paper, even to a woman as discreet as my wife. I crumpled the half-written letter into a tight ball, tossed it onto the fire and watched it blacken and catch and burn.

Then picked up my pen again.

My dear Amelia
   I shall be home late on Thursday night. Don't wait up.
                                                         W

4

YOU ARE Chief Superintendent Melville?"

"I am, Miss. Come in and sit down. Thank you, John."

Jenkins nodded and closed my office door behind him. The veiled visitor did not sit, but waited by the chair facing my desk, clearly expecting me to draw it back for her. I obliged, noting at the same time the stains on her coat and the mud around the hem of her dress. This was a genteel young woman, Italian by her accent, but down on her luck. All the same her posture was straight-backed and defiant; she was clearly aware of her shabby appearance and keen to make a good impression.

"Thank you for seeing me," she said.

"Not at all," I said. "Can I offer you some refreshment, Miss . . . Minetti, is it? Tea, perhaps?"

"Thank you, but no."

The officers manning the front desk at Scotland Yard knew they should never turn away anyone who claimed to have a tip-off, even on a day like today. It was Thursday; the royal funeral would take place in nine days' time, on the first Saturday in February, and there were still a million details to attend to—I had been at my desk since dawn. But my policy had always been that it was better to waste a few minutes indulging a fantasist than miss a crumb of real intelligence, and besides, I needed a break.

As I settled into my seat and took a more direct look at my visitor, I confess I felt ready to indulge her indefinitely, even if she did turn out to be spinning a yarn. She was in her mid- to late twenties, dressed in green, with a very fine figure. When she rolled up her veil, I saw she was strikingly pretty too, with large brown eyes set wide apart in a heart-shaped face, framed in thick honey-blond hair. But her olive skin was caked with powder and rouge; I suspected she had been making a living on the streets. Few streetwalkers I knew would approach a policeman for help unless they were desperate. And this woman needed help; the face powder did not quite conceal the bruise around her right eye.

"Are you sure?" I pressed her. "Something to eat, perhaps. I understand you've come a long way."

Whitechapel, Jenkins had said, a good hour on foot from our offices on the Embankment. And from the state of her skirt she had walked all the way rather than spend money on an omnibus.

"Later, perhaps," she said. "Thank you."

"I understand you have some information you wish to share." She had mentioned a plot of some sort to Jenkins, but against whom or what, I had yet to learn. Now she glanced down at her gloved hands; I recognised the tic of shame and waited for her to speak.

"I am teacher of Italian. I come to England four years ago, to work as governess. But I lose that position after a . . . misunderstanding. With my employer. His wife, she would not give me references, and I do not have money to go home to Napoli. Now I . . . I work from home. I give . . . private lessons." Comforted by how plausible that polite fiction sounded, she looked up at me, and I nodded.

"I see," I said. "Go on."

"Recently, I find a client, a pupil. He tell me he is Romanian."

"You were teaching him Italian?"

"English. He told me he just come to England, and he have not much money."

"When was this?"

"October, November. After a few weeks, he say he have no money at all, and nowhere to live . . ."

"And you offered him accommodation?" I prompted, as gently as I could.

"Yes. And soon he become, he became, more than my pupil. He gave me gifts—a beautiful fan—and he asked me to marry him."

She was blushing now and avoiding my eye. I picked up a pencil, partly to make notes, but mostly so she would not feel I was staring at her, judging her.

"Can I ask, what was your fiancé's name?"

"He say his name is Iosif Dalca. From Bucharest."

"Dalca . . ." The name meant nothing to me. "I take it you don't believe him?"

"He has friends now, who visit. Two men. They came last week, from Holland, they said, by a fishing boat. They talk in private, not in Hungarian or Romanian, but Russian. They think I do not understand Russian, but I do."

"How is that, if I might ask?"

"I learn it from neighbour, back in Napoli. I have, how do you say, ear for languages."

"And what is it these three men talk about?"

"The funeral of the Queen that will happen soon. There will be a great procession, with many nobles. Your King, and the Kaiser Wilhelm, and Leopold of Belgium? They plan to kill Kaiser Wilhelm."

I stopped scribbling and looked up. She met my stare directly, without blinking.

"Do they, now?" I kept my voice neutral. Even if her story was true, there were plenty of blowhards who blethered about revolution to their friends, in Russian, German, French and English, without ever getting off their backsides.

"These friends of the man called Iosif," I said, "do you know their names?"

"One is called Dimitri. The other one, the tall one, he is called Jean. But two nights past, they called Iosif something else, something strange. Dimitri called him Akushku." I frowned. Many anarchists, especially those with criminal records, used aliases to confuse the police. This sounded more like a code name. "It means, 'man who helps babies to be born.'"

"Thank you," I said, making a note. The term had an ominous ring to it.

"I think Iosif is not his real name," she went on. "I think he is not Romanian. I think he speaks English already. And I think he does not mean to marry me. And when I tell him this . . ." Her hand brushed the bruised orbit of her eye.

"He used me," she went on. Her voice shook, but there were no tears. This was anger—anger at her own naivety, and her lover's brutality. "He needed a place to stay where no one asks questions. And when he and his friends have finished their business, he will leave England. And leave me."

I kept an open door to informants precisely because it saved so much wasted effort. Over the decades I had learned to tell within a minute when I was being spun a yarn by some "concerned citizen" hoping to scrounge a few sovereigns, or some fantasist convinced their Jewish tailor was murdering his clients with poisoned needles. Minetti struck me as utterly sincere; with every calm, measured word she spoke, what had started as a vague sense of foreboding on my part was hardening into an iron fist of dread clenched around my gullet.

"This man," I said. "Iosif, the one his friends called Akushku. Can you describe him for me?"

"Tall. As tall as you. Not quite thirty years old. Blue eyes, fair hair. Strong. And his left hand—it has no, no . . . ring finger. From an accident as a boy, he said."

Mentally I scanned all the portraits-parlés—detailed written descriptions—of anarchists we had on file. None of them matched these details. Was this an elaborate fiction, after all?

"What about his friends? Can you describe them?"

"Jean, he is tall, but very thin, very pale, with bad teeth, black hair, but nearly bald. Dimitri, he is small. Small like me. Dark hair, dark skin, dark eyes, with, what do you say, a squint? I think he is from Bulgaria. He plays with knife, all the time—a hunter's knife."

The iron fist tightened its grip. *I knew those men,* I thought: the knifeman was a Bulgarian called Averbukh, his colleague the Serbian Bozidar. Two murderous thugs who sailed under an anarchist flag of convenience and were currently wanted by every police force in Europe. Each of them was vicious enough in his own right; from what sort of man would they be taking orders?

I took a deep breath to compose myself before I spoke again, for my own sake as much as hers. I had expected this, after all, and Special Branch had seen off countless threats like this before. Fast, hard, decisive action would tear this poison plant up by the roots.

"Miss Minetti, before you answer my next question, I want you to think about it very carefully. Does Iosif, or any of these men, suspect you have come to see me?"

"No." She shook her head insistently. "They think I am a stupid girl, infatuated. Iosif does not care where I go or what I do, during the day. At night, he wants me there." She didn't say what for, but it didn't take much imagination.

"And where are they at this moment?"

"Every day they go out, I don't know where. When they come home they make plans. I show you—"

She snapped open her handbag, drew out a scrap of paper with blackened edges and passed it over to me. It was a map of the West End, or rather the remains of a map, rescued from a fire; yet there was enough of it left to make out a line in red crayon heading north from Victoria Station along Park Lane—the proposed route of the funeral. I stared at it, chewing my moustache, and barely heard Miss Minetti's next remark.

"Iosif, Akushku, he writes nothing down. If makes pictures, he burns them, always. This one I saved. If he knew . . ."

He's thorough, this one, I thought. As if he's done this before.

"You will arrest them, yes? Before they hurt anyone."

"We will, I promise you."

"Iosif . . . will you hurt him? Beat him?"

"If it comes to that. And I expect it will. But rest assured, he'll never know it was you who helped us."

"I do not care if he knows," she said, and there was broken ice in her voice. "I want him to know. I want him to feel what it is like to be hurt. To be betrayed. By someone who said they loved you."

"AKUSHKU, YOU SAY?"

"It's a code name, sir. It means 'male midwife.'"

Anderson scowled. I rarely discussed my tip-offs with him, or sought his approval for my plans, but I needed Anderson's signature on a warrant for the action I had in mind.

"This terrorist calls himself a midwife?"

"I suspect it's by way of a black joke. He means to deliver a new world order—a process that will be bloody and painful. Indeed, for men like these, the bloodier the better."

"You suspect? And yet you haven't questioned this man, or even established that he actually exists."

"He exists all right. I visited the young lady's lodgings, this afternoon."

"Ah yes." Anderson nodded with an air of worldly wisdom. "This young lady. Tell me about her." As my old mentor Superintendent Williams used to say, the four essential qualities for a policeman are honesty, sobriety, punctuality and being extremely selective about what you tell your boss.

"She's a former governess, sir," I said. "Now making a living teaching languages. The suspect is a former pupil of hers."

"And did he by any chance become her paramour? And spurn her?"

I sighed inwardly. Prim Presbyterian as he was, Anderson hadn't ascended that greasy pole without some insight into human nature. "Her motive for coming to us, sir, is less important than—"

"There you have it." He sat back in his chair, smirking. "This is the tale of a woman scorned, William."

"She also mentioned two confederates, whose descriptions match those of two known criminals from the Continent."

Anderson waved my protests away. "So send a few detectives to detain these men for questioning."

"Sir, we're talking about violent anarchists who might well be armed—"

"Armed? Did this young woman mention any weapons? Did you see any, when you came calling on her?"

Calling on her? What was he suggesting—that I was some jealous client?

"I would rather go in with too much force than too little. If I'm wrong, the worst we'll suffer is some embarrassment."

"Some embarrassment? Chief Superintendent, half the crowned heads of Europe are arriving in London as we speak. This is a time of introspection, of national mourning—the last thing we need is a massive armed raid on a few foreign troublemakers, especially on such tenuous evidence."

"Sir, with respect—"

"Weren't you supposed to be in attendance upon His Majesty the King?"

"I returned with his permission, to prepare for the funeral."

"You said yourself, DCI Quinn has that well in hand. You have your orders. Send a few stout constables to round up these anarchists—half a dozen if you're worried about it—and return to Osborne House. Thank you."

By way of dismissal he pretended to busy himself anew with his papers while I stood there fuming, resisting the urge to bend and sweep papers, inkwell, blotter and all off his desk. But it was useless to object; Anderson was the sort of man who took the protests of his inferiors as proof of his firm leadership. My faith in Miss Minetti was based on instinct and experience, and it would be fruitless to try to explain that to someone with neither. I would have to slink back to Osborne House, though the King might well wonder why I had returned.

In fact, it occurred to me now, he almost certainly would.

PRINCE ALBERT—His Majesty King Edward, rather; I was still getting used to that—had never liked Osborne House and had usually spent his visits here hunting foxes or blasting pheasants out of the sky; but with the Court in mourning, now was not the time for noisy sports. All the same, horses and men need exercise, and I walked into the stable yard just as Edward, the Kaiser and their retinues were about to go out riding. Steinhauer was among the Imperial company and acknowledged me with a nod that conveyed a shrewd curiosity. By contrast His Majesty was oblivious to my arrival, at that moment lost in conversation with another rider—the younger daughter of the Earl Cadogan, seated sidesaddle facing him. A young lady in fine looks, with russet locks peeping out from under her riding hat, she seemed to be stifling a smile at the King's remarks, her comely face quite pink.

"You want to feel the beast between your thighs," Edward was saying quietly as I approached. "Less call for the whip. Unless you like that sort of thing, do you?"

The man's incorrigible, I thought. I cleared my throat. Edward turned, scowling, but only until he saw who had interrupted him.

"Melville! Back again, old man? Did you forget something?"

I would catch hell from Anderson. But, as my old super used to say, it's easier to get forgiveness than permission.

Back in the tack room, well out of earshot of the Kaiser and his retinue, I outlined the problem to His Majesty. I could hear the horses outside snorting and stamping impatiently and knew the German contingent was in much the same mood.

"This Akushku character, you say he's Romanian?"

"He claims to be, but he's been heard speaking Russian. We don't know enough about him yet to be certain either way. His friends, on the other hand, we know all too well."

"I'm surprised at you, Melville. I thought you were on first-name terms with all these European desperadoes."

"You flatter me, Your Majesty. I'll make this man's acquaintance properly when we have him under lock and key."

But the King did have a point. I had contacts among every anarchist club in London, shared weekly reports with my colleagues on the Continent, read countless radical newspapers—tedious dross though most of them were—and knew nihilist factions and fashions better than most nihilists did. But I had never heard of this Iosif Dalca, this Akushku; he seemed to have come from nowhere, like a character in Greek legend sprung from clay, and that fact alone made me uneasy.

"And you believe this woman?"

"Yes, sir, I do."

I liked her too. As I had gone through her story over and over again, probing for details, Miss Minetti had relaxed a little and gained in confidence; I'd glimpsed in her wit and spirit and even a mischief that reminded me of my first wife, Kate, God rest her soul. But that detail would not have impressed Anderson.

"But your superior Mr. Anderson does not?" said Edward. I made no reply.

Now we had come to the nub of it: the King certainly had the authority to overrule my boss, if he chose to. His mother had drummed into Prince Albert that he was never to abuse the powers of the Crown; but this was King Edward.

"Tell me what you have in mind." The King plucked a twig from his riding-jacket and tossed it into the fire.

"To put together a squad of Special Branch officers and local constables. To raid the anarchists' hideout, tonight, in force."

"And take them alive?"

"That would be my preference, but . . ." I shrugged.

Edward stared into the blazing logs in the hearth. I'd hoped for a simple nod, but sensed I was not going to get one.

"It is vital," said the King at last, "that not a word of this affair should come to the ears of the Kaiser."

"I'll do what I can," I conceded. "But with an operation on this scale . . ."

"My nephew is the most courageous of men," Edward continued, "but he considers himself divinely appointed to rule Germany, and for the sake of his nation he will not take any unnecessary risks."

I wasn't planning to ask him along, I nearly said. But I held my tongue. Gone, it seemed, was the easy-going Prince who chafed at ceremony; in his place was a king—cautious, closed and circumspect. I wasn't sure if I approved of the transformation.

"If the Kaiser were to learn that an attempt had been planned on his life, here in England," the King continued, "he might feel unable to attend the funeral. And that would be . . . damnably awkward." That was understating it. For the Kaiser to miss the late Queen's funeral would be a diplomatic disaster, a public humiliation for the royal houses of Britain and Germany both.

But then the public assassination of the Kaiser was hardly a viable alternative.

"When we apprehend these men, Your Majesty, we will eliminate the threat," I said.

"The immediate threat, perhaps. If word gets out that it was even attempted . . ." I waited patiently to hear Edward's proposal for an alternative course of action, praying inwardly that he actually had one. "This man Steinhauer," said the King. "The Kaiser's bodyguard. What do you make of him?"

"I'm sure he's a very capable young man," I said, wondering where this was going. "He would not have reached such a position otherwise."

"Discreet, do you think?"

"His first duty will always be to his Emperor," I replied, carefully.

"Hm. I'm sure you don't tell me the half of what you get up to, Melville."

"His Majesty always knows as much as he needs to."

"Well, the Kaiser does not need to know about this. I want you and Steinhauer to handle this matter yourselves, with the utmost discretion."

I was momentarily lost for words. True, with just Steinhauer I could move quickly, with the element of surprise on my side, but I would much rather have had the element of a dozen armed and experienced men on my side. Noticing my reluctance, the King smiled blithely. "Come on, old man, you're the equal of twenty anarchists. Young Steinhauer can go along to hold your coat."

"Your Majesty." I nodded. How could I argue? I had asked for new orders and received them, and now I had to damned well carry them out. On the bright side, if I failed, I would probably not be around to face the music.

As we emerged into the courtyard where the Kaiser's party waited, in their heavy coats and spurred riding boots, the jewelled knot of courtiers surrounding the Emperor unravelled. Steinhauer had already dismounted, sensing intrigue in the air and hoping to sniff out its nature. *You'll know soon enough, lad,* I thought. Edward, as relaxed as if he'd been discussing a grouse drive with his ghillie, beamed as he approached his nephew and launched into an anecdote. While all there focused on him I drew Steinhauer aside.

"Something has come up in London, Herr Steinhauer, and the King has asked that you and I deal with it ourselves. Could you spare me twenty-four hours?"

"I am sure that can be arranged," said Steinhauer without hesitation.

"I must warn you, our mission may be dangerous."

The young German merely grinned. "If I stay here, Herr Melville, I am in danger of dying of boredom."

5

WE HAD BARELY ENTERED our compartment before the stationmaster's whistle blew loud and shrill, and the London train jolted into movement. Steinhauer stowed his suitcase in the luggage net overhead while I reached for the window blind, scanning the platform quickly before I drew it down. It was more out of habit than concern: I didn't expect any dubious characters to be observing us, and I saw none. As I took my seat, Steinhauer produced from inside his coat a flat silver case and opened it to reveal a row of fine, plump cigars. He offered the case to me, but I shook my head.

"You're sure?" asked Steinhauer. "Cuban Imperadores. The very finest. Not easy to obtain."

"Perhaps this evening, after dinner."

He snapped the case shut and tucked it away again. "I shall wait until then. A fine cigar is best enjoyed in good company."

"You sound like a connoisseur."

"I used to sell cigars, when I lived in Chicago."

"And how did you rise from Chicago tobacconist to bodyguard to His Imperial Majesty? If you'll forgive me being so forward."

"Please. I was in my store one day, behind the counter, when two Pinkerton detectives came in and asked if they could use my premises for surveillance. I was intrigued and asked about their line of business. Very soon I realised it was not my destiny to sell cigars. I returned to Germany and joined the Imperial Navy. From there"—he shrugged—"it was largely a matter of luck."

"And do the skills of a cigar seller lend themselves to intelligence?"

"It sounds unlikely, I know, but you were once a baker, were you not?"

"You've done your homework, Herr Steinhauer." I wasn't surprised he knew that detail; the profiles in British newspapers that insisted I was "Europe's most feared policeman" seldom failed to mention my humble origins, in tones of wonderment I always found vaguely irritating.

"I have made a study of your career, Herr Melville," said Steinhauer. "And—forgive me if I sound obsequious—I feel privileged to be accompanying you."

"Hm. I hope you'll feel the same way tomorrow."

"I presume we are not going to London to take in the sights?"

"Sadly, no. And since we're going to be working together, perhaps we should drop the formalities. My colleagues generally call me William."

"My colleagues in the Imperial Court never call me Gustav. But I should be honoured if you did."

"Well, Gustav, our business concerns three visitors from the Continent. And they're not here to take in the sights either. Their leader calls himself Akushku." Steinhauer frowned, searching his memory and seemingly drawing a blank.

"Should I have heard of this man?"

"Probably not. I hadn't. He's currently lying low in the East End of London with two friends. We believe them to be the Serbian nihilist Bozidar and a Bulgarian called Averbukh. Have you heard of them?"

"I have. And this sort of sport I am used to. But why do you need me, William? Is Scotland Yard so short of men?"

"My informant says they plan to attack the royal funeral," I said. "And their target is your Emperor, Wilhelm."

Steinhauer's impertinent grin froze on his face as he saw how he had been railroaded. "Now I understand why you did not brief me properly before we boarded this train. I should have reported this to my master, immediately."

"His Majesty King Edward has asked that you and I handle this matter ourselves, as discreetly as possible. If your master needs to know, perhaps you can tell him when the job is done."

"If my master needs to know?"

"The thing about being a royal bodyguard, Gustav—the job is to protect not just the royal person, but his or her peace of mind. If I deal with a threat, without His Majesty ever even learning there was one, well—that's when I have done my job properly." Which was all true enough, though I'd only thought up that argument as we'd arrived at the station.

"And yet I notice you sought orders from your King," objected Steinhauer. But he seemed as much amused as indignant, as if I had hoodwinked him into an evening's folk-dancing. "And now you want me to help you to arrest these men, and to keep the operation secret? What if your press should hear of it?"

"Let me worry about that."

"That is most obliging of you, William, but your Emperor will not have you shot for keeping him in the dark. How will you stop the newspapers reporting? I thought there was no censorship of the press here."

"There isn't. But I doubt there will be any arrests to report. Akushku and his friends are likely to be armed, and they won't come quietly."

"Better and better. I have brought no weapons, apart from my natural charm."

"I'll find you something," I said. "And I don't want to sound too pessimistic, but have you made a will?"

"If you don't want to sound pessimistic, William, you need to try harder."

I laughed. "It's a precaution, is all. I have pen and paper here," I said, unbuckling my Gladstone. "And maybe a letter to your loved ones as well. We won't be in Paddington for another hour and a half."

. . .

BY THE TIME I showed Steinhauer into the offices of Special Branch it was nearly eight, and the place was almost deserted. I much preferred it that way; office hours brought a thousand pointless interruptions and a million interminable meetings, the purpose of which ever eluded me. Patrick Quinn handled most of that nonsense, thank God, and let me get on with the real business of confounding the Queen's enemies and keeping her peace. No, damn it, the King's enemies and his peace.

"None of these offices have names, or even numbers," remarked Steinhauer.

"Ah sure, we'll get round to it one of these days," I replied. But we wouldn't, as long as I was in charge. Those who needed to know their way around the Special Branch offices already did.

The door to my own office was as anonymous as all the others; unlocking it I let Gustav precede me. I noticed him quickly and covertly scan the room, but there was little to see, apart from the row of speaking-tubes and a pair of pistols mounted on a display on the mantelpiece. It was as poky as every other office on that floor, and my small desk bore only a blotter and two trays for correspondence, currently empty. I detest those knick-knacks and gewgaws that clutter some men's workplaces; I might work long hours, but I don't need photographs to remind me what my family looks like. Unlocking the third drawer down on the left I drew out a cloth bundle and passed it over to Steinhauer. When he unwrapped it, his eyes lit up in delight.

"A Colt! Excellent." Deftly he flicked the revolver open, checked it was clean, oiled and unloaded, snapped it shut again, spun the chamber and tested the action of the hammer and trigger.

"I thought you might appreciate that, after your years in America." From the same drawer I dug out a box of bullets and slid it across the desk. "And you might need a few of these."

While Steinhauer loaded the Colt and slipped extra shells into his pockets, I crossed to the hat-stand where several black scarves hung.

"Here you go, Gustav."

"I am warm enough, thank you." He slid the revolver too into the pocket of his coat.

"It's not to stop you catching a chill—it's to stop you catching a bullet. We need to cover up that shirtfront of yours." Steinhauer looked down at the spotless white triangle on his chest where starched linen met waistcoat. Was he not aware of what a splendid target it would make on a dark night like this? When he saw what I meant, he snatched the scarf from my hand.

"Very good," I said as he tucked the ends under his jacket. "And mind you don't fire the Colt from inside your pocket. The hammer—"

"Might catch on the lining. Please, William, this is not my first safari."

"Let's hope we bag some game." I tugged my pocket watch from my fob and looked at it. "But our quarry won't be at home for a while yet. What do you say to some dinner?"

"ANOTHER BOTTLE of the '98, sir? Or a glass of port?"

"Not for me. Gustav?"

"Thank you, no."

I drew deeply on the cigar Steinhauer had just lit for me and watched him light up his own, working away with a long match. He had declined the sommelier's offer of a spirit lamp—it would be sacrilege, the young German insisted, to taint such fine tobacco. As a purely amateur smoker I knew little about cigars, but I knew this one was exceptional, just as Steinhauer had advertised. The two of us sat back in a cloud of perfumed smoke savouring the moment as the silent waiters cleared our empty plates. Neither of us spoke until they'd moved off; Gustav seemed to know as well as I that waiters are a fine source of intelligence, gleaned from well-lubricated diners who ignore their existence.

"The last time I had a cigar this good," I said, "it was a J.C. Newman from Chicago."

"They do make excellent cigars," said Steinhauer. I waited for him to set me straight—Newman cigars came from Cleveland—but he did not. Interesting, I thought. Any cigar salesman worth his salt would have known that; his background story needed work. Or perhaps he was just being polite in not correcting me. I decided to have some fun probing the limits of his politeness.

"Tell me, Gustav, is the Kaiser a sympathetic employer?"

"I would say he is a model employer." Steinhauer beamed.

"An odd declaration, for a man so recently concerned his boss might have him executed."

"He is quick to blame when things go wrong, yes. But he is also quick to praise when things go right."

"So, if you get shot this evening, will he put up a statue in your honour?"

"If I get shot this evening, I shall neither know nor care. I see you are still trying to give me the creeps, William."

I laughed. "Apologies, Gustav. I find a little gallows humour can help to ease the tension."

"You don't seem tense, Chief Superintendent. In fact you seem remarkably composed."

"Sure what good did worrying ever do? Anyway, I see you cleaned your plate."

Steinhauer shrugged.

"I take it," I went on, "you didn't get to be His Imperial Majesty's bodyguard just by laughing at his jokes?"

"On the contrary, I have found a sense of humour is essential."

It was an interestingly subversive remark, but at that moment another waiter arrived to bring us an ashtray and brush down the tablecloth, and Steinhauer immediately clammed up.

"How so?" I pressed when we were once again out of anyone's earshot.

"His Imperial Majesty has all the qualities one desires in a ruler. He is the sun, and the rest of us merely reflect his glory. Certain gentlemen of his Court, however, believe they are stars in their own right. I think you, of all people, know what I mean, William."

"Human nature is the same the world over," I replied noncommittally. I wasn't about to step into the same snare I'd set for him. "Tell me about this lieutenant—Rolf, was it? How did you entice him back to Germany? When so many before you had failed?"

Steinhauer was silent a moment and tapped his cigar ash into the deep cut-glass ashtray, probably calculating how accurate to make his reply. I sensed that for all his discipline and discretion he loved a yarn, and that he was keen to make a good impression on a famous, if aging, policeman. In fact I had chosen a fine strong wine at dinner in the hope that it would encourage just such a performance, but even though Steinhauer had matched me glass for glass, so far he seemed to have said just as much as he meant to, and no more.

"We knew Rolf had found work in Antwerp, as an engineer," he said at last. "I contrived an encounter and befriended him. I took my time—it's a handsome city, and I was on expenses. I told him I too was German, but that I had been living in America to avoid military service. I had returned to Europe to sell trams."

"Trams? Why trams?"

"So I would not have to carry a case full of samples." Steinhauer grinned. "Anyhow, over the next week or so, my beloved Uncle Otto happened to come up in conversation."

"Ah yes, Uncle Otto," I said. "I daresay I know the man. Wealthy? Old?"

"Not merely wealthy and old. Wealthy, old and a widower, with two very fetching daughters. And as I confessed to Rolf, these cousins of mine had been brought up without the chastening influence of a mother and, as a result, were, well . . . rather too free with their affections."

"But wasn't it women and money that got this fellow Rolf into trouble in the first place?"

"This leopard had not changed its spots. It so happened my Uncle Otto lived in Neuss." I looked blank. "A small town near Düsseldorf, just over the border," Steinhauer explained. In fact I knew the place quite well. "And one morning, while I was having breakfast with the Lieutenant, I received a letter from Otto—beautifully composed, if I say so myself—insisting that I visit, and including a generous contribution towards the cost of my travel. Which I made sure Ernst noticed. And to cut a long story short, he said we should go."

"Ernst?"

It was almost imperceptible, but Steinhauer hesitated. "That was his name. Lieutenant Ernst Rolf."

I didn't let him dwell on his slip. "And of course you refused," I said.

"Point-blank. I told him I could not return to Germany—I would be conscripted. It took him two days to persuade me. Even on the train he kept reassuring me, insisting all would be well, and no one could possibly know about our visit." There it was again; his face had clouded, just for an instant. It looked very much as if Gustav been genuinely fond of this man. But he had delivered him to his death all the same. Admirably cold-blooded, young Steinhauer, I noted; not as boyish as he looked.

"At the first stop over the border"—Steinhauer noticed his neglected cigar had gone out—"I told him to wait on the platform, while I went to find Uncle Otto. I returned with two porters and placed him under arrest." He struck another match.

"How did he take it?" There was a pause while Steinhauer relit his cigar, and seemed to collect himself.

"Lieutenant Rolf swore an oath to our country and our Emperor. He drank too much, he whored and gambled his money away, and then he tried to save his own neck with treachery. He was a fool, yes, but he understood very well the risks he was taking." Steinhauer drew deep and blew out a long plume of blue smoke. He hadn't answered my question, I noticed. I could imagine this man Rolf, all bravado gone, hauled from the carriage with his knees buckling, pleading for mercy from a man he had thought was his friend. Perhaps Gustav found the memory too painful to recount.

Give it time, my lad, I thought. *You'll stop seeing their faces in your dreams.*

"I take it he was executed?" I said.

"By firing squad," said Steinhauer.

"Hm."

"Better that than the French way—a living death on Devil's Island."

"A soldier's death, at least," I said, glancing at the clock. It showed a quarter to midnight.

"Talking of which," said Steinhauer.

I grinned, and caught our waiter's eye.

6

I SLAMMED THE CAB DOOR SHUT as the driver wheeled the cab round in a tight U-turn, heading east along the Strand, still thronged with ladies and gents in silks and furs weaving their way through drunks and beggars and chestnut sellers. The glamour and clamour of the West End faded behind us as we entered the City, and the theatres and music-halls gave way to brightly lit pubs where the windows rattled with music and drunken revelry.

In the dimness of the cab Steinhauer rearranged his borrowed black scarf to cover his white shirt while I busied myself loading my old Webley Bulldog. Eventually our cab wheeled right and headed south across London Bridge, over the black churning Thames dense with smoking barges, and dived into a rabbit-warren of slums where tattered grey washing hung limply from lines across the street. The clop of our horse's hooves and the clatter of the cab's wheels seemed muffled by the sulphurous smoke that hung in a pall between the grimy houses. Before long we turned again, left this time, into a narrow cobbled avenue. I rapped sharply on the roof and the cab quickly came to halt.

"Two minutes, Gustav."

I stepped down onto the black beaten earth of the street and glanced around. Not a soul to be seen, apart from another cab, a little farther along. Its horse stamped and shook its mane while the driver huddled in his seat under a rug, waiting for a fare. I was the fare, as it happened. I'd often employed Jack Forte and his cab for jobs like this—he was one of my irregulars, discreet, reliable and always up for some shenanigans.

I asked our current cabbie to wait, just in case, then sought out a certain door. No streetlamps here; the only illumination was the feeble glow of paraffin lamps spilling from the dirty uncurtained windows high above. But I knew the house and found it quick enough— the premises of a professional lady who owed me a favour. This was where I'd arranged to meet Miss Minetti, far from the prying eyes of Akushku and his friends. I rapped lightly twice with the rusted iron knocker, as arranged, and the door was opened almost immediately by Miss Minetti herself, dressed and ready to go out, lacking only a hat.

"Mr. Melville. One moment, I am with you."

She stepped back to check her reflection in a mirror hanging in the hallway and picking up a pin fastened a shabby straw hat to her honey-blond hair. I stepped in, closing the door behind me. The bruising around her eye had faded, and now she wore no powder, but just a dab of rouge on her lips.

"Where are you planning to go, Miss Minetti?"

She frowned. "I am coming with you."

"You are not. All I need is your key to get into the house. Stay here until I send for you."

"Where are your men? Are they there now?"

"It's just the two of us."

"Two of you? Against Iosif and his friends?" She looked alarmed, as well she might.

"We'll have surprise on our side. Leave this to us."

"But . . ." The girl seemed to wilt in disappointment. Had she been looking forward to seeing her deceiver in handcuffs? Roughed up a little, perhaps? "I can help you," she said. "I can ask Iosif to come out and talk to me, away from his friends. You will wait outside, and take him, make no noise. Then when you go back in . . ."

"His friends will think we're him." I was silent a moment. It was not a bad plan, especially for one dreamed up on the spur of the moment. "No, it'd be too dangerous."

"It is less dangerous, surely!"

"I mean dangerous for you. If these friends of his are armed, as you said, and if they suspect you've informed on them—"

"They suspect nothing. They think I am a silly little girl."

"I can't permit it, Miss Minetti. You'd be risking your life."

"But you will be outside the door, Mr. Melville. I trust you. You will be there if I need you."

I hesitated, because it was a good ruse, and with only Steinhauer and myself involved we needed every advantage we could get. Miss Minetti had already shown plenty of courage, and even now she looked calm and composed, as if we were planning a picnic on Clapham Common rather than an armed ambush. Sometimes guile and nerve can get you further than mere muscle, and this young woman seemed to have plenty of both.

"Hang it," I said. "Yes. We'll do it the way you suggest."

Minetti laughed and clapped her gloved hands in excitement. Glancing in the mirror, she made some final adjustments to her hat, then turned back to me. "How do I look?"

She knew very well how she looked. But even so I sensed she needed reassurance.

"You look very fetching, Miss Minetti. We need to move."

Steinhauer was in the street, stamping his feet to keep warm. He had climbed down from the cab to smoke a small cigar, but seeing us emerge from the house he tossed the cigar-butt aside and ground it into the damp earth and bowed to Minetti, who nodded and smiled. I made no introductions but led her on down the street towards Forte's waiting cab, where I helped her aboard.

"Don't alight right by your front door," I said. "Get out one street early and walk the rest of the way. My colleague and I will be right behind you. Don't worry about losing us, and don't look back."

"I understand," said the girl, and settled calmly into her seat.

"You heard that, Jack?" I asked the driver. He nodded once. That was why I liked Forte; unlike most London cabbies he listened and kept his mouth shut. "Good," I said. "Off you go." Forte cracked his whip and the cab headed east. I trotted back to our own cab.

"Follow him, but keep your distance," I told our driver.

"Follow him? Right you are, guv'nor," he replied. Steinhauer scrambled aboard behind me, and the hackney moved off before we had even shut the door.

"How far from here?" asked Steinhauer.

"Whitechapel. Ten minutes or so."

North, we headed again, back across the Thames by way of Tower Bridge. Then east, and soon the massive elegant buildings around St. Paul's gave way to yet more grimy slums and the rutted streets of Whitechapel. Here the shadows teemed with life; I caught the flare of a match lighting up a huddle of beggars sharing a clay pipe, and farther on two shapes in a dark doorway that resolved themselves as we passed—a young woman with her hair cropped short, lifting her skirts for a soldier.

After a few minutes our cab slowed and stopped at the kerb.

"The other cab, sir, he's pulled up," our driver called down to us, but quietly, thank God. Steinhauer descended after me, and I flicked a sovereign to the driver. He caught it neatly, stared at it in disbelief and could not resist biting it, even while I watched. Then he grinned, with blackened teeth.

"Want me to wait, guv'nor?" He kept his voice down. "For this much I'll hang about all night."

"We'll manage, thanks. Good evening."

Angela Minetti was standing fifty feet ahead of us, fumbling in her handbag as if searching for the fare; she must have been watching us from the corner of her eye, for as soon as our cab moved away she turned and set off in the direction of her apartment without a backwards glance. Steinhauer fell into step beside me as we followed her along the deserted street of tall tenements, all veiled in a thin bitter mist.

"Is this the place?"

"Not quite. But two cabs pulling up right outside her home, a few minutes apart . . ."

"Would be as good as a fanfare."

"Indeed."

The smoke of ten thousand coal fires swirled in Minetti's wake as she strode up the street, and at one point even threatened to swallow her up, but I saw her turn left, and we quickened our step to close the distance. She kept up a brisk pace, without one look over her shoulder. Presently she slowed, and paused at the foot of a flight of steps leading up to a tall decaying town house. I knew the place from the reconnaissance trip I'd made shortly after Minetti had first presented herself at my office. I'd wanted to get the lay of the land before we raided the place in force; but of course Anderson had nobbled that plan.

Silently I caught Steinhauer's sleeve and drew him into the shadows on our left. The girl was fishing in her handbag again, and I saw the glint of a latchkey as she climbed the steps to the front door. Like all these houses, the place had been grand once, the home of some wealthy merchant; now it was rented out to scores of miserably poor tenants, sometimes with three generations crammed into one room.

As Minetti entered we followed and saw that she had closed the front door behind her, but not all the way. Laying a hand on Steinhauer's arm, I murmured, "Wait here, and cover the front door. Anyone comes out, you challenge them, and shoot if you have to. You're on His Majesty's service now."

Gustav did not argue but stood back as I ascended the steps, eased the Webley from my pocket and gently pushed the door. It swung wide, barely creaking, to reveal nothing but darkness. Stepping in, I pushed it shut behind me, again not fully, and edged forwards, listening to voices drift downstairs and letting my eyes become accustomed to the dark. The voices were coming from the first floor at the rear of the building—Minetti's apartment.

The hallway I stood in was a freezing black quagmire, but the dark was lifted a little by the light leaking in from the street. Faint as it was, it would be enough to silhouette me if anyone chose to look down from the first-floor landing. I crept forwards, towards the foot of the broad wooden staircase I had climbed just the day before, moving slowly, testing each floorboard before I placed my full weight on it in case a creak betrayed me. My thumb found the safety catch of my gun and flicked it on, and I turned the pistol in my hand to hold it by the barrel. As soon as Akushku reached the foot of the stairs, I would bludgeon him. A gunshot would certainly alert his accomplices.

If you were to ask me how long I stood there, I would say five minutes, or possibly five hours. At such moments one loses all track of time, focusing only on staying alert and ready for any eventuality, every nerve stretched taut, every sense extended. That was Minetti's voice, rising and falling; she had been pleading with her lover, but now by the sound of it she was starting to hector him. I cursed, silently— this was no good; if her charms were not enough to persuade him downstairs, nagging would not change his mind.

But why was he so reluctant to come out?

Abruptly the door on the first floor burst open and light spilled down into the hallway. I slipped back into the shadows, but the door shut again almost immediately, and I heard Minetti's footsteps tapping petulantly down the stairs. At the foot of the staircase she paused and whispered into the gloom, "He will not come down. He says whatever I have to tell him, I must say in front of his friends."

I weighed up my options. Was Akushku suspicious, or merely tired of obliging the girl? "Go outside," I whispered. "And ask my friend to come in."

She did not look in my direction but carried on to the front door while I kept my eyes fixed on the landing above. My thumb found the safety catch on my pistol again, and flicked it off. I heard the rustle of Angela's dress as she re-entered, and I glanced back quickly to see her leading Steinhauer by the hand through the gloom.

"Wait outside," I told her. "We'll do this my way."

"No, I know what to say to him now. This time he comes down, you will see." Before I could stop her, she was clattering up the stairs again, hitching her dress with her gloved fists. I cursed under my breath. What was it that Prussian general said? No plan of attack survives contact with the enemy. Steinhauer and I would have to take these men head-on, and the time to do it was while Minetti was distracting them. She opened the door to her apartment and went inside.

Then I heard footsteps, directly overhead, quickly pacing from the front of the building towards the back. Had someone been looking out the front window?

Abruptly the door at the top of the stairs was wrenched open again, and Minetti reappeared, her face pale and pinched with fear, her mouth a tight line. She had barely crossed the threshold when a pistol shot rang out, and she fell with a yelp of pain. A tall muscular figure stepped forwards to stand over her, raised a pistol and started shooting down the stairs.

As one Steinhauer and I raised our revolvers and returned fire. Fragments of plaster hit my face, blasted from the wall next to my right ear, but I kept shooting, and the hallway filled with thunder and gun smoke and the smell of cordite and dust. I felt my hat knocked back on my head and I saw the woodwork of the doorway where the anarchist stood shatter and splinter, but the man himself had the devil's own luck—he seemed untouched. Then his gun clicked on an empty chamber, and he calmly stooped down, grabbed the girl, dragged her inside and slammed the door shut again, even as Steinhauer and I raced up the stairs two at a time. I was first to the landing and heard on the far side of the door the rattle of a heavy bolt being shot home and the clink of a chain. I fired four shots into the wood and was rewarded with a man's yell of pain and a stream of Slavic curses.

I flattened myself against the wall to the left, Steinhauer to the right, moments before six shots from within smashed holes through the door while Steinhauer and I reloaded, scattering our spent shells on the floor. Now we could hear chaos in the room beyond—voices raised in panic and pain, babbling in Russian and German, scuffling feet, tumbling furniture. I caught Steinhauer's eye; he nodded and raised his Colt in readiness.

I stepped out, turned to the door and kicked it with all my strength, aiming for where I'd heard the bolt slammed home. Even splintered by gunfire the old door was solid, but the frame was flimsy, and on the second kick the door burst inwards. Steinhauer dashed in ahead of me, gun lowered; he jumped clean over two bodies prone on the floor—Angela Minetti and one of Akushku's accomplices—but the room was otherwise empty. I glanced down; the wounded man was Bozidar, clutching his bloody arm and groaning—the bones looked to have been shattered by my bullets. He had no weapon that I could see and was in too much pain anyway to resist. Angela was alive, but bleeding from her shoulder. All this I took in with a glance as Steinhauer swept the room, cursing in consternation.

"The window!" I said. I got to it first, and heaved it open in time to hear someone drop into the pitch-black alley below. The two remaining terrorists had clambered down using a drainpipe for support—an escape route they had clearly planned. I fired blindly into the murk only to hear my shots ring off stone, and the scuffle of fleeing footsteps.

"The mews entrance is back the way we came," I told Steinhauer. "Go, quickly—I'll be right behind you—"

Steinhauer hurried out the door by which we had entered and I heard him race down the stairs while I stooped to see to Angela Minetti. She was trying to sit up, her hair pasted to her temples and dark with sweat, her lovely face twisted in pain. I folded my handkerchief and held it to her shoulder where blood was blotching the fabric of her dress. "Lie still, lie still," I told her. "It looks like the bullet's gone through." She nodded, and pulling the handkerchief from my hand pressed it to her shoulder. "Go," she gasped, close to fainting. "Stop Iosif."

I needed no second bidding. Grabbing my handcuffs from my pocket I wrenched Bozidar's arms behind his back, heedless of his yells of pain, ratcheted the cuffs tight and dashed out the door after Steinhauer.

As I emerged onto the street, I could see our shootout had woken up most of the neighbourhood. Windows were being drawn up on every side, from which sleepy curious faces were emerging. Bad enough our quarry had fled our grasp, but now we had an audience. But by the look on Steinhauer's face as he ran back from the direction of the mews entrance, that was the least of our problems.

"They hailed a cab," he was saying. "Heading east. I just missed them—"

At that moment, as if summoned by wishful thinking, Forte's cab appeared. I had arranged that he should follow us here ten minutes after we left him. His hackney had barely halted before I wrenched open the door and Steinhauer and I scrambled aboard.

"East," I told Forte. "And hurry—we're after another cab."

The lurch of the hackney as Forte cracked the whip threw me back into my seat, almost on top of Steinhauer.

"How is the girl?"

"She'll live. It's these two I'm worried about."

"We have one man. He will lead us to the others, if it comes to that."

"Inspector!" Forte called down. I wrenched the window open and stuck my head out.

Half a street ahead of us was another cab, racing along.

"That's the one!" called out Steinhauer, from the other window. "I am sure of it!" I sat back in my seat, hurriedly dug more bullets from my pocket and reloaded. Steinhauer followed suit.

"He's slowing down!" called Forte. I stuck my head out the window again just in time to see a short dark man, bareheaded and without a jacket, swing from the open door of the cab ahead and hit the ground running. He almost fell, but finding his feet raced off down an alley to the left. The cab ahead picked up speed again and rattled on, its door swinging back and forth before slamming shut. "That's the Bulgarian, Averbukh," I snapped to Steinhauer. "You stay with Akushku—I'll take this one." Heaving our own cab door open, I leapt out without even a warning to Forte. I don't know how I kept my footing as I landed, except that I knew I must. Reaching the neck of the alley, I glimpsed my quarry stop at the far end. Before he disappeared off to the right, I raced after him, my heart thumping in my chest and my breath roaring in my ears. He was heading towards the warehouses that served the East India Docks, and for the first time in this fiasco I felt a glimmer of optimism. The docks were securely fenced, the warehouses were patrolled by night watchmen, and once upon a time this had been my beat. I knew it better than my own face.

But tonight there were no coppers or even civilians around that I could call to my aid; the alleyways were deserted and every shop shuttered and dark. I paused, and over the rumble of a passing goods train heard the crack of hobnails on cobblestones off to my left. Drawing my revolver again, I peered around the next corner. The street was formed by two warehouses that faced each other, lined with blank brick recesses in the shape of windows, with a deep double doorway every fifty feet or so, and at the far end a tall blank brick wall ran the width of the street. I knew the place: Penny Street, a dead end with only one way out—back past me.

Halfway down, high above the cobblestones, a single large gaslight gleamed, hissing. Above each warehouse door jutted a loading girder, and their long shadows probed like grubby fingers into the alley below. I calmed my breathing, feeling a trickle of sweat run down my back, and waited, listening and watching.

There—a glimpse of pale linen. Averbukh had been concealing himself in the farthest doorway on the right and had leaned forwards, hoping to see if I was still following. I had him.

"Come out." I paced slowly down the alley, my gun raised and ready. No answer.

"*Venez, immédiatement, ou je tire,*" I called. And now the vague pale figure I had glimpsed in the doorway stirred again and took shape. It was indeed Averbukh, matching precisely the description I had on file, courtesy of my contacts in the Sûreté: short, slight, in his late twenties, with curly black hair, swarthy skin, heavy eyebrows and a squint that could make it hard to tell which way he was looking. At this moment it was clear enough he was looking at me as he stepped out from his hiding place and raised his empty hands wide from his sides, almost level with his shoulders, as if to offer me a hug.

"Keep those hands where I can see them," I said. "And hold still."

"What will you do? Will you shoot me, and tell everyone I was trying to escape?" His accent was thick, but his English was excellent, and he was smiling wolfishly.

"If I shoot you, friend, I won't have to tell anyone anything." I reached inside my coat for the specially tailored pocket that held my second set of handcuffs. The Bulgarian raised his hands until they almost touched behind his head. "I told you to hold still," I said. "Turn around, and kneel down."

Averbukh shrugged. "I want no trouble," he said, almost affably.

"I know what you want," I said, pacing slowly towards him. "And if you try it, I'll shoot. Turn around."

He grinned again, with a look of injured innocence, and neither turned nor knelt, but brought his hands together behind his neck. I saw the muscles of his shoulders tense, and I pulled the trigger—once, twice, in quick succession. By now it was less than fifteen feet from the muzzle of my gun to Averbukh's chest, and the impact of my shots hurled him flying back onto the cobblestones. I watched him fall, keeping my finger on the trigger, ready to fire a third time, but there was no need. The anarchist's arms were flung wide again, and his left leg was kinking slowly, in a death reflex.

I went down on one knee beside him, grasped his right arm and lifted his body up a little. There it was—the throwing knife with its long gleaming blade, half-drawn from the scabbard he had been wearing between his shoulder blades. A party trick of his, one that had taken the life of a French policeman. That too I had read about in the Sûreté files.

From the entrance to the alley I heard more racing footsteps and stood, my gun at the ready—but it was Steinhauer, panting, with a sheen of sweat on his cheeks.

"William! I heard the shots—are you all right?"

"I am. What about Akushku?"

"It was a ruse, a decoy. I am so sorry—"

"What do you mean?"

"We stopped the other cab, but it was empty. He must have jumped before we caught up with it—"

"Sweet Saviour," I said, taking to my heels, back the way we had come, yelling over my shoulder, "he'll have doubled back! For Bozidar, and the girl!"

7

BY THE TIME we returned to Minetti's house a crowd had gathered on her doorstep, jostling and gossiping, exchanging exaggerated versions of events they had not seen. Pushing through them, I climbed the stairs again to the apartment. Other tenants had gathered on the landings above, and questions and appalled whispers in half a dozen languages were drifting down the stairwell—but nobody, it seemed, had approached the shattered door, which still hung open. Entering I found my handcuffs lying discarded on the bed, not broken, but picked; apart from bloodstains on the floor there was no sign of the wounded Bozidar, nor of Angela Minetti.

"Can I ask what you two gentlemen are doing?"

The police sergeant nearly filled the doorway behind us, slapping his palm with his truncheon, red-faced, beefy and spoiling for a fight. He was late to the ball, I thought, but that was hardly his fault. I showed him my warrant card—it was all the explanation I felt inclined to offer—and his attitude immediately changed to one of servile deference and eagerness to impress. At that moment I found it immensely irritating.

"Sorry, sir—Sergeant Launceston, at your disposal."

"Go out and blow your whistle—we need more men here. And talk to the crowd, ask if any of them saw three people fleeing the scene, two male, one female."

"Begging your pardon, sir, I already have. I'm told two men flagged down a cab not five minutes ago. One of them was bleeding. Said they'd been robbed and were off to find a doctor."

"There was no woman with them?"

"No, sir."

"Did anyone hear them give instructions to the driver?" said Steinhauer. Launceston grimaced—it hadn't occurred to him to ask.

"Find out, please," I said. "Oh, and by the way"—the burly sergeant paused on the threshold—"there's a dead man in Penny Street, east of here, near the docks. Pass the word when you get the chance."

"Dead, sir?"

"Shot while resisting arrest. Quick as you like, Officer."

Launceston nodded and headed downstairs, his boots thundering on the wooden treads. What a God-damned disaster, I thought. Why hadn't I gone after Akushku and sent Steinhauer after Averbukh? Because I'd have lost both of them, I told myself. Steinhauer would have fallen to the Bulgarian's knife, and at this moment would be lying dead in Penny Street with his blood soaking the cobblestones. I turned back to survey the room.

It was chilly and damp and cheaply furnished, with a chaise-longue against one wall draped in a patchwork quilt that touched the floor, and a double bed, neatly made up, against the far wall. The fire had gone out, but a few embers still glowed, and some singed fragments of pastel-coloured paper—tickets for the music-hall, by the look of them—lay on the hearth as if they had fallen from the grate. A few decorative touches, like the artificial flowers in a tin jug on the dresser, showed where Angela Minetti had tried to brighten the place. Pasted onto the wall above the bed were slightly less respectable decorations: a collection of photographs, some of famously beautiful actresses, others of less distinguished performers, the latter wearing very little—a display presumably intended to stimulate the appetites of Miss Minetti's callers. Above the head of the bed hung a fan, spread out in a semi-circle, that caught my eye. I had not noticed it on my first visit.

Its large panels of lace in delicate shades of blue matched nothing else in the room, and although I was no expert in fashionable accessories, it looked to me worth more than all the furniture in the place put together. Hadn't the girl mentioned receiving a fan from Akushku as a gift? Reaching up I eased it from its nail for closer inspection.

Then I heard something—a mewl or a whimper, as if from a wounded animal.

"What was that?"

"What?" said Steinhauer, looking about. I heard it again; a faint, muffled groan, from somewhere close to hand—in the very room.

"My God," said Gustav. "The girl, she's still here—"

He rushed to the chaise-longue behind us, knelt down and flipped up the worn patchwork quilt to reveal the hem of a familiar green dress and Angela's pale, perspiring face peeping out. She'd squeezed underneath like a little girl playing at hide-and-go-seek and had almost passed out from pain. I hurried over to help.

"Don't move her," I urged him. "Help me lift up the chaise—"

A FEW MINUTES LATER Minetti was in Forte's cab—he was earning his fee tonight—with a constable to look after her. "I knew he would come back," was all she'd managed to say.

"The nearest infirmary, Jack, and be quick about it," I said. Steinhauer and I watched the cab set off at a brisk rattle and turned back to the scene of our failure. Now it was under control, at least: Launceston had rustled up half a dozen constables who had helped to seal off Minetti's apartment and were taking witness statements from those onlookers who hadn't already gone back to bed.

Gustav sighed. "I am sorry, William. I should not have been so easily duped."

"You were only following my orders." I stared up at the building. "It was I who misjudged this Akushku character. I should have come here with twenty men, and to hell with His Majesty's orders. But thank you for your help tonight, Gustav. You acquitted yourself admirably."

That was no idle flattery; it'd been years since I'd worked with a partner, but in the heat of that battle it had been almost as if he had read my mind.

"I am glad the girl is safe, at least."

"She is. No thanks to me."

"We should take that room of hers to pieces," said Steinhauer. "Lift the floorboards."

"My men will. But I doubt they'll find anything. This Akushku character is scrupulous about burning evidence. And if he's building a bomb, it won't be here, where the girl would have seen him. They'll have a lockup or a shed somewhere . . ."

I noticed Steinhauer was smiling wryly and looking at a spot above my head.

"You need a new hat," he said.

I slipped off my bowler and inspected it; a neat hole had been punched in the crown. The bullet must have parted my hair. I remembered it now—that shot that had knocked my hat back, in the dark hallway, a lifetime ago.

"I have another at home," I said, putting it back on my head. "What about you? Can I lend you a coat?" I nodded at his right sleeve, and looking down Steinhauer saw a ragged hole, just above the elbow.

"Hm," he said. He dug in the hole with a finger, and after a moment dug out a spent, crumpled bullet.

"A ricochet," I said.

"A souvenir." He offered it to me. I took it and threw it away.

"I won't want to remember this night, Gustav," I said. "You should head back to Osborne House." I would have instructed him to keep our misadventures to himself, but I was in no position to give him orders, and I was not going to beg—tonight had been embarrassing enough. But Steinhauer would have none of it.

"I can't leave now, William, with the job only one-third done. I can still be of use to you. I have friends, here in London, who may be of assistance."

"Do you, now?"

"Besides, if I return to the Isle of Wight, His Imperial Majesty is bound to ask where I have been and what I got up to." Steinhauer grinned. "And if I do not return, I won't have to tell him." Reaching into his pocket he drew out the Colt and offered it to me, grip first.

"Keep it," I said. "If you're going to help out, you might well have need of it."

8

O N THOSE RARE OCCASIONS when I've had to reprimand a member of my team, I find a certain coolness and an air of deep disappointment are all that's needed to make my point. I've heard of bosses who hurl inkpots and rant and rave to the verge of apoplexy, but in my opinion that merely demonstrates impotence and lack of self-control.

Assistant Commissioner Anderson used neither technique, preferring to let me stand before his desk while he scrutinised official papers. This was meant to convey how much more valuable his time was than mine, but it reminded me of a provincial bank manager carpeting a clerk for having an ill-tended moustache. I would have minded less if there had not been a room full of detectives downstairs waiting for a briefing. Eventually Anderson scratched his signature at the bottom of a letter, put it carefully aside, laced his fingers and peered at me over his half-moon glasses.

"Detective Chief Superintendent." My full title? That was a bad start. "When I come into work on a Saturday, I don't appreciate having to spend that time cleaning up after you. I presume you have a good excuse for ignoring my direct instructions regarding these anarchists."

"I have no excuse, sir. His Majesty the King gave me an order and told me to act upon it immediately."

"And how, pray, did His Majesty the King come to hear of it?"

The King has his own sources, I could have said, but it would have been evasive, and I had no intention of squirming or shifting the blame. "He asked me directly, and I told him. He felt that sending me and the Kaiser's man Steinhauer to confront these anarchists would nip the problem in the bud, with the smallest risk of bad publicity."

"That's not exactly how it turned out, is it?"

"No, sir. But I took to heart your concern about newspaper reports. I've let it be known to my contacts in the press that the suspects were three notorious bank robbers. Which is true enough—that was Averbukh's speciality." Anderson seemed momentarily mollified, so I pressed my advantage. "And just as I'd feared, the suspects were armed and violent. If we'd sent in uniforms we might be looking at four dead constables this morning, and that would have been a sight harder to play down." I didn't have to mention that that had been Anderson's idea of a plan; by the way his lip curled in distaste I could see he didn't care to be reminded.

"According to your report, two of these three suspects escaped."

"We killed one, and badly wounded another. There's a chance we've scared them off altogether."

Anderson snorted. "I would hardly depend on that, DCS Melville."

"I don't intend to, sir. Hence my request for eight extra officers from the CID to augment my team."

Anderson dug around for the note that had accompanied my written report and scowled at it, pondering. As if he had any choice in the matter.

"I've taken the liberty of already calling them in," I said.

"Yes. Yet another fait accompli." He drummed his fingers on the desk, weighing up his next words. "This raid you led was an utter failure. And now you're asking me to pour in more resources to prevent it becoming a catastrophe. I'm surprised you're not considering your position."

"My resignation is yours if you want it, sir." I met his gaze and held it. His words stung—the truth often does—but by threatening me he'd overplayed his hand, and now I stood there waiting for him to realise that. Seven days before the Queen's funeral with two violent anarchists on the loose was hardly a good time to fire me, and I was certainly not going to quit. If I succeeded in tracking them down, there'd be no glory—few people would ever hear of it—but such was the nature of my profession. If on the other hand I failed, the whole world would know. In the former case, Anderson could take the credit, with those who mattered, and in the latter, he would need a scapegoat—me.

I could see Anderson working this out, already composing the memorandum that would cover him in either eventuality. The man was as predictable as one of those vending machines you find in railway stations; I'd dropped the coin in the slot and turned the handle, and now at last the postcard popped out.

"That's a matter we must consider at a later date," said Anderson, setting my note down and picking up his pen. "But you would go a long way to redeeming yourself if you tracked down these two villains and arranged for them to meet their Final Judgement at the earliest opportunity."

"Point taken, sir."

Anderson scribbled his signature on the requisition request and held it up, slightly out of my reach, so I had to lean over to take it.

"Then best get on with it, Melville."

USUALLY WHEN MY MEN assembled for a morning briefing there was a certain amount of horseplay and banter. I didn't encourage it, but I didn't disapprove either: a cheerful crew is a willing one. This Saturday, however, was different, and the atmosphere was muted and expectant. A few officers had already been scheduled to come in, but the rest—including my hand-picked "volunteers" from the Criminal Investigation Department—I had summoned by runner, telegram and penny post. That had been enough for recipients to understand the urgency of the matter, and the office gossip had confirmed it. Over my years as head of Special Branch these men had come to see me as all-knowing and nigh-infallible, but I took care not to believe it myself, and there was nothing to be gained by whitewashing the previous night's fiasco.

"Gentlemen"—I paused to let the murmured conversations subside—"as some of you already know, last Thursday I got a tip-off from a member of the public, to the effect that three anarchists from the Continent had set up shop in Whitechapel and were planning to attack the royal funeral, with the intention of assassinating Kaiser Wilhelm of Germany."

The room was so silent now I could hear in the middle distance the mudlarks calling out on the banks of the Thames.

"Last night, with the help of the Kaiser's personal bodyguard, I raided their hideout, in the hope of taking the terrorists by surprise. We shot and killed one, the Bulgarian anarchist Averbukh, and wounded his colleague Bozidar. But their ringleader, a man calling himself Akushku, escaped with Bozidar, and the two of them have gone back into hiding.

"The task ahead of us is to stop these two men. Arrest them if we can, kill them if we have to. Their descriptions are on the board—memorise them. Bozidar some of you know already, but the other—the one who calls himself Akushku—do not underestimate him. From first-hand experience I can tell you he's damned smart and he's damned dangerous. If we don't catch him and Bozidar, they will attack the funeral, and if they succeed—I hardly need to tell you the consequences. Sacrilege would be least of it. Butchery and bloodshed and war."

The room was utterly silent now. It was my habit to pepper my briefing with jokes, to project an air of swagger, of relaxed confidence; not this morning. There was nothing to laugh at.

"All leave for the next fortnight has already been cancelled, but now you'll be working weekends too, and every hour God sent until these two men are caught. Forget about sick leave, I don't care if you're at death's door. I don't care if you're dead. We have seven days, and I want an arrest in two.

"And it goes without saying, but I'll say it anyway: not a word of this to anyone. We will find these men, we will put an end to their scheme, and we'll do it before the Great British public gets even a whiff of it." I nodded to my deputy, Patrick Quinn, a dour, dogged, indispensable Ulsterman. "Inspector Quinn will take over the arrangements for security at the funeral. I will lead the hunt for the two anarchists. Ellis, Baxter—"

I allotted my two oldest hands to help Quinn. The rest I split into teams, each with its own assignment—some combing the streets around Minetti's lodgings, asking questions door-to-door; others checking every infirmary, hospital, clinic and doctor in the East End, in case Akushku had tried to get Bozidar patched up. "Keep your eyes and ears open. Whatever contacts you have among the dissidents and refugees, use them. Bribe them, threaten them, I don't care, but somebody knows these villains and where they've gone to ground.

"Johnson, Connolly—I have a job for you." I produced from my pocket the fan I had taken from Angela Minetti's apartment and held it up for all to see. The lanky, lugubrious Johnson—who always reminded me of Markey, my foul-tempered old schoolmaster in Sneem—elbowed his way to the front of the room, followed closely by Connolly, a stocky, balding Glaswegian. They were two of my best men, with a knack for asking the right questions.

"This was a gift to my informant," I said. "From Akushku." I spread the fan out. Someone at the back whistled. "My thoughts exactly," I said. "Belgian lace, I believe, and these are pearls and topaz."

"That will have cost a few guineas. Easy," said Connolly.

"Genteel sort of gift, for an anarchist," said Johnson.

"So where did he get it?" I asked. "Start with the department stores in the West End. And sharpish, before they close this afternoon."

"Sir," said Johnson, taking the fan from me with a delicate touch. If he was wondering why exactly this fan was so important, he didn't ask, and I couldn't have answered him if he had. Akushku had almost certainly stolen it, so even if we traced the owner it would do us no good. But the fan's presence in Angela's shabby apartment felt to me like an anomaly, a loose end, and I wanted it tied off.

I raised my voice again to address the room.

"Next briefing eight o'clock tonight, gentlemen. If anything comes up before that, send a runner here, double quick." This was going to cost the department a fortune in overtime, but I'd let Anderson worry about that. As the room cleared, I stepped down and headed back to my office, Quinn at my elbow with a long list of queries.

"Sir? Word from Dover. That Italian agitator Domenico arrived last night from Paris, and was followed to his sister's house in Isleworth. Do you think there might be a connection?"

"No," I said. "Domenico's a windbag. We needn't worry about him. Anything else?"

"The funeral arrangements—the pressmen are demanding ringside seats, as it were. And separate platforms for the photographers and kinematographers."

"And what?"

"The men who take moving pictures. They say they'll need extra space for their equipment."

"Let me see the list when I get back," I said, entering my office. I plucked my coat and hat from the rack.

GREY WINTER LIGHT seeped through the high windows of Whitechapel Union Infirmary, illuminating the neat rows of iron beds arranged on either side of this long room. Its whitewashed brick walls were bare except for a plain wooden cross high up at one end, big enough for a fresh crucifixion should the need arise. The place was clean, at least, if the eye-watering reek of carbolic was anything to go by. At the far end of the ward two nurses had just entered with a trolley and were moving from bed to bed ladling out bowls of soup. Beside me Angela Minetti sat up, tugging impatiently at the high frilled collar of the worn grey nightdress she had been given. She had regained much of her colour, and her fair hair tumbled loose around her shoulders in a manner so fetching I suspected the ward sister would disapprove. The bentwood chair I had pulled up by her bed groaned under my shifting weight.

"How's the wound?"

Minetti glanced down at her shoulder and blew out her cheeks. "Is nothing," she said. "I have had worse." She glanced at the nurses. One of them was shaking awake a patient who looked too weak to even sit up, scolding her to eat her soup.

"I hate this place," said Angela. "They treat me like a fallen woman."

Well, strictly speaking, I thought. But I said, "Not so long ago it was a workhouse. I suppose old habits die hard. It was the nearest place that could patch you up."

"I want to go home." She looked at me, almost pleading. It was my turn to drop my eyes in embarrassment.

"That might be a tall order," I said. "My officers are in your rooms now, going over the place for evidence." Taking it to pieces, in fact. I forbore to mention that a man claiming to be her landlord had appeared that morning, a seedy character in a greasy frock coat, demanding compensation for the damage and swearing "that Italian trollop" would never be allowed back. I planned to pay him a visit after this interview, to suggest he reconsider his decision.

Angela had turned her face away, and when she spoke her tone lacked its usual assertion. "I do not want strangers searching my possessions." And sniggering, she probably thought, at the sad trappings of her trade.

"Your possessions are safe," I assured her. "I've had them properly packed up. But we'll be a while yet. Is there a friend you can stay with in the meantime?" She said nothing, and that was answer enough. I cursed inwardly. "I'll see what I can arrange. Just rest for now. But tell me—I found the fan. The one you said Iosif gave you?" False as it was, it seemed more tactful to call Akushku by the name he had used when they were lovers. "Do you have any idea where he obtained it?"

She shook her head, and winced at the pain from her shoulder. "What happened last night?" I persisted. "After Gustav and I left?"

"I try to help him," she said. "The one called Jean. He was bleeding. I tie up his arm with belt, from my robe."

"That was good of you."

She snorted in reproach. "I was not being good. I thought, if he die, you cannot ask him questions. And then I heard him, on the stairs."

"Iosif?"

"I know his step. And I have no time. If he find me, he kill me. So, I hide, under the *divano*. Jean, he—how you say—he pass out, he see nothing."

"Did Iosif say anything to him before they left?"

"He say, *Prikhodite, prikhodite na klub*."

". . . *klub?*"

"It means, 'Come, we go to club.'"

"What sort of club? Where?"

"Is all I hear. I am sorry. The pain was bad. I want to cry, but . . ."

Good Lord, I thought, *this girl is made of stern stuff.*

"Away out of that, Miss Minetti. I'm the one who should be apologising."

And now the two nurses with their trolley arrived at the foot of the bed and thrust at her a battered pewter spoon and a blue enamel bowl filled with greasy water. If it smelled of anything, it was hard to tell— the stink of disinfectant drowned out every other scent in that place. The young Italian turned her head away in revulsion.

"What is that stuff?" I said.

"Skilly," said the pale, pinch-faced nurse, moving on. My gorge rose at the very word. Indian corn mixed with hot water, the same slop that had been doled out to my starving countrymen during the Famine. Minetti handed the bowl to me and with her good hand started tugging at the bedsheets, struggling to get up.

"Miss Minetti—Angela—sit still," I said. "You've been hurt—"

"I will not stay here. I cannot."

"Sure where will you go?"

"I do not care." She glared at me defiantly. "I make my way. Is not first time."

Damn it, I thought. This girl had tried to help us, risked her life and lost the little she had—and this is her repayment?

"Hold on," I said.

"BRIGID, OUR HOUSEKEEPER, is in Ireland, looking after her mother," said Amelia as we ascended the stairs. "And Dorothy, the girl covering for her, doesn't live in, so . . ."

She pushed open the door of Brigid's room and entered. Amelia was usually the most warm and welcoming of hosts, but she preferred a little notice, and my turning up on our doorstep and decreeing we find room for an attractive young woman, without warning or explanation, was testing her patience. For now she hid it well, but I feared I'd get a grilling later.

Miss Minetti paused on the threshold. "Come in," said Amelia, beckoning. Entering the little box room, our guest looked around at the flowery wallpaper and the ruched pink curtains and the single bed and the religious statues Brigid liked to collect lined up upon the dresser. I hovered outside the door—Brigid's room was barely big enough for three people—as my wife gathered up the rosary and missal from Brigid's nightstand and tucked them away in a drawer. Our houseguest shook her head.

"I am very grateful, Mrs. Melville, but I cannot—"

"You can and you will, Miss Minetti," I insisted. "And there's an end to it."

The girl turned to look out the window, and though there was little to see except our overgrown pear tree and the neighbours' washing lines, the place must have seemed like a Tuscan palazzo after the stew she'd been living in.

"Perhaps for a day or two, until I am well again." She met Amelia's eye at last. "Thank you, Mrs. Melville."

"Not at all," said Amelia, but with little conviction. But when Miss Minetti sat on the bed and closed her eyes, clearly exhausted and in pain, I could see Amelia thaw a little.

"Are you hungry? We have some cold mutton."

"That would be most kind of you."

"And we need to see to that dress of yours."

Minetti glanced down at the bloody stain on her shoulder that showed almost black on the ripped green silk of her dress.

"Is nothing. A needle and thread, and some cold water, I mend."

"It's a bit far gone for that," said Amelia. "You may wear something of mine for the time being." She glanced down at Angela's figure, before adding with the hint of a sigh, "Though we might have to take it in at the waist."

"I'd better head back to the office," I said. "Make yourself at home, Miss Minetti." I clumped down the stairs and plucked my hat from the rack. Amelia came down after me.

"You don't often bring your work home, William." Her soft voice had an edge to it. Surely she didn't think I was the sort of scoundrel who'd take his floozy home to meet his wife?

"I'm sorry," I said. "The girl had nowhere else to go, and I owe her a great debt. I couldn't just stick her in a lodging house when she needs looking after."

"She has no family? No employer?"

"Not anymore, no."

"Might I ask what she does for a living, precisely?"

"She's been working as a language tutor," I said, brushing invisible dust off my hat. "Freelance."

"And now she's here, with no belongings, in a ragged dress soaked in blood." She raised a sceptical eyebrow. "Teaching languages must be a riskier occupation than I'd imagined."

I sighed. Perhaps I could have thought up a better story before we'd arrived, but it would have been futile—Amelia could read me like a tuppenny novel. When I leaned down to kiss her, she reluctantly proffered her cheek.

"Don't wait up," I said. "And tell no one she's here."

"I wouldn't dream of it. Though I daresay your children might notice."

BEFORE RETURNING TO SCOTLAND YARD I dropped in on a few dubious acquaintances—fences, dips and buttoners—who owed me a favour or wanted to get in my good books. Our ordinary decent criminals, with their own quaint codes of propriety and honour, despised foreign agitators even more than the "respectable" classes did.

But none of my shady contacts had information on our fugitives. I wasn't entirely surprised—Akushku was no common criminal, and this club Miss Minetti had heard him mention was clearly part of a fallback plan. Before we'd even left the infirmary I'd sent a note back to the office telling my team to check out radical clubs within a mile of our encounter, and as soon as I got back to my desk I set about compiling a list of every other sort of club in the East End—social, religious, chess clubs and sports clubs—but I'd barely started when there was a rap on my door.

"Chief—visitor for you, sir." Constable Lawrence manned reception in rotation with Jenkins, and though he was going on twenty-two he was so fresh-faced he could have passed for fifteen.

"I've no time for visitors," I growled.

"German chap, sir, name of Steinhauer?"

I FOUND GUSTAV waiting on one of the hard benches by the street door, reading the *Times*. Looking up at me he beamed.

"Chief Superintendent! Hello again." He rose and shook my hand firmly. "How goes the search?"

"It's in hand, thank you, Gustav. How was that hotel I found for you?"

"It is excellent, a home from home."

I nodded at the neat repair on the upper arm of his topcoat. "You didn't buy yourself a new coat?"

"Oh!" Steinhauer glanced down at the rip the bullet had left in his sleeve, now neatly mended. "I changed my mind. This one is much too good to throw away."

"Your tailor did a good job. You must let me have his name."

Steinhauer smiled; he knew I was fishing. The Jewish German tailors of the East End, exiles from their homeland, were socialists almost to a man, and so pure of principle they would not even hire assistants, employment being by its very nature exploitation. They had little love for British policemen, and even less for the Kaiser's—hence their presence here—but, of course, Steinhauer would hardly have identified himself as an Imperial official.

"William," chided Steinhauer. "A man of your resources, who knows London like the back of his hand, hardly needs me to recommend a tailor. But I did hear some gossip you might find interesting. Shall we talk in your office?"

"You know, I fancy some fresh air. Let's go for a walk."

"Fresh air" in London is a relative term, of course. We strolled west along the Embankment, where the fumes of the barges steaming up and down the Thames hung heavy in the air. Dusk was gathering and it was damnably cold; we walked with our hands buried deep in our pockets and our shoulders hunched, as the redbrick battlements of Scotland Yard receded into the smoky mist.

"Have you reported to your King on our adventures of last night?" asked Steinhauer.

"Not yet," I said. "Though I shouldn't put it off much longer. What about you?"

"His Imperial Majesty would rather hear about solutions than problems, and I would rather oblige him by waiting until we have some good news. After all, the threat is no greater than it was yesterday. It is one-third less, in fact, since you killed Averbukh."

"Except that now Akushku knows we are on to him."

"He knows, yes, but what practical difference will that make? He may have gone to ground, but he was not exactly advertising his presence before. And now he has a wounded colleague to worry about."

"True."

"They will be seeking medical attention soon, if they have not already. Perhaps that is an avenue your people could pursue?"

"We're not totally incompetent, Gustav, though after last night you'd be forgiven for thinking so. No, we're on to that, and now we have another lead: Akushku and Bozidar may be hiding out at a place they referred to as 'the club.'" I didn't mention my source was Angela Minetti. He didn't need to know, and the fewer who learned the girl was lodging with my own family, the safer she would be.

"But this is excellent! Are there many clubs in the area?"

"Only about a thousand," I said. "And that's presuming it's not a reference to some secret society, or even a private joke. But what's this piece of gossip you mentioned?"

"Ah yes. Our man Akushku, I think he is not what he seems. He and his friends spoke in Russian, and he uses this Russian nom-de-guerre, but . . ."

"You think that's intended to throw us off the scent?"

"I am told our man is Latvian. And the Latvians, as you know, have little love for their Russian masters."

"Indeed," I answered vaguely, trying to disguise how much my mind was whirling.

Because Jakob Piotr was a Latvian, and in the Lyons Tea Room he had told me about a stranger at that last meeting of his dissident countrymen: a man in his thirties, possibly American, with a military bearing. And beside me at that moment walked a man who fitted the description all too well—Steinhauer himself. Yes, the stranger at that meeting had sported a moustache, but that was easily faked.

What mischief might Steinhauer have been up to there? Long before the Kaiser's yacht had even docked in England?

"This gossipy source of yours," I said. "I don't suppose he told you Akushku's real name?"

"No, and it would be worthless if he had. Radicals like Akushku change their names as often as you and I change our shirt-collars."

"True enough. Latvian, eh? I'll make some enquiries." And not just about Akushku, I thought.

9

W HEN CONAN DOYLE'S fanciful nonsense first appeared in the *Strand Magazine*, I had tried to enjoy it, but soon gave up. The British public, on the other hand, took Sherlock Holmes to their hearts, and who could blame them? Ingenious detectives catching ingenious villains makes for splendid entertainment— unlike the daily grind of genuine police work. Real-life coppers nail criminals by knowing their patch, asking endless questions and getting tip-offs from informants. It helps that so few criminals are geniuses: instead they are, for the most part, sloppy, boastful and/or stupid.

Akushku, however, seemed to be none of these. Late last night I had sent telegrams to my counterparts on the Continent, asking if they'd ever heard of him; no joy. And this evening, as my men reported in at debriefing, it became clear they'd had no more luck than me. The officers I had sent to comb Minetti's neighbourhood had knocked on every door in her street and for three streets in every direction, and spoken to every family crammed into those ramshackle old mansions. They had visited every clinic, infirmary, doctor and nurse within a two-mile radius, asking if they had treated a patient suffering from bullet wounds. They had visited a dozen political clubs, and invented pretexts to search their premises, but there was no sign whatsoever of our quarry.

I told myself this was progress of a sort. If the two fugitives had not obtained medical help by now, they would be weaker and more desperate, more likely to make mistakes—they might even try to flee the country. I made a note to tell my men stationed at Britain's ports to keep an eye on departures as well as arrivals.

Last to make their report were Johnson and Connolly. From the eagerness on Connolly's face—even the gloomy Johnson was wearing a faint smirk—I could tell they were bearing good tidings, and I'd left them until last on purpose; ending this debrief on a positive note would boost morale. When I called on them, Johnson started to flick through his notebook, but Connolly couldn't contain himself.

"That fan you took from the young lady's lodgings, sir," he blurted out. "It was part of a range of fans imported from Budapest. In Hungary."

"I know where Budapest is, Sergeant," I said.

"Yes, sir, sorry," he said, face reddening. "They ranged in price from ten to fifteen guineas, not the sort of item a tart"—he corrected himself, reddening some more—"I mean, a young lady in her walk of life would normally afford, sir."

"Rather than go from shop to shop, trying to find out where they had been sold," butted in Johnson, without deigning to look at Connolly, "we thought we would talk to the importer, and take it from there."

"Good thinking," I said. "And?"

Johnson consulted his notebook. "The importer and distributor were one and the same—a Mr. John deLauncey of Eastern Enterprises Limited, with offices near Smithfield. He told us that he had supplied only a few dozen of these particular fans, to Whiteleys of Bayswater, Pratt's, Swan and Edgar in Piccadilly and Marshall and Snelgrove on de Vere Street. We've been to the first two, and the management let us see their ledgers, so we have a full list of their purchasers."

"But Marshall and Snelgrove had closed, sir," said Connolly, to Johnson's irritation. "We plan to call in there first thing Monday."

"Good work, both of you," I said. I rounded up by expanding our new line of enquiry—finding this "club" where Akushku had taken

Bozidar. I named teams that from tomorrow would start checking out my list. "I know it won't be an easy task, especially on a Sunday, and there are a few dozen candidates within reach of Whitechapel, but if we work hard and methodically we will track these men down.

"And whichever of you does, you are to keep them under observation and summon reinforcements right away. Do not on any account try to tackle them by yourselves."

A few of the men were discreetly checking their watches, looking forward to hearth and home after a long day. I felt a stab of pity for them, but stifled it. I would see little enough of my own bed while this crisis was upon us, and neither would they, and that was what we'd all signed up for.

"Gentlemen, you've done sterling work today, and you can all be proud of yourselves." There was a muttered chorus of thanks, but I carried on, talking over it. "And none of us are done just yet. Report for duty in the yard in twenty minutes. The Committee for Latvian Liberty meets tonight in Brewer Street, and we're going to pay them a visit."

I STOOD PATIENTLY WAITING as O'Brien, the custody officer, unhooked the keys from his belt, unlocked the cell door and pulled it squealing open. I was carrying a tin plate draped in a cloth, by way of a peace offering to my guest. "That'll be all, thank you, Sergeant," I said. "I think I can manage."

O'Brien nodded and stepped out again, and the heavy door clanged shut behind him. I placed the dinner plate on the steel table bolted to the floor and lifted the cloth. "I brought this for you, from the canteen," I told Jakob. He eyed the raw steak with little interest, and leaned back in his chair with his handcuffed wrists resting in his lap.

"I am not hungry," he said. His jacket was filthy, the collar was half-torn from his shirt, his left eye was swollen half-closed, and he had a fat lip.

"It's for your eye, you buck eejit." I pulled back the chair facing him, sat down and stretched out the fingers of my right hand. I'd scraped my own knuckles raw against the pavement helping to restrain one young firebrand. Our visit to the Latvian Liberty meeting had not been warmly received; several chairs, one window and two noses had been broken in the fracas. It was pretty much the outcome I had expected—in fact had counted on. When Jakob was dragged from the building and chucked in the back of our Black Maria, then hauled from his holding cell to this interrogation room, his fellow radicals would have seen nothing suspicious.

"I'm sorry about your injuries, Jakob, but they are your own fault. You didn't have to make such a song and dance about resisting arrest. Indeed, some of your friends might have thought you were protesting too much."

"I was not making a 'song and dance,'" Jakob spat, with real indignation. "We were having a peaceful political meeting and you had no right to break it up. You are always boasting that England is the country of free speech—is this free speech?" He gestured to his purple eye socket.

I shrugged. "Freer than most."

"You told me that here, as long as there was no incitement to crime, a man could think and say what he wanted. There was no incitement to crime at our meeting. Ask anyone. Ask the policemen you had planted in the audience. No one was proposing violence or even disobedience—we were discussing the rights of man."

"An admirable concept, I'm sure."

"Is it because we are foreign that we have no rights? So much for equality under the law."

"You have precisely the same rights as any of the King's subjects," I said. "Which are whatever rights the Crown sees fit to allow, at any particular time."

Jakob snorted in derision. "Then your freedom of speech is a fiction. Your men are thugs, just like the Tsar's thugs, but with better manners."

The lad was starting to annoy me. It occurred to me I could enhance his credibility with his fellow anarchists by blacking his other eye for him, but that would only have proved his point. I took a deep breath instead.

"Freedom of speech," I said, "is an ideal to which we aspire. And on occasions we fall short, because our hospitality is sometimes abused, and our tolerance is mistaken for licence. We're not like the Tsar's secret police. You and your friends will be free to go home in the morning—at least, the ones who didn't take a swing at my officers. If we were the Okhrana you'd be on your way to a Siberian salt mine, or a firing squad, right now. So don't give me any more of your nonsense."

He fell silent and stared at me, glowering.

"Maybe no one was discussing violence or sedition tonight, I really don't care. We raided that place to remind your friends who's boss. And because I needed to talk to you, and it couldn't wait until next month."

Now Jakob tilted his head to one side, curiosity mingling with his contempt. "I am not in the mood for conversation." The look on his face saddened me. All those high ideals and the noble ambition of youth, unsullied by harsh reality and impossible choices.

"I can have this cooked if you'd like," I said, nodding at the bloody steak. "I'd go for rare if I were you. The canteen meat is so tough you could sole your boots with it."

"I am not hungry," Jakob insisted. I sighed.

"Jakob, Her Late Majesty Queen Victoria is being laid to rest next weekend. There's going to be a state funeral, and half of Europe's royalty will be there."

"Sadly, I have a prior engagement," said Jakob—with the ghost of a smile, at last.

"Will any of your friends be attending?"

"To laugh, maybe. For myself . . . I have never cared much for the circus."

"What about Akushku?" I said, staring him straight in the eye. "Will he be coming?" I saw his eyes widen, in what looked like surprise or apprehension. Then he frowned in incomprehension, slightly too late.

"Who is this Akushku?"

"Don't pretend you've never heard of him, Jakob. He's a nihilist, a terrorist. He was planning to attack the funeral cortege with two comrades. We nearly had him last night, but he and one of his friends escaped. They've gone to ground somewhere in London, and I need to know where."

"You expect me to know?"

"I'm told this man is Latvian. Like you." I watched him closely. Jakob snorted. "You know everybody in the movement," I said.

"I do not know him. And even if I did, even if I knew where this Akushku was, why would I tell you?"

"Because of the man you are, Jakob. You're a revolutionary socialist, and you're an idealist, but you're not cruel and you're not a fanatic. You're not the sort who would slaughter women and children and working men and claim it was for their own good. This man Akushku wants to start a war in Europe, and I mean to stop him."

Jakob nodded, listening, a smile slowing growing clearer on his face. He leaned forwards, placing his wrists on the table as if to display to me his chains, though it was I who had put them there.

"Chief Superintendent Melville . . ." He concentrated, as if about to explain a challenging concept to a child. "You think you know me. But you do not. You know nothing about me, or what I believe in, or the sacrifices I am prepared to make. Yes, I am an idealist—I want to remake the world so there is no need for men like you, so that men like you will not have to exist. You and I meet, and we talk, and you come to our lectures and you read our magazines and you listen to our plans, but you do not hear what we are saying. You cannot see the simple truth. And this is because you cannot understand it, any more than a dog could understand astronomy, any more than the bricks in these walls understand that they are part of a prison."

I waited, listening.

"If this Akushku really wanted to kill the Kaiser or King Leopold or your King or any of that gang of fat, lazy parasites, I would gladly help him, in any way I could. You say you want to stop a war, but we are already at war. The ruling classes have declared war on the workers, and very soon the workers will start fighting back. You are a general for the ruling class. I fight for the workers. I am not on your side."

He fell silent, watching me, his body tensed, waiting for the explosion, for the punch that would knock him out of his chair. He had called me a dog to my face, after all, and this time we were not sitting in a tea-shop hemmed in by genteel bourgeoisie.

"What do you mean, if he 'really wanted to'?" I said.

Jakob blinked. He had expected a thump, not a question. "If?" he echoed. "What?"

"You said, 'If this Akushku really wanted to kill the Kaiser or King Leopold . . .'"

"I am sure he does. I would, given the chance."

"Yes," I insisted, "but you said, if he 'really wanted to.' Why did you put it like that?"

"My English is not so good."

"Your English is not so bad, Jakob. Your English is excellent. You're telling me that Akushku isn't planning to attack the funeral?" I wasn't entirely sure where I was headed with this. But Jakob's turn of phrase had puzzled me, and the more I focused on it the more agitated he became, so I kept going. "Then why is he here? Taking pot-shots at me and my officers?"

"Why are you asking me?" Jakob tried to wave his hands in exasperation, forgetting his handcuffed wrists. "I have never met this man, I have no idea where he is, I don't know what he intends—"

"You see, Jakob, this is what I meant by 'protesting too much.' I don't believe you. Oh, I know you want a revolution, and that's no skin off my nose, as long as it's back in Latvia and not here. And I don't believe you're helping this man Akushku. In fact it looks very much like you're afraid of him. But that's what bothers me. Why would you be afraid of him, when you're on the same side? Are you worried he'll find out that you and I have been talking? That he'll think you're working for me as an agent provocateur?"

Jakob snorted with laughter. "Me? *I* am not the agent provocateur!"

I had to fight to hide my astonishment. "You're saying that *he* is?

That Akushku is working for the Russians?" The young Latvian laughed and shrugged and shook his head, but this time it was fake—hopeless playacting. He could not take it back now. My own mind was whirling at the implications. "Mother of God, if you think Akushku's an Okhrana agent why the hell didn't you say so, instead of giving me this blasted runaround?"

"I am not here to help you!" snapped Jakob. "I don't work for you. I told you, I am not on your side! You, the Okhrana, you are all the same—if you want to waste your time chasing each other's shadows, why would I stop you?"

"How do you know this?" I blustered, before I could stop myself. It made me sound like an idiot, but I already felt like one and had little to lose. "That he's a Russian police agent—do you have any evidence?"

Jakob practically giggled at my discomfiture. "An anarchist who emerges from nowhere, a Latvian with no family back home, no record? Who has plenty of money, who manages to outwit the great policeman Melville? And you want me to show you proof!" He was laughing in my face now, as if my predicament made his black eye worthwhile.

"God damn it—" I kicked back my chair and stood, so furious at the lad I briefly envied the Okhrana their firing squad. I strode to the door and thumped it with my fist.

"Don't forget your steak, Mr. Melville," sniggered Jakob.

I had a good mind to betray him to his comrades, the brat, but I knew I might yet have need of him. "Away and shite, Jakob," I snarled. The key rattled in the lock and I was out of that damned place, striding down the corridor. Jakob's mocking laughter rang in my ears until the metal door slammed shut.

QUINN WAS UPSTAIRS at the custody desk, flicking through the logs of that evening's raid. "Do you want to question any of the others, sir?" he said.

"I do not. Send them home."

"Including Piotr, sir?"

"Especially him, the little gobshite. And don't give him his shoe-laces back."

THE NIGHT-TIME ROOFTOPS of Whitehall loomed around me like hard-edged hills shrouded in smoke. I had climbed the maintenance staircase to our roof, where a small patch of gravelled felt, half-hidden among the chimney stacks of Scotland Yard, offered the only solitude I could ever find around this place. The gaslights in the street lit the smoky air from below, so the gaps between the buildings were like glowing canyons—or like a glimpse into the pits of hell, tonight. I took a deep breath to calm myself; the air was almost clear, the building's boilers having been banked for the night. Beyond Whitehall the dark sprawling mass of London stretched out farther than the eye could see, or the mind conceive: the world's greatest, wealthiest city, at the heart of history's greatest empire. I liked it up here; the streets of Whitehall never slept, not entirely, but up here there were no distractions and nobody pestering me for orders or opinions. I hadn't been up here for a year or two, but by God I needed to be here now.

I sighed. It wasn't Jakob I was angry at, but myself, for missing what should have been obvious. Everything the boy had said about Akushku made sense. Most anarchists were incompetents, who shared their plans with a dozen informers, or whose shots went wild, or who blew themselves up with their own bombs. But the man I sought spoke multiple languages fluently, shifted between identities and had rescued his wounded colleague from under our noses, after picking my handcuffs. All of this was field-craft. Akushku had been trained, by professionals.

God knows, I'd used agents provocateurs myself in the past. A decade before, in the so-called Walsall affair, I'd locked up several Fenians who had planned to bomb the church where Queen Victoria worshipped. It was I who had planted the germ of the plot, and I'd even sketched out the device they could use. When the truth about my involvement came out—as I'd known it would—it sowed panic and mistrust among terrorists of every stripe, not just the Fenians. Any radical too fierce, too eager for action, was immediately suspected of being in the pay of the police, and the ones too timid to break the law were just as suspect. Anarchists ended up fighting among themselves like rats in a sack, denouncing and informing on one another; persecution mania did much of our work for us.

It had also become a favourite tactic, I knew, of Rachkovskii, head of the Okhrana. If Jakob was right, and Akushku was an agent of the Tsar's secret police, then this anarchist conspiracy was a hoax—a trap for exiled Russian dissidents. In a few days Rachkovskii would bring me the whole story of Akushku's plot, name the conspirators who had helped him and demand that they be arrested en masse and deported back to Russia to face the tender mercies of the Lubianka. While the supposed ringleader, the "terrorist" Akushku, would mysteriously vanish—only to pop up again elsewhere in Europe with plans for a fresh atrocity.

If Jakob was right.

10

I T WAS WAY PAST MIDNIGHT when I reached my front door and dug in my pocket for my latchkey. The house was dark and quiet; everyone was in bed, I didn't doubt. Miss Minetti needed rest, but I hoped all the same she hadn't sat all day in that poky little bedroom hiding from Amelia's disapproval; I knew how the girl hated to be judged.

But when I stepped into the hall and slipped off my coat I heard voices from the kitchen, and saw the warm glow of a lamp beyond. Somebody was burning the midnight oil. I had shut the front door softly so as not to rouse anyone, and now I tiptoed down the hallway and paused at the top of the steps.

And there they were, Angela Minetti and my wife, sitting at the kitchen table with a bottle of sherry between them, chatting away like a couple of conspirators. As if I didn't get enough of those at work, I thought.

"Ladies," I said, entering. Amelia nearly jumped out of her seat.

"William! You almost gave me a heart attack!"

Miss Minetti, I noted, had not even flinched. She was wearing a blue dress I'd seen before—one of Amelia's—and her smile lit up the room.

"Have you eaten?" said Amelia.

"I have," I said. "But I haven't had a drink."

"I'll fetch you a glass." She bustled off to the parlour while I pulled up a chair at the head of the kitchen table. With the heat from the stove the kitchen was cosier than the parlour, if not as comfortable. But kitchens have always been the place where women can exchange confidences. I worried briefly what confidences Amelia might have shared, then chided myself for fretting; my wife never asked about my work, and I never discussed it, and what little she deduced she was shrewd enough not to pass on.

"So how are you, Miss Minetti? How's your day been?"

"I am well. Mrs. Melville has been very kind to me."

"Am I Mrs. Melville again?" came Amelia's voice from the hall. "I thought we'd dispensed with that, Angela." She set a glass before me and poured me some sherry. The bottle had been full a few days ago, I remembered—now it was half-empty.

"What about the shoulder?" I asked.

"Is much better. I want to help in house, but Amelia—"

"You're here to rest, and there's an end to it," insisted Amelia. "And you have helped, with James's German homework."

"Your son is a very clever young man."

"News to me," I said, sipping my sherry. James was my younger boy, and though I loved him dearly, or tried to, he was an awkward adolescent—truculent, contrary and opinionated. "Hold on—" I said. "German?"

"Angela speaks fluent German, didn't you know?" Amelia beamed. Miss Minetti went pink, like a little girl. It had been a long time, I could see, since she had simply sat at someone's hearth and felt welcome and had had to fend off compliments.

"Not fluently," she said. "But is easier than English."

I grunted. "Well, I hope the boy minded his manners."

"He was good as gold," said Amelia. "Quite tongue-tied, for a change."

You mean smitten, I thought. And who could blame him, with such a girl leaning over his shoulder? Even in that old blue dress I'd often thought so dowdy, Minetti would turn any young man's head.

And an old one's too, I realised. Had I been staring? I busied myself with my sherry glass.

"And how was your day, Mr. Melville?"

"You're in my kitchen—I think you may call me William," I said.

"And you must call me Angela." She smiled.

"Well, Angela, there's not much to report."

"You have not caught Iosif?"

"It's only a matter of time. His friend will need medical help." Amelia said nothing and asked no questions, but clearly she had already heard the whole sorry story from Angela herself. "The local hospitals know to look out for them," I said. "And the doctors too."

"Anyway, it's late," said Amelia. She knew how much I hated discussing my work, and perhaps she sensed that the day I'd just been through had been worse than most.

"Iosif will not go to a doctor," said Angela.

"Then his friend will lose his arm," I said. "Or likely die of infection."

"I mean—" She looked down. Again that tic of shame; Amelia saw it too.

"I'll just go and turn your bed down, Angela," she said, and slipped out of the room. Angela waited to hear her footsteps ascend the stairs.

"I mean," said Angela, "Iosif will go to a doctor the police do not know. One who does not advertise."

I confess I stared at her, only slowly realising what she was referring to, and when I saw it I nearly kicked myself for not thinking of it first. Rising from her chair, Angela gathered up the sherry glasses and turned to rinse them at the sink, so she would not have to face me. "The other girls in Whitechapel told me of a man they would go to when they were . . . in difficulty. He is American, I think." Her back was still turned to me, and her voice was barely audible. "His name is Remington. If I was Iosif, I would seek this man."

CHURCH BELLS WERE CHIMING all across the West End and the City as I rode a hansom up to Bloomsbury, moving at a brisk pace through the near-deserted streets. After my conversation with Angela

I had caught a cab straight back to Scotland Yard—to Amelia's dismay—and set the night relief to the task of tracking down this dubious Dr. Remington. No easy task in the early hours of Sunday morning, but with six days to the funeral we had to seize every lead. I had snatched a few hours' sleep on the couch in my office, and now I was off to chase up a contact of my own, splashing early churchgoers with gutter-water in my haste.

My thoughts drifted briefly back to Angela, wondering how long this cosy domestic arrangement could last. Amelia seemed to be enjoying her company, but eventually our maid Brigid would return, and what then? I could hardly turn the girl out on the streets to resume her former trade. The obvious solution was to provide her with a reference, find her decent employment and lodgings, and with luck all else would follow—a husband and a home, either here or back in Italy. I had done a lot more for informants who deserved a lot less. The hansom clattered to a halt.

Antoinette de Bosanquet's Bloomsbury domain was in a quiet, tree-lined backstreet; wide granite steps led up to a tall, handsome Georgian building, its elongated windows lined with green velvet curtains. In the summer flowers cascaded from troughs on every windowsill, and even today, in the depths of winter, clumps of jasmine and hellebore brightened the building's sooty redbrick façade and scented the air. I hammered twice firmly on the front door with the great brass knocker and waited, listening to the echoes die away within. Every afternoon and evening a string quartet or a pianist entertained the clientele; at this early hour however there would be no clientele and no music, and the staff would be abed, recovering from their night's exertions.

The door was opened by Susanne, a slight and modest serving-maid who rarely spoke, conscious of her harelip. She kept her eyes cast downwards as she took my hat and coat; no need to send her for the woman of the house, because Madame de Bosanquet herself, wreathed in smiles, was descending the grand marble staircase.

"Monsieur Melville! It has been so long since we had the pleasure!"

She glided down as gracefully as a ballerina, wearing a magnificent dress of claret silk, blond curls piled high upon her head. I made a deep bow; though she was nearly my own age, the lady never failed to impress. She had led a hard life, I knew, but she had the complexion of a thirty-year-old, and her brown eyes danced with mischievous promise.

"Can we offer you coffee, or something stronger?"

"Alas, Antoinette, it's a little early for me. And I'm on duty."

"William!" She pouted prettily. "You are always on duty. Someday you must allow us to show you some proper hospitality."

"Someday, maybe. But today all I need is a few minutes of your time."

She had opened her mouth to reply, only to be interrupted by a scream from upstairs—not one of pleasure or excitement, but fear. Madame's smile was instantly replaced by a snarl of indignation and anger.

"But who is still here?" she hissed at Susanne.

"The gentleman with Alice, mum," the girl squeaked. "He paid for the night." Now came a male voice raised in anger, and the sound of glass breaking.

"Where's your man Harold?" I demanded.

"He hurt his knee, dealing with a difficult client—"

I did not wait for an invitation but pushed past her and took the stairs two at a time, heading for what was now a stream of female screams, mingled with drunken male roaring. The racket was coming from the room at the farthest end of the first-floor landing, and as I passed the padded bedroom doors several of them opened and anxious young women peeked out, a few in flimsy peignoirs, most in less.

I didn't bother to knock, but flung the door open just in time to see a gilded chair go flying into the mirror of a gilded dressing table, smashing it into shards of glass and wood. In the corner by the window a girl of barely twenty with a bloody nose was trying to drag a curtain over her nakedness, cowering from the muscular young man who was standing over her clad only in a pair of linen drawers. His left hand had seized her hair, to drag her sobbing back into the centre of the room; around his right was wrapped a leather belt, the buckle on the outside.

He was too angry and too drunk even to notice I had entered, and as I strode over to him he raised his right fist to punch the girl in the face. It was the work of an instant to grab his wrist, wrench his arm back and force it up between his shoulder blades. His turn to yell; releasing the girl's hair he writhed in my grip, trying to turn and clawing at my face with his left hand. I spun him round and slammed his comely face into the wall panelling so hard it bruised the wood. He roared in pain and indignation.

"Damn it! Take your hands off me, you ignorant oaf!"

"I will, just as soon as you've calmed yourself down."

Madame de Bosanquet entered and was immediately so incensed at the sight she forgot her accent and blurted out in broadest Geordie, "Oh bloody hell, not again!" Plucking a handkerchief from her sleeve, she rushed to comfort the girl and wipe the blood and snot from her nose.

"I am calm, damn you!" the lout snarled at me. "Look, I paid for the little bitch, I can do what I like!"

"You're in the wrong establishment for that," I said. "That dish is not on the menu."

"For Christ's sake, you're going to break my arm!"

"Damned right I will, unless you promise to behave."

"Yes, yes, blast you . . ."

He wouldn't honour his promise, I knew. He was an aristocrat, a spoilt vicious brat, and any promise to an inferior such as myself would mean nothing anyway. I caught Madame de Bosanquet's eye, and she nodded, so I unwound the belt from the man's fist, tossed it onto the bed and stepped back, releasing him. He turned, flexing his twisted right arm and massaging it with his left, face pale and eyes wide with injured pride. His mouth worked, and he hawked and spat on the carpet at my feet. "You ignorant Irish ape, do you have any idea who I am?"

"Nobody gives a tinker's curse who you are," I said. "Get dressed and leave." His nostrils flared. For a moment I thought even he wouldn't be stupid enough to take a swing at me, but I had given him too much credit. He was young and strong and fast, but I've been knocked about by bigger and better fighters, men who didn't telegraph their intentions. I had only to lean back for his fist to swing wild, and it was the work of a moment to grab his arm, tilt him off balance and kick his feet out from under him. He landed with a thump on the rug and, as luck would have it, face-first into that gob of his own phlegm. If I'd planned it I couldn't have planted him more neatly. Too bad the rug was deep and soft, so it broke his fall—he tried to get up again until I brought my right boot down hard on the elbow of his outstretched arm. I felt rather than heard the bones crack, and he screamed, and when the women turned away in revulsion I realised I'd probably over-done it. I'd let frustration get the better of me—I was treating this drunken idiot the way I wanted to treat Akushku. Then again, better him than someone who didn't deserve it.

While the young buck lay on the floor, snivelling and clutching his arm, I crossed to the wardrobe and wrenched it open. His clothes were all there, neatly hung up; de Bosanquet's offered all the luxuries of a West End hotel, but with hot and cold tarts on tap. I pulled the trousers from their wooden hanger and tossed them at the injured man.

"Stop whimpering," I told him.

"You'll regret this!" he wailed. "You have no idea who you're dealing with!"

"I have a very good idea, Lord Trevithick," I said. "And if your father the Earl finds out you've been up to your old tricks again, he'll probably ask me to break your other arm, and your valet will have to wipe your arse. Now get up, get your clothes on and get out. And count yourself lucky I don't make you get dressed in the street."

"WILL THE GIRL BE ALL RIGHT?"

"Jenny? Oh yes, nothing broken. It's not her first time either, poor thing. I've given her the night off. Sugar?"

"None for me, thank you."

We were sitting by a low table in Madame's library, a long elegant room facing east, lined with deep soft sofas and mahogany shelves filled with leather-bound volumes. A temple to literature, except nobody ever came in here to read. This morning, however, the pale winter sun washed the room with light and lit up very prettily the wisps of steam rising from my tea.

"You sure he won't make trouble? You were rather rough with him, Mr. Melville." After the morning's fracas, Madame Antoinette de Bosanquet—alias Sally Porter from Gateshead—had dispensed with the French accent, and to be honest I was glad of it. Playacting was part of her business, of course, and her clients went along with it, but I had always found it a seedy sort of charade that quickly grated.

"He won't," I said. I didn't mention that I knew the family well; having already paid out a small fortune to hush up one scandal, they would have no time or tolerance for another. "But if he tries anything on, you let me know." It was lucky for me Trevithick had been here that morning and the club's bouncer had been off sick. Sorting out that wretch had put Madame in my debt, and it would make the task ahead that much easier.

"Well, suppose you tell me why you're here? Seeing as you never indulge us with your custom."

The tea was too hot for my taste; I put the cup back in its saucer till it cooled off. "You might have heard," I said, "of an incident last night just down the road from here. A police raid on a gang of bank robbers. There was some shooting."

"I did hear something, yeah, but I didn't know it were bank robbers. You there, Mr. Melville?"

"As it happens I was. The blackguards blew a hole in my best hat."

"God almighty. Mind—didn't think that were your department. Bank robbers, I mean." She said it casually, as if daring me to elaborate, but I merely looked at her, until she blushed and cast her eyes down and stirred her cup urgently.

"It isn't, usually. But I was passing by."

"Well, I'm glad you weren't hurt."

"I wasn't, thank God. But one of the men we were after was injured."

"I don't follow you." Sally frowned. "They didn't come here."

"No, of course not. But they would have gone somewhere. They were in need of medical assistance. Probably still are."

"Oh yes?" Sally sounded studiously vague.

"Professional medical help, from someone qualified." Now it dawned on her where I was going with this, and her mouth puckered into a hard pink line. "Qualified, that is," I went on, "but not practising. Not openly, anyway. I've heard tell of an American chap, by the name of Remington, and I need to get hold of him."

My tea had cooled enough now, I found as I sipped it, and I brushed a few drops from my moustache while I waited for Sally to reply. In the silence I heard the grandfather clock in the hall chime a stately half-hour.

"I know what you are getting at, Mr. Melville, but that is not a practice I countenance. My girls see the nurse every month and take every precaution to avoid such misfortune. We do have mishaps now and again," she conceded, "but in those cases we send our young ladies away to the country—"

I replaced my cup in its saucer rather too hard, and she flinched, but my patience with all this fake gentility was wearing thin. "Name of Jaysus, Sally, I didn't come down in the last shower of rain. You're not running a convent here, and you don't spend your tarts' earnings on country retreats. So where do I find this lock picker?" She winced at my use of the street term, but I charged on. "I'm asking you as a friend, but I have no time for flannel."

Her shoulders sagged a little. "I do know him. Remington. He's discreet and he's obliging and he does the business, well enough, when he's sober."

"And where would I find him?"

ON THE WAY BACK to Scotland Yard I asked the cabbie to drop me on the north side of Green Park and walked from there in the direction of Whitehall. On so chill and damp a day there were few families *en promenade*, but all the same I was nearly run down by an overenthusiastic little boy in a sailor suit driving a hoop twice his own size. It was just after noon, and a silver band had assembled on the bandstand, swathed in heavy coats, their faces red from the cold. The first tune they struck up was Wagner's *Rienzi*, a suitably sombre piece for this period of national mourning, but it lifted the spirits all the same; a solemn sort of joy seemed to spread across the park, putting a spring in every step. I paid an attendant threepence for a deckchair, which I inspected carefully before I sat down, in case it planned to collapse under me. That had happened once before, to the great amusement of all assembled.

"I do hope they play *Moses in Egypt*," said the young man seated to my right. He was pale and skinny, with a neck so thin his scarf went around it three times, and glasses so thick they made his eyes look too big for his head. "They have an excellent arrangement."

"I hope so too. Sure who doesn't love a bit of Rossini?"

We weren't looking at each other, but we could hear each other perfectly well, and there was no one close enough to eavesdrop, even if they had been able to make out our words under the grunt of the tuba.

"Though there is much to admire in your English composers. Herr Elgar's Enigma Variations. Superb."

"I prefer his choral stuff myself. But then Amelia says I have no taste."

I heard him chuckle. "How have you been, Herr Melville?"

"Fine, thank you, Walther. Thanks for coming."

"My pleasure. Your note suggested the matter was urgent."

"Well, it is and it isn't. I'm working with a compatriot of yours. His Imperial Majesty's new bodyguard."

"Ah yes. Herr Steinhauer."

"You know him?"

"I have met him." Walther worked as a clerk at Prussia House, the German embassy. I had formal police contacts there, of course, but Walther was an informal contact, and a sight more useful. We'd been friends ever since he'd tried to bring his young fiancée across from Germany; I'd helped him resolve some complications with her papers, and in return he'd taken to doing me the odd favour. As it happens,

I had been the one who originally caused those complications, but Walther was not to know that.

"He's an interesting character," I said. "I'd like to know more about him."

"In what respect?"

"Who recruited him. Who he answers to. The scope of his duties."

Walther paused to listen to the soaring flight of a cornet. "I shall have to enquire," he said at last.

"Don't put yourself out on my account. I'm just looking for some background, is all." I was hoping the remark sounded enough like a warning.

"I shall be discreet, Herr Melville, don't worry."

"Good. And how's the lovely Mathilde?"

"She is well. Expecting a baby shortly."

"Lord help us, how many's that now? Two?"

"This will be our third."

"You must be a glutton for punishment, Walther. Good luck with everything. I'll send along a gift for the christening." I'd be sure to send money, as well as baby clothes; Walther was an excellent investment.

"You are too kind. Ah!" He grinned with delight on hearing the opening bars of *Moses in Egypt*.

"I must be getting along. Enjoy the concert. Drop me a line, when you can." I extricated myself, with some difficulty, from my deckchair and strode off south-east.

WAITING ON MY DESK were replies from the police chiefs of Europe to my latest questions about Akushku, pursuing the agent provocateur possibility, but even though Angela's description of the man had been superbly detailed—right down to his missing finger—yet again my enquiries had drawn a blank. Which was, I confess, not entirely unexpected; those government officials who commissioned agents provocateurs did so at arm's length and routinely denied all involvement. If I wanted the truth, it seemed, I would have to twist some arms in person.

There was a rap on my office door—Constable Lawrence, who knew better than to enter unbidden before I had secured my papers.

"Come."

"Herr Steinhauer to see you, sir."

Steinhauer strolled past Lawrence beaming, like a gentleman of leisure visiting his wealthy maiden aunt.

"Thank you for seeing me up, Constable. It would be all too easy to get lost in this maze of unmarked doors." I took that with a pinch of salt: I'd wager Steinhauer memorised the layout on his first visit here. Then I recalled with a jolt how that had only been the night before last.

"Gustav, good afternoon," I said. "Jim, wait—Gustav, would you like tea or coffee?"

"You are very kind, William, but I have just had an excellent breakfast."

I nodded to Lawrence, who stepped out smartly and shut the door behind him. "A bit late for that, surely? I thought you Germans liked to be up with the lark."

"I was up with the lark, as it happens. I did not go to bed until six."

"Ah yes. Another of your mysterious sources."

"You know how it is. Some sources needed to be cajoled. Others can be persuaded with oysters and a good champagne. Particularly younger, female sources."

"Oh aye? And was your investment worthwhile?"

"Oh, I learned a great deal. Sadly none of it was relevant to this case."

Was he trying to shock me? I wondered. I didn't bother to tell him I'd just come from one of London's finest bordellos—this wasn't a competition. Besides, I wanted to know a little more about young Steinhauer before I shared too many confidences with him.

"So what can I do for you, Gustav?" I slipped the unmarked folder of telegrams into a drawer of my desk.

"My report to His Imperial Majesty is now long overdue. And I hoped you might have some good news I could share with him."

Was that a threat, or a genuine plea for help? More likely the latter, I decided; Steinhauer had as much to lose in this business as I had.

"We're making some progress, but not enough to report. Maybe you should tell His Imperial Majesty about these contacts you interrogated last night; I'm sure he'd find that entertaining."

"Have you managed at least to confirm what I told you?"

Was Steinhauer stringing me along? Or were his so-called sources stringing him along? What was his game anyhow? I could not send him back to the Kaiser—I did not want word of this affair to spread before I caught Akushku—but I didn't want to leave the young German to his own devices either.

"Let's discuss it on the way," I said, rising from my seat.

"On the way to where?"

"Ah now, that would spoil the surprise."

II

WE LEFT SCOTLAND YARD through the eastern entrance this time, past the stables and out into Whitehall's Parliament Street, where I flagged down a cab. I wanted to have a discreet conversation—and in a cab, over the rattling wheels and clattering of horseshoes, nothing could be overheard, not even by the driver, unless he were to lean over backwards and press his ear to the window.

"Langham Place," I told the cabbie. "Since you ask, Gustav, no— I haven't been able to confirm what you told me yesterday."

"Don't you have sources among the Latvian exiles?"

"I have. But they tell me the man we're after is not Latvian. He may claim to be, but in fact he's Russian. And no anarchist." I observed Steinhauer closely. "Rather, he's an agent provocateur, in the pay of the Okhrana." Steinhauer blinked, and stroked his bare chin, very much like a man quite taken aback. "And if all that is true," I went on, "this whole conspiracy could be a sham."

Steinhauer nodded. "And this," he said, his grin creeping back, "is what you call having little to report?"

"If it's indeed a hoax, there's no point in reporting it at all," I said. "I don't know about you, but I don't waste my master's time with false alarms."

"Are you so sure of your sources?"

"This one has been reliable in the past."

"But even if Akushku were an agent of the Russian police, it does not follow this plot is a hoax."

"Surely you're not implying the Russians want to assassinate His Imperial Majesty? He's the Tsar's cousin."

"When has that ever made a difference? How often in history have brothers gone to war over a crown? Besides, even if a ruler embraces peace, the men who surround him sometimes think they know better."

Is that how it is in the German court? I wondered. But I said, "You're suggesting it's not the Tsar who is behind this, but his generals? Or the Okhrana themselves?"

"I am suggesting nothing—I am merely asking questions, weighing up the possibilities. And in the end"—he held his hands out wide, palms up—"it does not matter what you or I believe. Our job is to manage risk. And I am sure you would agree there is a risk. There is certainly no evidence that would justify us sitting back and doing nothing."

"Akushku nearly blew my brains out the other night, Gustav. I have no intention of sitting back and doing nothing."

"So why are we in this cab, exactly?" asked Steinhauer.

"There's a backstreet butcher called Remington," I said. "An American, who fled his homeland under a cloud. And he now resides somewhere in Whitechapel, offering his services to embarrassed ladies of the parish."

Steinhauer sat up, like a hound that has caught the fox's scent. "Of course. Who better to extract a bullet or sew up a wound for a criminal on the run?"

"Are you a fan of the kinematograph, Gustav?"

"Moving pictures? Not particularly. If I want melodrama I go to the opera, where at least they have a decent orchestra."

"I'm of your mind entirely. But it seems Dr. Remington is fond of novelty. It's how he likes to spend his Sunday afternoons."

Even on a Sunday the traffic along Regent Street moved slowly, and this afternoon it was jammed solid; two delivery carts had collided in Piccadilly, and the drivers had come to blows. Rather than wait, Steinhauer and I jumped out at St. James's and walked north to Regent Street. Fifteen minutes later we were admiring a huge banner covering the entire façade of a building just south of Langham Place, advertising the latest kinematographic sensation.

"That does not look like a music-hall," said Steinhauer.

"That is the Royal Polytechnic, an educational establishment. With its very own auditorium, designed especially for displaying moving pictures."

"OUR NAVY AND OUR ARMY," Steinhauer read aloud from the banner. "SHOWING DAILY FROM ONE P.M. The same presentation every day?"

"And a very popular one, I'm told."

Steinhauer shook his head as if baffled. "The English do like to congratulate themselves."

"They have a lot to congratulate themselves about," I pointed out.

We crossed the street through a slow-moving tangle of cabs, pantechnicons and omnibuses to the far pavement and skipped up the steps to the foyer, where I purchased two tickets for the back of the stalls at a shilling each.

"Is Scotland Yard so strict about expenses?" Steinhauer grinned. "Why don't I buy us both seats in the Royal Circle?"

"We're not here for the show, Gustav." I handed the pastel-pink paper tickets to the usher.

The auditorium was darkened for the exhibition, a tub-thumping celebration of Britain's Imperial might. I'd seen it myself a few months earlier, and it was stirring stuff indeed, but I had no great desire to watch it a second time. I seemed to be in the minority, however—customers were coming to see it again and again, every few days, and according to Sally Porter the disgraced Dr. Remington was one of them.

We stood to one side in the aisle near the front, scanning the faces by the flickering light reflected from the screen. Well, I did; Steinhauer seemed to be admiring the auditorium. He seemed impressed, not just by the scale of the place but its modern, unconventional design. The hall was plainly decorated, with an elegant wrought-iron balcony, but none of the gilt and velvet found in theatres, nor any pillars that might block the view for the audience. It held about seven hundred people and, even now, at lunchtime, was half-full. The audience was male for the most part and enraptured by the moving images of Britain's fearsome battleships and their well-drilled naval crews. The patriotic fervour of the assembly was encouraged by stirring martial music performed by a small orchestra concealed behind the screen.

It was no damn' use. "I can't see him," I said, in exasperation.

No one there matched the description of Remington I'd shared with Steinhauer—a man of five foot eight or so in height, early forties, with reddish hair and a bushy, untended moustache. Sally was of the opinion he had once been striking, but a fondness for drink had seen to that. Steinhauer, I noticed to my irritation, had given the audience no more than a cursory glance.

"How often does this man Remington come here?" He had to raise his voice to be heard over the orchestra and drew several dirty looks from nearby customers.

"Most days, I'm told." I ignored the dirty looks.

"To see the same moving picture? Every day?"

"What's your point, Gustav?"

"You say he is American, not British. Why would he be interested in your navy? Unless . . ."

"Unless what?"

"Unless his interest is less in the British navy . . . than British sailors." I stared at Steinhauer a moment.

"Damn me for a fool," I muttered.

I set off across the front of the auditorium, throwing shadows on the screen, ignoring the boos and catcalls of the audience. I was headed for the alcove halfway up the far aisle closed off by a curtain that concealed the door to the public lavatories.

Steinhauer and I entered the gents' and paused a moment, dazzled by the harsh electric light bouncing off the white porcelain. A line of urinals along the left-hand wall gave way to a row of four wooden cubicles, each with a polished brass lock. There was no sign of any attendant, but a delicate young man with fair hair falling over his face was loitering by the washbasins, as if waiting for a servant to bring him a towel. He smiled fetchingly at me; and I gave him my hardest glare in return. He hurried out wordlessly, his face burning.

The first three lavatory cubicles were empty, but the last was occupied, its door shut and locked. The door did not reach all the way down to the floor, and I only had to bend down briefly to glimpse a single pair of scuffed brown shoes draped with trousers that had been pulled down. A man was clearly seated on the lavatory, and beside him on the floor rested a bag of the stoutest brown paper. The bag was a large one, and its contents bulged against the side. That old codology, I thought. Straightening up I thumped on the door with my fist.

"This stall is occupied!" snapped an angry American voice.

"Dr. James Remington, is it?" I said. "A moment of your time, if you please."

I heard a stifled gasp, then silence. When the American spoke again, his tone was not quite so defiant.

"God damn it, you blind? I'm otherwise engaged."

"The name's Melville, Dr. Remington, Detective Chief Superintendent Melville of Special Branch, and if you make me force this door I'll arrest both you and your friend with his feet in the paper bag, and you can talk to a judge in the morning."

More stifled gasps, and a frantic theatrical shushing beyond the door. When I caught Steinhauer's eye, he was trying not to laugh out loud.

"This is much better than the kinema-show," he whispered.

"Just a moment," said the American, his voice quavering. There was an urgent rustling of shirt-cloth and a fumbling of buttons, and the brass latch clicked open.

I PULLED THE CAB DOOR SHUT and took a seat on Remington's left, with Steinhauer seated on his right, sandwiching Remington between the two of us.

"May I ask where you are taking me?" His voice cracked with fear.

"That depends on how satisfied we are with the outcome of this conversation," I said. Remington, pale and apprehensive, swallowed and stared at the grubby cab floor. Steinhauer gazed out of the window, as if admiring the noble sunlit town houses of Park Crescent. We must have looked like three old pals setting off on a sightseeing tour of London.

"With respect, I fear you might have misread the situation," piped up Remington. *Here we go,* I thought. "That man was an employee of the Polytechnic who wished to consult me about an . . . intimate complaint," Remington continued. He swallowed to steady his voice, hoping to reassert some of his authority as a doctor of medicine. "I can see how this misunderstanding occurred, but I assure you—"

"Isn't Bow Street Police Station in the other direction?" said Steinhauer, addressing me.

"You're right, of course," I said. "I'll tell the driver to turn around."

"Look—please," protested Remington, "we were doing no harm to anyone—"

"I believe in this country it is called 'outraging public decency,'" said Steinhauer. "Personally, having served in the German navy, I know such things go on. But the Chief Superintendent here was raised as a good Roman Catholic in the west of Ireland. I am sure he was appalled by what he witnessed."

"Oh now, you'd be surprised, Gustav," I said. Folding my arms I leaned over just a little towards Remington, so he felt even more trapped. "I'm not as green as I'm cabbage-looking, Doctor. I don't give a damn what you chaps get up to, as long as everyone involved is old enough to make up their own mind, and you don't frighten the horses.

"If I did want to send you to prison, sure I already had enough evidence to put you away for twenty years. And that was before I caught you offering consultations in a public convenience. I'm told you're in what's commonly known as the lock-picking business."

"Who told—I don't—I'm not sure I know what you mean," stammered Remington.

"You know very well," I said. "But I'm not arresting you for that either. Not yet, anyway. You're more use to us at liberty."

"Indeed," chipped in Steinhauer, "if you are useful enough, my colleague might contrive to lose the charge sheet."

"Lose his whole damned file, for that matter," I added.

"My file?" quavered Remington.

"What would you say to that?" I put to him. "A chance to set up shop again with a clean slate?"

"What—what would I have to do?" Remington, God love him, was no fool; he already suspected that the task we had in mind might be even more dangerous than the work he was already doing.

"Your duty as a subject," I said.

"Dr. Remington is an American," Steinhauer reminded me.

"His duty as a human being, then. We're looking for two anarchists, Dr. Remington. Terrorists. One of them shot in the arm. Have you been approached at all?"

"By—by terrorists?" stammered Remington. "No, absolutely not. I know nothing about any terrorists—"

"All the better," said I. "You can still help us catch them."

"But, but—I am a doctor," protested Remington. "I have obligations, of confidence, towards my patients—I have taken an oath."

"Of course you have. I must say I'm impressed by ethical principles. Aren't you, Gustav?"

"Deeply," said the German. "Remind me, what is the penalty here for performing unnatural acts?"

"Prison, with hard labour. But he'll be out in five years, with good behaviour. If he doesn't get murdered in the meantime."

"Dear God," said Remington.

"But I don't like to see a man jailed just for indulging his unconventional affections," I went on.

"That's very broad-minded of you," said Steinhauer.

"Not when I could bang him up for performing abortions." Remington shut his eyes and shuddered. In truth, I'd never arrested or reported anyone for that offence, apart from one vicious old witch twenty years ago who'd been doing more harm than good. But Remington was not to know that.

"The Zoological Gardens!" exclaimed Steinhauer, looking out of the cab window again. "I have always wanted to visit."

"You should, Herr Steinhauer," I said. "It's a grand day out altogether."

"I didn't—didn't mean—" stammered Remington, "—of course I will do my civic duty—"

"Good man yourself," I said, beaming.

"What exactly do you want me to do?"

"Just . . . go about your normal business."

"My normal business? But—you know my normal business."

"I do," I said. "But I have bigger and meaner fish to catch than you, and you're going to be my bait."

"SERGEANT LOVEGROVE."

Lovegrove looked up from the map of London on his desk. A big fleshy man in his forties, he'd often been mistaken for me, and in happier days we'd speculated in jest about how he could provide me with an alibi should the need ever arise. But this was no time for jesting.

"There's an American doctor sitting in Interview Room number one, name of Remington. He's based in Whitechapel, and he offers certain medical services off the books. I'm betting our man Akushku is going to come looking for him. Pick three men, take Remington home to his lodgings and find premises nearby from where you can keep an eye on him, discreetly and at a distance. Work out a rota among yourselves. If or when our suspects come calling you are to send here immediately for reinforcements, and I or Inspector Quinn will raise an army. And on no account will you try to detain these terrorists yourselves, understood?"

"Sir," said Lovegrove, rolling up his map.

"Thanks for your help today, Gustav." We were heading downstairs towards the Embankment exit.

"That is why I am here. Besides, it was quite enjoyable. If I might say so, we make a good team."

"You think so?" For all my misgivings about Steinhauer I was inclined to agree. I preferred to work alone, and had thought myself set in my ways, but I had enjoyed the young German's company that day. Even if browbeating and blackmailing a backstreet abortionist was not exactly the noble vocation I had signed up for. "Well then, I hope you'll join me tomorrow."

"I shall report for duty at seven."

"I shall be at my desk at six. But by all means, treat yourself to a lie-in."

THERE WAS A WARM inviting glow from the front window of my home as I fished in my pocket for my latchkey, and the strains of a familiar hymn played on piano and violin in a ragged duet. Kate was a gifted pianist, but William, God love him, was less accomplished. He might make a living at the violin, I reflected, if we ever brought back the custom of torturing prisoners. I wondered if Angela was in there, pretending to enjoy the performance.

But she was not. "She went out for the day," was all Amelia said as she laid before me a plate of lamb chops and cabbage.

"Out where?"

Amelia shrugged, but her face betrayed real concern. I set to my dinner, but I could hardly taste it. Where could Angela have gone, barely recovered from that bullet wound? She'd been safe here, I'd thought, and happy too. Surely she wasn't missing her old existence? Friendless, impoverished, at the mercy of every—

Then I heard a soft tread upon the stairs, a tread that had become familiar over the last few days, and the lady herself appeared in the hall, swathed in a blue scarf, cheeks flushed with the cold and eyes gleaming beneath the brim of her borrowed hat. She'd entered silently by the back door. Amelia hurried to help as if Angela was her own prodigal daughter, taking her coat and her scarf and fussing over her— "You haven't even eaten? Well, I've a plate put aside for you, William's at his dinner now . . ."

As Amelia bustled away, Angela came to sit by me, pulling off her gloves. Sensing me watching, she drew herself up, straight-backed and defiant.

"You know he is still out there," I said. "Iosif." From the parlour I heard the sound of Kate and William laughing over some private joke. They would not overhear us. "He'll know it was you who betrayed him."

"Who do you think I was looking for?" She met my gaze and held it.

"That's not your job, Angela. I was thinking, I could find you a position as a governess—"

"That did not work out so well, last time."

"As a teacher, then. What would you like to do?"

"I would like to help you."

"That's not possible. It's too dangerous."

She laughed, and gestured to her shoulder. "You think I have forgotten?"

"There's nothing you can do that we can't."

"William, now you are being foolish. Iosif—Akushku—" She tilted her head to one side, searching for a delicate expression. "He has a . . . vigorous appetite. Without me, he will find himself another woman. He must, it is like breathing for him. I talk to the street girls." No tic of shame anymore, I noticed.

"We're already doing that."

"Yes, but you are men." She smiled, and I had no answer for her. She stroked the creases out of her gloves. "I cannot be a governess or a teacher. I hate children."

"That is something of a disadvantage," I conceded.

"But I will not go back to the gutter."

"Then let me find you a position, and a place to live."

She smiled, radiantly and sadly. "I would be your . . . kept woman?"

"That's not what I meant."

She rose from the table but, before she turned to go, placed her hand softly on my shoulder.

"You are a good man, Mr. Melville. I am glad I came to you."

12

I HADN'T BEEN CODDING STEINHAUER; I was at my desk by six on the Monday morning. Five days to the funeral, and still no word on Akushku and Bozidar, either from my counterparts on the Continent or from the team watching Remington's lodgings. That might be to the good, I told myself. Maybe Bozidar had died from loss of blood, or succumbed to infection from his shattered arm. Until I could kick his corpse, however, I had no intention of curtailing the search.

The morning newspapers had made no more mention of the "bank robbers" who had fired on the police on Friday night; the cover story had done its job. Was it worth planting another, I wondered, to keep the hue and cry alive, to turn the screws on Akushku? Or would that merely sow unease among the public? I drummed my fingers on the desk. Not just yet, I decided.

At the bottom of my heap of correspondence was a sealed envelope addressed to me by name and marked "personal." Inside was a letter on a single sheet of paper, unsigned and undated, but I knew the handwriting well: it was from my young friend Walther at Prussia House. His letter was brief by necessity: his casual enquiries about this latest recruit to the Kaiser's staff had been met with shrugs or cold stares, and the only files he could find on Steinhauer were slim indeed, with gaps that posed too many uncomfortable questions. According to those records Gustav had indeed travelled widely in the USA and Mexico, but there was no mention anywhere of cigar-selling or Pinkerton detectives. On his return to Germany he had been recruited to the Imperial Navy—not as a common seaman, but as an Offizier-Stellvertreter, a commissioned officer, attached to the staff of Admiral Von Tirpitz himself. After distinguishing himself in that role—notably by bringing home the traitor Ernst Rolf when all before him had failed—Steinhauer had been promoted to his current position. But that position was not officially bodyguard to the Kaiser, even if the Kaiser himself was under that impression. According to his file, Steinhauer was now attached to the German General Staff, Section IIb.

The Intelligence section.

I struck a match and held it to the corner of the letter, then to the envelope, and dropped them both into my litter bin, to watch them blaze and writhe and shrivel into ash. Walther had confirmed what a small nagging voice in my head had been suggesting from the start of this affair—that there was more to Steinhauer than met the eye, and more than he was telling. Indeed, ever since our first encounter he had been parsimonious with the truth, where he had not lied outright. I felt a twinge of regret. I liked Gustav; I admired his wit and valued his pluck.

But what to do? How to keep an eye on him? I could not park him at a Special Branch desk, still less send him back to the Kaiser.

AT SEVEN SHARP I started the briefing; Steinhauer stood at the back of the room, relaxed, attentive, and somehow making himself so inconspicuous my team barely noticed him. Now the weekend was over, I told my men, we could begin a proper sweep of the clubs and premises that had been closed over the weekend, assuring them we'd have the villains in cuffs or coffins by the end of the day. The men seemed heartened by my certainty, and oddly so did I. No one asked after Lovegrove or the other officers who were at that moment staking out Remington's lodgings, and I offered no explanation. Only those who needed to know about the vigil did.

"Johnson, Connolly?"

"Still tracking down the fan, sir," said Johnson.

"Any progress let me know immediately. And those of you with contacts among the demi-monde—have a quiet word. It seems our man Akushku can't go long without female company. Nothing exotic or specialised, which is a pity for our purposes, but there we go. You have his description, pass it along."

I saw Steinhauer raise a curious eyebrow, wondering where this tasty tidbit had come from. But my men knew better than to ask.

"Finally, some of you are already acquainted with our guest, Herr Gustav Steinhauer, bodyguard to His Imperial Majesty the Kaiser." Steinhauer acknowledged the curious looks and friendly nods with his usual short bow. "Herr Steinhauer has kindly offered to assist on this case. He'll be working with me, but I hope all of you will offer him the warm welcome and full co-operation due to a brother officer.

"That's all until tonight. Get to work, and Godspeed."

In a matter of moments the room was clear except for myself and Steinhauer. "Gustav," I said. "Have you met Colonel Rachkovskii?"

"Head of the Okhrana? Long ago. He may not remember me."

"If you met him, he'll remember you. He pretends to be a buffoon, but Rachkovskii forgets nothing. I plan to ask him if Akushku is indeed one of his agents."

"To his face? And you expect him to tell you the truth?"

"I expect it to be an interesting conversation."

How did Shakespeare put it? *Those friends thou hast, grapple them to thy soul with hoops of steel.* I would keep my friend Gustav close—the better to keep an eye on him.

THE GREAT GILDED HALL of the Criterion, with its massive pillars and stained glass, always seemed to me more like a cathedral than a restaurant. There were few worshippers present—it was just before ten—so it was easy to spot the grey-haired Colonel seated alone in one corner, perusing a French newspaper. As the waiter led us over to him, the Russian noticed our approach, laid his paper aside and rose to offer his hand. Slight of build, he was shorter even than Steinhauer, but his piercing grey eyes missed little.

"Chief Superintendent Melville!" He beamed. "So good to see you again. I am just arrived yesterday from Paris—I was about to come and pay you my respects." That was bunkum, I knew very well—he'd been in the city a week. But Rachkovskii was always saying such things, even when he knew his listener was certain he was lying. The purpose of such an approach baffled me; telling lies continuously and keeping them all consistent must call for enormous effort.

"Welcome back to London, Colonel," I said. "You've met Herr Inspector Gustav Steinhauer, I believe?" The two men shook hands, Steinhauer with his customary half bow and heel click.

As we settled back down in our seats a waiter offered us menus.

"We're not eating, thank you. Just two coffees."

"So it is true, then?" Rachkovskii smirked.

"So what's true?"

"That a previously unknown terrorist is abroad in London. One who calls himself Akushku. And that your men tried to intercept him, and failed." So much for my efforts to keep the matter *sub rosa*. I should have known Rachkovskii would have his own informants.

"My men did not fail, Colonel," I said. "I did."

"To be precise, we did," said Steinhauer.

"Presumably, he means to strike at the royal funeral," said the Russian, and sighed theatrically. "Well, I hate to say I told you so, but . . . your British approach is utterly unsuited to the threat these anarchists pose. Every day the disease of nihilism infects more of Europe's populace, and the only remedy is amputation. We are the surgeons—we must cut off the infected limb, and burn it." This was a favourite topic of his; the idea of tolerating dissent was utterly alien to him. "I know what you will say," Rachkovskii went on. "Permitting free speech lets you easily spot troublemakers and separate the dreamers and the doers. But when you give these terrorists and murderers a platform, you make doers of dreamers. You have sown the dragon's teeth, and now . . ." He glanced at Steinhauer. "Since you have brought along our young friend here, I take it the assassin's target is the Kaiser himself?"

"That is what our sources have suggested," I said.

"And of course that too could be misinformation," said Rachkovskii. "Leopold of Belgium is equally hated by these anarchists. And then there is Franz Ferdinand, of Austria. Or have you considered, the target might even be your new King, Edward? Oh, I know you think he is too beloved of his people to be in any danger, but the more popular the ruler, the more these fanatics despise them, precisely *because* the people love them."

I liked Rachkovskii, but not enough to sit and listen to a lecture. "One way of better identifying the assassin's target," I said, "would be to know who sent him."

"Sent him?" Rachkovskii chuckled. "Do I need to explain to you the principles of anarchy? Nobody sent him."

There was a lull in the conversation as the waiter served us coffee, and we fell silent, like a family that had just had a row over dinner.

"Except if the man we seek is no anarchist at all, but an agent provocateur employed by a foreign government," I continued, when the coast was clear. Rachkovskii frowned at this, as if trying to take it in.

"Your sources told you this? Tell me, would this source of yours, by any chance, be another anarchist, who hopes you will drop your guard? Chief Superintendent, you and I both know that agents provocateurs are a waste of time. Your own people end up spying on each other or, worse still, the agent manufactures conspiracies from thin air, simply to justify his wages. Provocateurs!" He snorted. "I never use them." That was a whopper, but I let it pass. "If this anarchist you seek was in fact working for us—and I take it that is what you and young Herr Steinhauer are implying—I would recall him, and tell him to stop wasting your time. Alas, he is not."

"But he is Russian?" asked Steinhauer.

The Colonel did not look at him, but stirred sugar into his coffee. "I am sorry, but my information about this Akushku is no more reliable than yours. In fact—and I admit I have no evidence for this, merely an instinct—I suspect he is French. Perhaps you should speak to the

Sûreté. Though might I suggest"—he smiled at me as he nodded at Gustav—"that if you do, you leave Herr Steinhauer behind?"

AS WE MADE OUR WAY BACK to Scotland Yard in a hansom, we did not discuss Rachkovskii's last barb. No need: we both knew what he was getting at. Thirty years earlier Germany and France had fought a war, a very short one; the Germans had utterly routed the French, the Emperor Napoleon III had fled, and the citizens of Paris had risen in a revolt that came to a predictably bloody end. To rub salt into French wounds, Germany had annexed the border territory of Alsace-Lorraine, with its wealth of coal-mines and steelworks. The war had been a national humiliation for France, one which her people—particularly her military—had neither forgotten nor forgiven.

"Will you talk to the Sûreté?" asked Steinhauer.

"I might. But I'm pretty sure Rachkovskii is giving us the run-around. All that nonsense about not using agents provocateurs—he has more of them than regular officers."

"This is common knowledge. So why lie to our faces like that?"

"Because it amuses him to project an air of intrigue." I sighed. "The Colonel is like a bad actor's version of a secret policeman. Perhaps he thinks it will make us underestimate him."

"Do you believe anything he told us?"

We were just passing the Crimean War Memorial at the corner of Regent Street and Pall Mall, the figure of Honour spreading her wings over three British Guardsmen. Even when the Russians were not openly at war with Britain, I reflected, they were never wholly at peace with us either.

"There are other ways using an agent provocateur can go wrong," I told Steinhauer. "If he's one of your trained officers, it takes a while for him to get accepted. If he's ever exposed he's dead. He has to immerse himself in the world of the men he is targeting, prove to them he's more committed to the cause than any of them. That can mean taking part in the very outrages he was hired to prevent. You end up funding terrorist atrocities with public money."

"Awkward indeed, if the press ever got wind of it," said Steinhauer.

"Awkward indeed. And it can get worse."

"How could it get worse?"

"The most effective undercover agents are those who immerse themselves completely. They live in poverty, starve themselves, live and breathe and preach anarchy. They become more radical than the radicals they're infiltrating. And sometimes they forget who they really are and how they got there. The British call it going native."

"You think"—Steinhauer looked genuinely disturbed—"that this is what has happened with Akushku? That he is a Russian agent who has turned his coat and joined the anarchist cause?"

The hansom wheeled right into Cockspur Street, the cabbie bawling out some hapless pedestrian who'd crossed his path.

"If a skilled agent provocateur, acting on behalf of a foreign power, is caught by the police, he surrenders," I said. "He might put up a token resistance, perhaps, to maintain his cover. But once in custody, he reveals himself, co-operates and waits for his handler to vouch for him.

"That first night you and I went after Akushku he tried to kill both of us, and nearly succeeded. No one is coming to vouch for him, and he'd hang even if they did. No, Akushku has gone rogue all right. He is a trained assassin, and he means to kill your Kaiser."

13

WE HAD BARELY DESCENDED from our hansom opposite Scotland Yard when another pulled up behind us to disgorge Johnson and Connolly. Johnson hurried over, pulling his notebook from his pocket, while Connolly fished for the fare.

"Sir," said Johnson, passing me his notebook. "Five customers purchased that same fan at Marshall and Snelgrove."

I skimmed the list of names; the final entry caught my eye. This might call for some diplomacy. "Good work. Find Jenkins and Baum, and the four of you call at those first four addresses. Ask if the fan is still in their possession."

"Sir."

"And if they say yes, ask to see it. Don't just take their word for it. The last name on there, I'll handle."

"Sir."

With the hint of a sideways glance at Steinhauer, Johnson went indoors. "This is about the fan you took from Miss Minetti's lodgings?" asked Steinhauer. "I had wondered why you thought it significant."

"It might not be," I said.

"May I ask, what is the last name on that list?"

"You can come with me, Gustav. I'll introduce you."

. . .

BERKELEY SQUARE seemed somehow sunnier than the rest of the city; it was as if London's common fug did not dare pollute this idyll, a tree-lined private garden surrounded by elegant town houses. Even the birds among the bare winter branches seemed to sing more tunefully. The hansom dropped Steinhauer and me outside Number 40, halfway up the western side of the square, and we ascended the broad granite steps to the massive front door painted shining black. There was a tradesman's entrance a little farther along, through the railings and down an iron staircase to the basement, but I was not here to talk to the servants. I gave the bell-pull a sharp tug, stood back with Steinhauer at my shoulder and waited. I had heard no bell ringing inside the vast house and started to wonder if the thing was working. Even our reflections in the mirror-like paint of the front door seemed diminished somehow, as if we had climbed a beanstalk to the castle of a foul-tempered giant. But after a minute, there was a hefty clank and rattle, and the door swung silently open to reveal a tall, strikingly handsome young footman in impeccable livery. He eyed us with an expression that was neither welcoming, deferential nor particularly intelligent.

"Chief Superintendent Melville of Scotland Yard, and Herr Inspector Steinhauer, a servant of His Imperial Majesty the Kaiser, to see Lord Diamond," I said.

"Do you have an appointment?" The footman's voice was as fine as his features, but his perfect diction sounded slightly contrived. I suspected the boy had been chosen for his looks rather than his gravitas.

"We do not," I said, "but he'll see us all the same." I held up my warrant card and gave him a warning look—the one that silently promised a nightmare of disruption and indignity and toxic gossip if he chose to defy us. The young footman got the message and stepped back to allow myself and Steinhauer to enter. I heard sharp footsteps farther up the hall, approaching with urgency, as if someone senior to this skivvy had smelled trouble and was coming to head it off. Sure enough here came a man who must have been Diamond's head butler—my age and almost my size, but with a stiff military bearing, a mane of snow-white hair over a deeply lined face and watery blue eyes under bushy white eyebrows. He paused a few paces away, and the footman hurried to his side and whispered his report. The butler listened, nodded calmly and turned to us with frost in his glare.

"May I tell His Lordship the nature of your business here, sir?"

"No need," said I. "I'll tell him myself."

"His Lordship is currently reading."

"Good. Then he can spare us half an hour. Let him know we're here, there's a good man."

The butler blinked as if I'd slapped him. Of course he had meant that we were to wait for His Lordship for as long as His Lordship fancied, but I would be damned if I was going to put up with that sort of nonsense. I held out my calling card, and the butler accepted it, sealing his defeat. But he still managed to add a good dollop of contempt to his invitation. "If you gentlemen would care to wait in the morning-room . . ."

The morning-room did not live up to its name; it was gloomy, with heavy green velvet drapes so bulky they blocked the light from the windows even when they were open. The walls were lined with pressed flowers and plants set in dark frames—lilies, roses, ferns and grasses laid out in starched, lifeless arrangements. It was the sort of decor one might associate with a particularly old-fashioned maiden aunt.

"It is like the Botanic Gardens in here," observed Steinhauer, sotto voce.

"Melville? What in God's name do you want?"

Diamond, swaggering into the room in his shirtsleeves, was all indignation. I'd half expected him not to recognise me, or to pretend not to recognise me; I might be a servant of the King, but I was still a servant, and a gentleman such as Diamond would never acknowledge the existence of servants if he could help it. Now he had been forced to abandon that rule and was making up for it by addressing me like a beater who'd turned up drunk for a grouse drive.

"My Lord," I said, "thank you for seeing us. We have some questions we would like to put to you."

Diamond was tall, pale and wet-lipped, with receding fair hair and eyebrows so blond and thin they were barely there. At thirty-one—I'd checked his entry in Burke's Peerage—he was half the King's age, but today as before his dress aped that of Edward, down to the lowest button of his waistcoat left undone. Edward needed to make room for his ever-expanding paunch; on Diamond's scrawny frame it was a silly affectation.

"And who's this?" Diamond was staring at Steinhauer as if he were a vagrant who had followed me in off the street. Even when I'd made the introductions, his attitude did not thaw. "Steinhauer? Not one of our Jewish brethren, are you?"

"No, sir. I do not share that honour."

"No. Didn't think the Kaiser allowed those creatures on his staff, thank God. So what is it you want, Melville? I've got no time to waste, even if you have."

I dug Minetti's fan out from inside my coat and opened it. Diamond glanced at it with little interest. "Have you seen this fan before, my Lord?" I said.

"Why on earth would I have any use for a fan?"

"So you haven't? Seen it before?"

"I might have done," he snapped. "Many ladies have fans. They're not items in which I take a particular interest."

"This fan was purchased at Marshall and Snelgrove, the department store, five weeks ago. And the sales ledger names you, my Lord, as the buyer."

"Really." It wasn't even a question; Diamond already seemed bored with the whole business. "And because some shop-girl writes my name in a book, I get a visit from the police?"

"Are you saying you don't shop at that particular store, my Lord?"

"Well, I do, as it happens, but rarely in the ladies' department."

"Why doesn't His Lordship take another look?" I suggested, in a tone designed to make clear it was not a suggestion. Diamond hesitated, then licking his thin lips reached out and took the fan from me. He peered more closely at it and flipped it over, his pale face starting to colour.

"Well, actually . . . I might have bought one like this, as a gift. I buy a lot of gifts at Christmas. It's pretty enough."

"One *like* this?"

"Well, yes, presumably, if that's what their books say. Though frankly I don't see—"

"Who was it intended for?"

"My . . . my . . . my wife of course," stammered Diamond, with a nervous smile, as though it were a stupid question.

"And is the fan still in her possession?"

"Well, em, no. As it happens, I mislaid it. Before I gave it to her."

"Mislaid it? Mislaid it how, my Lord?"

Now Diamond looked from one to the other of us, calculating, I suspect, if this was the proper time to become indignant about being interrogated in his own morning-room. But Steinhauer's presence unsettled him, as I had hoped it would. Unsure why exactly the German was there and what influence he might have, His Lordship was reluctant to resort to an aristocratic tantrum.

"Well, I put it away—as one does with Christmas presents—and when I went to retrieve it, it wasn't there."

"I see. Is it possible," I pressed him, "that it was stolen by a member of your staff?"

"Absolutely not. I mean, dash it all, Melville . . ."

The longer this went on, with every new morsel of information that had to be teased out of him, the less assured Diamond became. His swagger had evaporated; he was as nervous as a cow being led to an abattoir. In my experience, the reaction of the guilty under questioning was nearly always the same, whether the charge was stealing a loaf of bread or murder.

"Then what do you think became of it, sir?"

"I have no idea. It might still be in the house for all I know."

"Perhaps we should speak to Lady Diamond," I said, taking the fan back.

"Out of the question," said Diamond. He bit his lip, aware of how sharply he'd spoken. I said nothing, but let the silence curdle, waiting for Diamond to explain himself and thereby wade farther into the swamp. Steinhauer, God bless him, recognised the tactic and played along.

"That is, she's indisposed," blustered Diamond at last. Still neither Steinhauer nor I spoke. "My wife is of a nervous disposition," Diamond went on, "and I would rather not upset her with matters I can dispense with myself. And in any case, I am not even sure she's at home at present."

"Geoffrey?"

The three of us turned towards the double doors at the other end of the room, through which an imperious and stocky woman a little older than Diamond had entered. Lady Diamond's mousy maid was closing the doors behind her. How long had the two of them been loitering there? I wondered.

I recognised Her Ladyship from her occasional visits to Court, although she had never been one of the brightest stars in that firmament. Her square-shaped face seemed to wear a constant expression of disappointment; her finest feature was her gleaming chestnut hair, which she customarily wore severely pulled back and fastened down, as if it had a life of its own and at any moment might break free and embarrass its owner.

"Ah, my dear, you are home after all," said Diamond, smiling. There was something glassy and fixed about the smile and the greeting that made me doubt he was pleased to see her, or indeed that he was ever pleased to see her.

"You did not inform me that we had guests," said Lady Diamond. As ever her accent was hard to place—Prussian, I had always thought—and her words were perfectly polite, but the cold tone of rebuke in her voice was hard to miss.

"These gentlemen are trying to trace the owner of a lost fan," explained Diamond helpfully. "I was just explaining to them—"

"Chief Superintendent Melville of Scotland Yard, my Lady," I interrupted. Diamond fell silent, and chewed his lip.

"I have seen you at Court, I believe," she acknowledged with an imperious nod.

"And my colleague here is Herr Steinhauer, in the service of His

Imperial Majesty Kaiser Wilhelm." Again she nodded, with the merest glance at Gustav; she did not seem overly impressed. "Has Her Ladyship seen a fan like this before?" I continued, spreading the fan out once more.

"I am not sure. May I please have a closer look?"

"My dear!" Diamond laughed, too loudly. "You won't have seen it before. I bought you a fan just like this one as a gift last Christmas, but silly ass that I am I mislaid it somewhere. This can't possibly be the same one."

Lady Diamond looked up from the fan and tutted at her husband, "Why, Geoffrey, you are so forgetful. You did give it to me, don't you remember?"

Diamond blinked and smiled, as if searching his memory. His lips worked, but no words came out.

"And I lost it," she continued, "at the opera. I did not have the heart to tell you."

"You silly thing," Diamond almost simpered. "As if I would have minded!"

"Which opera?" Steinhauer cut in, addressing the question to Diamond.

"What?" grunted Diamond.

"If His Lordship can remember the opera in question, that might narrow down the dates," offered Steinhauer, pretending to be helpful. "Which opera house do you and Lady Diamond usually attend?"

"None of them," said Diamond. "My wife goes. I can't bear the opera." He laughed, unamused. "All that damned caterwauling—gives me a headache."

Lady Diamond smiled indulgently at her husband, then turned to Steinhauer. "It was a few weeks ago, at the Grand. A silly little piece called *The Princess Chic*. I felt unwell and left early. A day or two later I realised I had left my fan there. This might be it, I suppose."

"Did you make enquiries at the opera house?" asked Steinhauer. Registering his accent Lady Diamond peered at him sharply, as if trying to place him.

"Really, what would have been the point, after all that time?" she said, with a languid shrug. "But I am grateful you have returned it. Might I offer you a reward?" She sounded quite sincere.

"That won't be necessary," I said. "In any case you cannot have it back just yet."

"But why not?" protested Diamond.

"It's evidence in a criminal enquiry, my Lord," I said. "But rest assured, now we know it's yours, we'll be sure to take good care of it. And we'll return it in due course." I watched them both closely as I spoke, to see which of them squirmed. Diamond did, I noticed, but then he seemed prone to squirming when events strayed beyond his aristocratic control.

"You can buy me another, Husband," said Lady Diamond, lightly; her spouse flashed her a smirk utterly devoid of affection.

"Thank you for your assistance, my Lord. Lady Diamond." I bowed.

"Might I just be so bold—" said Steinhauer. "Your accent, my Lady. I pride myself on my ability to tell anyone's homeland by their manner of speaking, but when I listen to you I confess I am at a loss."

Lady Diamond gazed at Steinhauer with much the same disdain she had shown her husband, as if pondering whether to bark at him for his impudence or merely ignore him. "I grew up in Odessa," she said at last. Steinhauer nodded, and waited for her to elaborate, but it quickly became clear she wasn't going to. The German snapped his heels together and bowed.

"Thank you, Lady Diamond. I have learned something new today."

THE HEAVY DOOR swung shut behind us, and Steinhauer and I donned our hats as we strode south. Neither of us spoke until we were well clear of the Diamond residence.

"Lady Diamond is the most indulgent of wives," said Steinhauer. "To cover for her husband like that. I would swear he never gave her that fan."

"He did seem remarkably ill at ease."

"You brought me along to unsettle him?"

"And you did a fine job of it, Gustav."

. . . .

"ALL THE OTHER FANS are accounted for, sir," Johnson reported. "Present and correct." We were back at Scotland Yard; the daylight was already failing, and Sergeant McCarthy was lighting the gas mantles in the hallway outside my office.

"So our purchaser was indeed Lord Diamond," I said.

"And somehow the fan he bought ended up in the possession of Akushku," said Steinhauer. "Who gave it in turn to Miss Minetti."

"Should Johnson and I visit the Grand Opera House, sir?" offered Connolly. "If that's where Lady Diamond says she lost it."

"Lady Diamond is lying," I said. "She's protecting her husband. Never mind the opera house, I want Diamond's household watched. Where he goes, who he meets. Take Jenkins and Baum to assist you."

"Sir."

Steinhauer shut the door behind them, then planted himself in the seat facing my desk. "Shouldn't you bring Lord Diamond in for further questioning?"

"His Lordship is a Privy Counsellor, and a friend of the King," I said. "One does not *bring* such men anywhere they would rather not go. Not without substantial evidence. Which hopefully my men will uncover."

"Given time, he might concoct a better story."

"I pray he does. The more lies a man tells me, the more rope I have to hang him with."

"Do they hang lords in this country?"

"Not often enough, I admit."

IT WAS PAST MIDNIGHT when I climbed into bed beside my sleeping wife. Diamond was reported to have spent the evening at his club, and come rolling home roaring drunk at eleven; Remington had had two appointments, one with a girl barely old enough to have children, the other a matron swathed in veils. No men at all had been seen entering or leaving his lodgings. The snares were set; I just had to wait.

But it was the waiting that tormented me. One day closer to the royal funeral, it felt as if I was the one being hunted, and that if I dozed for a moment I would be caught in my own snare, at the mercy of the wolf.

"Brigid wrote," said Amelia sleepily. "Her mother's better. She'll be back on Friday."

"I'll arrange lodgings for Angela," I said.

I heard a catch in her breathing and sensed bad news coming. "Angela's gone," she said. "She left this morning, hasn't come back."

Just like that? I wanted to ask. No explanation, no word of thanks? But I just grunted, and after a little while Amelia's breathing regained its steady deep rhythm.

God help the girl, I thought, remembering what she'd said about seeking out Iosif herself. It was a madcap notion—the man had tried to kill her once already. Should I send men after her? Impossible. We were stretched to the limit as it was, without chasing after a wilful young woman obsessed with revenge. *You did your best*, I told myself. *She's not your problem anymore.*

But I slept uneasily, dreaming of wolves and snares and a girl in a blue hood lost in dark woods.

14

G OOD OF YOU to see me so early, Pierre."
Colonel Blanc grunted as he dabbed his croissant into a
blob of raspberry jam. I had not meant it as sarcasm; Blanc
was a creature of the night, and this was the crack of dawn for him.
We were seated in the dining room of the Coburg Hotel, Blanc in his
military uniform, a crisp white napkin tucked into his collar at the
neck. Blanc was maybe a decade younger than me, with a thick mane
of fair hair he wore swept back, and we were of much the same size.
More of his bulk was round his midriff, although his uniform was so
beautifully cut it was hard to tell. A fine bit of tailoring, I thought, as
I watched the Frenchman polish off his croissant in one bite and lick
his thumbs. He and I were old acquaintances in the intelligence trade,
but the last time we had spoken was at the 1898 conference in Rome,
where ministers and policemen from every state in Europe had met to
discuss the anarchist threat. The Frenchman had been less interested
in the task at hand—hammering out a definition of "terrorism" on
which all nations could agree—than finding the best brothel in which
to blow his expenses.

As it turned out, Blanc was the only one not wasting his time. After
more than a week of discussion, debate and furious argument none
of the illustrious ministers or coppers present could settle on a satis-

factory definition of "terrorism," and none of them could admit why, though radical newspapers were quick enough to oblige. The tactics certain governments used against their own people, these commentators observed, could all too often be classified as atrocities. If defining "terrorism" required some rulers to hold up their own bloody hands, they would rather it went undefined.

"I am up early," Blanc said at last, "because half the nobility of France is coming to this funeral. And every one of them expects a full military escort, armed and on horseback."

"What are they so afraid of? The English don't start fights at funerals. The Irish, now . . ."

"It is not about personal safety, Melville, it is about looking important. These people are not coming to mourn. This is a chance to mingle, to be seen in gilded company." He slurped his coffee. "It is a *promenade.*"

"Perhaps you should send to Paris for extra men." I sipped my own coffee and ignored the empty plate in front of me. I had been hungry, but the sight of Blanc's table manners had stunted my appetite.

"*Bof!* That would take weeks. I would have to put in a request to Gonn, he would demand to requisition men from Jeaume, Jeaume would appeal to Duvalier for more funds . . ." He picked up the coffeepot and, finding it empty, gestured impatiently to the waiter. "The more men my colleagues have working for them, the more important they feel. We are all competing with each other, keeping secrets from each other, chasing each other's operatives, more often than not. That damned Jew Dreyfus has done more damage to France than a whole army of Germans."

I stifled an impatient sigh. The Dreyfus Affair—when the French army was found to have rigged the trial of a Jewish officer falsely accused of spying and let him rot for years on Devil's Island—was a hobbyhorse of Blanc's, and I didn't have time to watch him cantering round the same old paddock.

"Him and the chorus of Jewish newspapers," Blanc continued. "The Hebrews have no sense of discretion or patriotism—and why should they, when they are not of our race? They will not be happy until they have pulled our civilisation down around our ears, so they can climb up on the rubble and crow. And sell the ruins back to us at a profit."

"Pierre, I am not here to debate the Jewish conspiracy. I am looking for a man they call Akushku—L'Accoucheur, in your language."

Blanc stopped chewing, but only momentarily. "I have heard that name." He nodded. "And that he was here, in London."

"He's a hard man to track down. We're not even sure of his nationality. Some say he's a Frenchman."

"Frenchman! He is no Frenchman."

"What is he, then?"

"He is probably another Jew." Blanc sniffed. "All these anarchists and terrorists, they are either Jews or the dupes of Jews."

I let that nonsense pass. I had long since given up arguing with otherwise intelligent men who allowed mere bigotry to colour their judgement.

"What else do you know of him? L'Accoucheur?"

Blanc shrugged. "Troublemaker, terrorist, revolutionary—these are, how do you say, mere flags of convenience. The Jews serve no cause and are loyal to no one but their own race." He spoke loudly, oblivious to the waiter at his shoulder swapping the empty coffeepot for a full one. I let him carry on ranting until the man had moved on. "You should ask Duvalier in the Sûreté, he has all the files."

I had done that, of course, days ago. For an intelligence officer Blanc was utterly lacking in guile; he didn't even enquire why I was asking. The French intelligence services were clearly in an even worse mess than I'd thought.

"I hear you have been working with that German, Steinhauer," said Blanc abruptly.

"We've been co-operating on security arrangements for the funeral."

He snorted. "How generous of the German Kaiser to lend you one of his officers."

"The Kaiser was Her Late Majesty's grandson."

"Of course, of course," said Blanc airily. "But if I were you, I would be careful what I allowed young Herr Steinhauer to see."

"Why would that be, Pierre?"

Blanc shrugged again, as if it was a matter of the utmost indifference to him. "When the Germans offer to help, when they say they share your interests as neighbours, that is the very time you must be on guard." He lowered his voice and leaned forwards until I could smell sour breakfast on his breath. "Thirty years ago I was a mere lieutenant, still—*comment cela est-ce que se dit?*—wet behind the ears, but even then I could see them, insinuating themselves into our society, our culture, even our court, every part of our daily life. I reported my concerns, but, of course, our people insisted there was nothing to worry about—these people were under observation, our own spies had infiltrated the German government, and so all was well. And then, in 1870, came the war, and our army fell apart like papier-mâché, and our agents . . . poof! They evaporated. As if they had never been. And they never had been, because they were never our agents, they were German agents. The Germans had been preparing for ten, fifteen years, waiting for their moment." Blanc drained his cup and wiped his moustache. "I do not trust any German, however helpful they may seem to be. And unless you want Great Britain to fall, as France fell, neither should you."

IN THE CAB back to my office I mused on Blanc's parting shot. He had merely been echoing my own misgivings about Steinhauer. But hearing them from the mouth of that small-minded buffoon made me wonder if I had been too long in this job and had started imagining conspiracies where there were none. So Steinhauer the Imperial bodyguard really worked for the Intelligence section—so what? The same, after all, could be said of me. So Walther could not find much in Steinhauer's files—well, Gustav had not been in military service all that long.

Britain was not France. The Germans were our ancient allies. Albert the Prince Consort had been German; the new King and all his siblings were half-German; the army had a German battalion; we had German cultural exchanges, German-owned businesses. Were they all elements in some brilliant plan to infiltrate Great Britain, played out over centuries? The idea was preposterous.

Almost certainly Steinhauer had been at that meeting of Latvian radicals. But Latvia was a thorn in Russia's side and, as such, of strategic interest to Germany. Steinhauer, surely, was just doing his job.

If only I knew what that job was, exactly.

As I pushed through the doors of Scotland Yard, all thoughts of Steinhauer vanished from my mind. There was something terribly wrong; I could sense it in the very air of the building. The constables on duty at the front desk were grim, conferring in hushed tones with Patrick Quinn, who turned to me with a face as pale as death.

"Sir," said Quinn, "I was about to send for you."

"What's happened?" I said. But somehow I already knew.

OUR TWO CHARABANCS, crammed with uniformed men and every officer we'd been able to muster, swayed wildly as they took the corner into the narrow street in Whitechapel where two squat terraces of blackened brick faced each other across a dirt road in the shadow of a railway bridge. As our vehicles rocked to a halt a train thundered overhead, filling the air with sooty smoke, steam and noise. I jumped down, looked around and saw the stocky figure of Dubois, vomiting into the gutter outside a small shabby house—the house where Lovegrove and his team had been stationed, directly opposite Remington's lodgings. As I approached, Dubois straightened up, wiping his mouth with a handkerchief.

"Where are they?" I said.

"Inside, sir. We found them at seven, at the change of shift."

He led me through the front door along the short gloomy hallway to the back room. From the look of the place the usual inhabitants were poor but fastidious; their furniture, though meagre, was spotless, and the kitchen stove neatly blacked. This I took in at a glance, before my eye fell on the body lying crumpled in the farther doorway. It was Sergeant Harry Bishop, in his waistcoat and shirtsleeves; the tail of his shirt was stained red with blood that had spilled from a single stab-wound to his left kidney, but most of his blood was on the floor, in a large puddle under his prone body; after he had fallen, it seemed the killer had lifted his head by his fair hair—it was still standing up in a tuft—and cut his throat. Bishop had died clawing at the oilcloth flooring, fingers stained red with his own life's blood.

"Any footprints?" I asked.

Dubois shook his head. I looked around; the killer had waited behind the dresser, I guessed, for Bishop to come downstairs, stepped out from behind him, stabbed him, then slit his throat and hurried out before blood stained his boot-soles. Out the way he had come, through the back alley.

"Lovegrove's in the outhouse?" I said. Dubois nodded, wondering how I'd guessed. But it was how I would have done it, if I had wanted to murder two policemen keeping surveillance from a house. I would lie in wait until morning, when one of them would come out to use the toilet. I would kill the first man there, in the dark, as quietly as possible, and stash the body out of sight. And when his companion missed him and came looking . . .

Lovegrove had been garrotted with a wire. His purple tongue protruded through his purple lips, and his eyes bulged painfully from his face. He was leaning forwards slightly on the toilet seat, held in place by the wire that had been secured around the down-pipe from the cistern. The tension had pulled the garrotte so tight it had disappeared into the flesh of his neck. Oddly, in death, he looked more like me than ever. I felt a pang of savage pain for the loss of a man I'd known and liked and trusted, and I felt rage boil up in my belly. To hell with defending the Kaiser or the kingdom—Akushku had made this personal. Silently I vowed that very soon I'd have the villain alone in a cell under Scotland Yard, longing for his own pit of lime.

"What about the subject?" My voice was more gruff than I'd expected. Dubois looked blank. "Remington," I said. "Is he dead too? Has anyone checked on him?"

Dubois ran a hand through his hair. "He's gone, sir. Vanished."

"I am with the Chief Superintendent."

It was Steinhauer, at the back gate, addressing the constable on guard. The man turned to me for permission, and I nodded.

"Dear God," said Steinhauer as he joined me at the outhouse. He slid his hat off his head. "I am sorry, William."

"They had families," I said. "Bishop had three young children."

"The alley out there leads off in both directions," offered Steinhauer. "And it is heavily used. I looked for footprints, but there are too many."

"I can't believe it," said Dubois. "That Akushku sniffed them out and did this. They were two of our best."

"And yet," I said.

But I didn't believe it either. Akushku, for all his fearsome skills, could not have sniffed them out.

Not without help.

"THIS IS GRAVE NEWS, WILLIAM." Anderson had for once come to my office rather than summon me to his. Whether he wanted to be close to his troops at a time of crisis, or merely wanted to keep this disaster away from his desk, I did not care enough to guess.

"It is, sir. They were good men, and well liked."

"My sympathies to you, and to their colleagues, of course." He made a show of cleaning his spectacles while he moved on to the practicalities. "Have the next of kin been informed?"

"It's in hand."

"And what about the press?"

"They've been sniffing about. I want to let them know what happened."

"That would merely spread panic. We should say nothing to the newspapers until Saturday."

Of course: Sunday's newspapers would be crammed with accounts of Saturday's funeral and tributes to the Queen; a story on the murder of two detectives on duty would be scarcely noticed. Trust Anderson to think of that.

"On the contrary, sir," I said, "we should raise a hue and cry. If the general public is asked to look out for vicious bank robbers who murdered two policemen in the line of duty, it will make it that much harder for Akushku to stay concealed. Let's use the press to our advantage, invoke public outrage."

I watched Anderson fish for reasons to overrule me, and find none.

"Very well," he conceded irritably. "But not a word about our quarry's true intentions."

"Of course not, sir," I said.

"Perhaps," said Anderson, replacing his glasses and gazing at a point somewhere over my shoulder, "we ought to consider bringing in more reinforcements, from CID. Officers of greater seniority." I nodded, as if considering the idea. He meant either to replace me or line up more scapegoats to suffer when this affair was over. I was not prepared to countenance either option.

"We already have their best men. And enough of them."

"Nevertheless, this chap Akushku seems to be running rings around us." *Around you*, he meant; that was clear enough.

"Every move he makes brings me closer to him, sir. And I have a new line of enquiry to pursue." *Don't ask me what it is, and I won't have to lie to you*, I thought. But Anderson merely shook his head and sighed.

"I am not as a rule a gambling man, William."

"I know that, sir. And I appreciate your support." He stood.

"Keep me informed."

"I will," I lied.

15

"G ENTLEMEN . . . earlier today we lost two good men. Good friends. Men with families, men who served their King and their country, men who—gave everything they had." I took a deep breath, to compose myself. "Their sacrifice—it won't be in vain, I swear to God."

The faces watching me were grim and solemn and silent; I'd rarely made such a speech. But not rarely enough. "Four days from now the state funeral will take place. There was a chance that Akushku and Bozidar had given up or fled. Now they've murdered two of our colleagues, we know that's not the case. They mean to assassinate the Kaiser, and if they succeed, if there is any defilement of that ceremony, the consequences . . . they're unthinkable. We must stop these men, and we will, by any means necessary.

"The man who calls himself Akushku is the most ruthless, the most bloodthirsty and the most dangerous we have ever sought. We're going to redouble our efforts to find him, bring in uniformed officers, search every workers' club and social club and political club again, along with every lodging house, every bawdy house, every lean-to and every shed. And every one of you will carry his weapon, close to hand, loaded and ready to use. If for one moment you fear for your life or for the life of a colleague, do not hesitate—shoot, and shoot to kill. Whatever happens I will stand by you, and answer to anyone on your behalf, because you are my brothers. And because the stakes could not be higher."

From the corner of my eye I noticed Steinhauer, grim and solemn, but watching neither me nor my officers; rather he seemed lost in some dark, comfortless world of his own.

"Descriptions of Akushku and Bozidar will go out to every newspaper in this country, and on the Continent. But fear and horror are the terrorists' stock-in-trade, and I want to deny them those weapons. As far as the press is concerned, they are bank robbers who murdered two policemen while evading arrest, and that's all anyone outside this room needs to know. Not how they died, nor the atrocity they gave their lives to prevent. I don't have to remind you, but I will: we do not discuss our work with anyone, not our colleagues, not our sweethearts, not our families—no one. Yes, at times like this we need friendship and we need solace, but let us find it in each other. We are men, and we are warriors, and when our comrades fall in battle, we honour them by marching onwards. When this battle is won we will mourn them, and we will remember their sacrifice, and honour it. But for now we will honour them in our hearts, and avenge them with our actions. We will work every hour the good Lord gave us, and we will hunt down these savages, and we'll see them hang or we'll kill them ourselves, but by Christ's holy blood they will pay for what they did today."

I fell silent a moment; my voice was shaking. I wasn't ashamed of my anger and grief, but there was still business to attend to.

"The team that went with me to the East End today," I went on, "is staying there to comb the area for witnesses and evidence. Quinn here has the assignments for the rest of you. Your work is vital. Next briefing here tomorrow at seven a.m. Till then, God be with you, and with all of us."

"WHERE DID YOUNG STEINHAUER GO?" I asked Quinn as I headed for my office.

"Down to the canteen, I believe. Said he hadn't eaten since this morning." He followed me in, and cleared his throat. I guessed what was coming. "Sir . . . The families, of Lovegrove and Bishop, they've yet to be informed. Would you like me to see to that?"

"Thank you, Patrick, but no," I said. "I'll do it myself, this afternoon. God forbid they should find out some other way."

"I don't envy you that."

"Before I go," I said, "I've a job for you. I'm meeting a source tonight in Bedford Square, at two in the morning."

Quinn was puzzled. I never told anyone I was meeting an informant, still less shared the details.

"Sir?"

"I need you to make a note of it."

TWENTY MINUTES LATER I emerged from my office shrugging on my coat, and saw Steinhauer just up the corridor, handing Quinn a piece of paper my man had let slip from the teetering stack in his hands. Seeing me the German smiled solemnly and sauntered over.

"Gustav, hello," I said. "I'm just off to see the families of the men we lost today."

"I am sorry, William. I would not wish that task on anyone. Would you like me to come with you?"

"No, no. I know these people; it wouldn't be appropriate to bring a stranger along. And you've done enough for one day." I locked the door of my office and slipped my keys back into my pocket. "Come, I'll give you a lift to your hotel."

"Thank you, but I do not think I will return to my hotel just yet."

"Off to see the tailor, or the tarts?" I said. Steinhauer merely smiled. "Good," I said. "I'll be chasing up a lead of my own, later."

MY BREATH was condensing in clouds around me as I strode towards Bedford Square; I heard a grandfather clock chime two o'clock from a hallway nearby. Town houses loomed on each side of me, massive as cliffs, shuttered now and silent. Even the scullery maids would be abed, I thought, snatching a few hours' sleep before they rose at five to rake out the grates and light the household fires. For myself, I couldn't have slept if I'd wanted to. When I'd called at Bishop's house, I found the maid-of-all-work had the night off, so Edith Bishop had answered the door herself. Seeing me on her doorstep she had known instantly what it meant, and all the colour had drained from her face. We had not met since her wedding; Amelia and I had attended as guests of her husband. I had danced with her that day, I remembered now, and tonight I had held her in my arms again, but in grief; her slight body racked with sobs. As I had left, an hour or so later, I had found myself shaking with anger, that this Russian had murdered her husband, my friend and colleague, in cold blood, and left him sprawled on the floor like a worthless drunk.

Much of that anger I directed at myself, because it had been I who had sent Lovegrove and Bishop to their deaths. I had known that Akushku was lethal, and warned them; what I hadn't known was that they would be betrayed.

When the street opened into the square, I was the only living soul to be seen, and that was how it should be, I thought. Let the gentry and the merchants and their servants sleep soundly in their beds; it was my task to ensure they could. But I promised myself when this business was done I'd sleep for a month.

The garden at the centre of the square was surrounded by iron railings eight feet tall, but the massive gates at the eastern end lay wide open as if the park keeper had forgotten his duty. As I passed through it seemed that I was entering a primeval forest. Yes, the trees that towered above and around were leafless, but the paths were edged with evergreen bushes of holly and laurel that soaked up the streetlamps' glare and absorbed the noises of the distant city, so I walked in black shadow, with only the sound of my boots on gravel for company. As I headed south, towards the drinking fountain, I picked up a faint rustling off to my left. I paused and waited; the sound came from low down, and moved off quickly, with a scrabbling of claws—a rat, perhaps, or a feral cat on the hunt.

The black shape of the fountain loomed out of the darkness so abruptly I nearly walked straight into it. I knew how it looked in daylight: a pink granite plinth crowned with a Gothic-style arched turret. In each of its four alcoves was a tap and a basin, with a brass cup chained to one side so visitors could drink. Now it was just a mass of stone, to be felt rather than seen. I turned my back on it, and waited, and listened.

In less than a minute I heard it—the screech of metal hinges and a heavy clang on the eastern side, followed moments later by the same screech and clang to the west. Now hobnail boots were clattering on stone, and there were urgent shouts, and in the middle distance a flicker of hand lanterns like French fireflies. I stood and waited; I had no lamp of my own, and if I had run into the bushes to see what was going on I might have impaled myself on a branch. Besides, I had a good idea what was going on, and only needed to attend the outcome.

There was a constable's whistle, thirty feet or so away to my right, and the shouts and ruckus seemed to gather and focus there. So much for the unbroken sleep of the gentry—the rumpus was echoing all around the square. Now I started to move towards the locus of the noise, back the way I had come. Perhaps it was the lamplight glinting through the bushes, or perhaps my eyes had become more accustomed to the darkness, but I fancied I could see more clearly now. On the lawn beyond the next row of shrubs, by the light of half a dozen lanterns, a mass of heaving shadows resolved itself into solid shapes: four of my detectives—in heavy coats but hatless now—wrestling a man to the ground and pressing his face into the grass so that his yells of protest were stifled. He appeared to be heavy-set, with a long beard and hair cut short in a military style.

"Easy, lads, easy, let him breathe, now," I said. My men lifted some of their weight, and their captive raised his head, gasping and gulping for breath.

"Gustav," I said. "Small world."

16

STEINHAUER WAS MANHANDLED, none too gently, into the rear of a Black Maria, Dubois and myself clambering after him. He struggled to get up—having lost the padding that had helped to disguise him, he kept getting tangled in his oversized coat.

"William, this is absurd—"

"Dubois, keep your gun on him." I hauled Steinhauer up onto the bench farthest from the door. Dubois took a seat at a safe distance and propped his revolver on his knee, pointed squarely at Steinhauer's chest.

"You think it wise to bring a witness?" said Steinhauer, but his attempts at dignified indignation fell flat. With his fake beard hanging half off his face and his hat trampled in the struggle he cut a pathetic figure. "I will report this!"

"You'll report nothing, Gustav. And take no comfort from the presence of Sergeant Dubois. He won't witness anything, even if he has to shoot you. Which he will, if you make one sudden move."

Steinhauer's mouth worked. He was trying to figure out if I was bluffing, and decided that I was not, which was shrewd of him, because two of my friends had been murdered and I was full of cold fury. When he finally spoke, his usual air of detached amusement had evaporated. He raised one hand slowly and started to peel off his fake beard.

"I have no idea what you are hoping to accomplish with this—"

"How long have you been working with Akushku?"

"Working with him?" Steinhauer almost stammered. "I do not— I have never met the man, never communicated with him, even indirectly—"

"There's an informer in our ranks, Gustav, and it's not one of my men."

"You think I have been feeding information to a terrorist—?"

"They were waiting for us that night, at Minetti's lodgings. They knew we were coming. That's why they had a lookout at the front of the house. You were the one who told me they'd escaped in a cab, then told me you'd lost him. When all the while he'd doubled back to rescue Bozidar."

"This is absurd—" Steinhauer glanced nervously at the muzzle of the gun.

"Two colleagues of ours are dead, Gustav, and the only one who knew they were watching that house was you."

"Akushku must have spotted them, then—"

"Lovegrove had done that job a hundred times," I said, "and never once given himself away. He and Bishop were murdered, butchered in cold blood, by a man who knew just where they were and how many." I glanced at Dubois, who cocked the hammer of his gun.

"Then I am not the only one who knew!" insisted Steinhauer, raising a hand to shield himself, as if his fingers could stop a bullet.

"One last time, Gustav, who is Akushku?"

Steinhauer opened his mouth, and closed it again, and exhaled, long and deep. When he spoke his voice was full of disappointment and resignation. "William . . . your man may as well shoot me, because I cannot help you. I am sorry, but I think the strain of this affair has broken you—you have lost your mind."

"It's you who will lose your mind, Gustav. It will be all over that wall." Dubois raised the muzzle a little higher.

"What will you tell my master?"

"Whatever I damned well please," I said.

Steinhauer sighed. "I am not working with Akushku. I am trying to stop him, like you. I stood by your side in that hallway, have you forgotten? You think he was shooting only at you? He nearly blew my arm off. You know this is true."

"You haven't told me the truth since the day we met," I said. "You never sold cigars in America, or you'd know that Newman cigars are made in Cleveland. And you're not just the Kaiser's bodyguard, or you wouldn't have been hanging around at a meeting of Latvian anarchists in London a few weeks back, wearing a disguise, just like the one we caught you in tonight. Or am I mistaken about that as well?"

Steinhauer hesitated, clearly taken aback by how much I knew of his activities. I left out everything I'd learned from Walther's letter— I couldn't mention that without compromising Walther. But I didn't need to; tonight I'd caught Steinhauer red-handed, and he knew it.

"Yes, I was spying on you tonight," he blurted. I could see sweat beading on his brow. "But if our positions were reversed, you would have done the very same. I did this because for some reason you do not trust me, William, and I have to know what you know. I want to catch these men as badly as you do. If we fail, you may be embarrassed, forced to retire with a gold watch and a pension, but all I will be offered is a blindfold and a cigarette."

"Not if I shoot you first."

Steinhauer paused a moment, then actually smiled.

"You will not," he said softly. "Or you would have done it by now."

He was right. But only a few moments earlier I would gladly have given Dubois the nod. In those moments at least Gustav had believed he might die, which was one reason I now believed his protests.

The other reason had just occurred to me.

There were two others besides Steinhauer who had known of my plans, and had known that Lovegrove and Bishop had staked out Remington's lodgings. I had told both of those people myself.

I turned to Dubois. "Put that away, Sergeant. Tell John to head back to the nick." Dubois uncocked the hammer of his pistol, slipped it back into its holster and clambered out of the rear door. We heard him bark an order to the driver.

"Your man Quinn," said Steinhauer, "he dropped that memorandum deliberately?"

"I'm surprised you fell for that one, Gustav."

"I am embarrassed, I confess."

The Black Maria jolted into motion, and the circles of yellow light cast by streetlights shining through the portholes started to flick across our faces. Steinhauer leaned his head back against the metal wall.

"It is ironic, is it not?" he said. "We talked about using agents provocateurs to sow mistrust among our enemies. And here we are, fighting among ourselves." He sighed. "I shall rejoin the Emperor tomorrow, and report to him all that has happened."

"By all means do," I said. That took the wind from his sails, and he looked at me in disbelief. I wasn't scared of his Kaiser's wrath, but that wasn't why I'd called Steinhauer's bluff. "His life will be in grave danger at the funeral. He needs to be aware of it, and take appropriate measures," I said.

"But your own King forbade you to tell him that," said Steinhauer.

"He did," I replied. "But he also said I should take you with me on that raid, instead of a squad of men, and look how that turned out. Tell your Emperor everything and let him decide what he wants to do. You don't answer to my King, and I don't answer to yours."

"William, you must believe me. In this business, we are on the same side."

In this business. I couldn't help noticing that. "I do believe you, Gustav. Mind, if you actually got yourself shot by Akushku, I would have believed you sooner."

Steinhauer took his hat off and tried again to push the crown back out.

"I don't believe you would have ordered your man Dubois to shoot me."

"Don't you?"

"You are too good a man," said Steinhauer. "Too honourable. Not ruthless enough, I fear. Not for this new century."

The cheeky young whelp, I thought. Did he mistake me for a gentleman? But I merely grinned politely. "I suppose we'll never know," I said. "Now, should I drop you at your hotel? Or take you to the German consulate at Prussia House?"

"Wouldn't you rather I was somewhere where you could keep an eye on me?"

"What makes you think we don't keep an eye on Prussia House?"

"Our mission is not accomplished, William. I would still like to help."

"What I have to do next, you can't help with."

"Then send me out with your men. I have some ability, I think you will allow me that. Even after tonight."

I pretended to ponder for a while, though we both knew what my answer would be. "I'll drop you at your hotel. Get some sleep, and report to Patrick Quinn in the morning."

"What about you? Are you going home?"

"No point, at this time of night. I'll probably bed down in a cell. God knows I might have to get used to it."

BUT I HAD NO INTENTION of bedding down, either in a cell or the couch in my office. I found Patrick Quinn at his desk, wading through a flood of paperwork as he waited to hear what our trap had snared.

"It's not Steinhauer," I said.

"Then it's Anderson," he said. "No one else knew in advance about the raid on Akushku."

"It's not Anderson either. One other man knew," I said. "I've written a report to him every day since this started."

"You don't mean . . ." Quinn could not bring himself to say it.

"His Majesty the King has known every detail of our every operation. And he's not very discerning about the company he keeps."

"But, sir—how can you be sure it's not Anderson?"

"I have my own sources, Patrick. Better you don't ask."

"So what's to be done? Will you tell His Majesty that someone in his circle is passing information?"

"I can't. The King's no actor—he can't bluff. If he knows, his whole circle will know, and the jig will be up. No, we have to keep His Majesty in the dark if we're to catch our man in the act."

"It's only three days until the funeral."

"Yes, so we must set up the surveillance and the postal intercepts straightaway. Before first collection this morning. I'll plant some misinformation in my next report, see where it reappears."

Quinn cleared his throat. "Sir . . . some of the King's circle are Privy Counsellors. If it ever gets out that we opened their letters . . ."

"We'll all be fired. Disgraced. Thrown in jail. I don't give a damn. If we don't catch Akushku in the next three days we'll face a lot worse."

17

LORD DIAMOND left his house this morning at nine-oh-seven, sir, on horseback, and headed for Hyde Park, arriving there at nine twenty-six. He exercised his mount on Rotten Row until ten thirty-five, when he fell into conversation with a lady out walking with her maid, whom we later identified as Lady Florence Randall."

Johnson read from his notebook in his usual quiet, droning voice. I fought back the urge to tell him to hurry up and get to the point.

"At one point Lady Randall had words with her maid, who thereafter kept a distance of about ten paces behind the couple."

"I see," I said. "And did you manage to overhear what Diamond and Lady Randall were saying?"

"Connolly managed to get quite close, sir. He tells me they appeared to be discussing a new exhibition at the Marlborough Gallery. Nude portraits, sir, supposedly of quite a shocking nature." Johnson's drone made even these salacious details vaguely soporific. "Lord Diamond mentioned similar exhibits he'd seen in Paris."

"I see. Frankly this sounds more like a flirtation than anything sinister."

"That was our impression, sir. And indeed, although the subject and Lady Randall parted at eleven-oh-five, fifteen minutes later Lord Diamond left the park and went directly to Lady Randall's house."

I guessed where this was headed. To London's aristocracy Rotten Row was more than just a venue to exercise their horses.

"Lord Randall is in India at the moment, isn't he?"

"Yes, sir." The respectable Johnson seemed unwilling to meet my eye. "Bangalore."

"Was Lord Diamond admitted to the residence?"

"He was, sir. And the bedroom curtains on the second floor were closed a few minutes later. For over an hour, sir."

"I see."

Johnson looked back to his notebook. "At twelve forty-five p.m. Lord Diamond emerged and rode to the Liberal Club where he joined the Lord Eden for lunch. At two o'clock they were still there, and had started on their third bottle of wine. Shortly after two p.m. Masterson and Jones took over the surveillance."

"I suppose there's no point in my asking, but any sign of Akushku?"

"No, sir. And we didn't see him post any letters or make any written communication, sir." Johnson flipped his notebook shut, and hesitated. "Might I make an observation, sir?"

"By all means, Inspector."

"Lord Diamond is well known to be, pardon me, somewhat louche. He drinks, he gambles, he's unreliable, indiscreet. Frankly, he's a man with no moral fibre of any sort."

"That sounds like a fair assessment."

"Which would make him a target for blackmail."

"It might," I said, "if he made any effort to keep his vices secret." I remembered Lady Diamond, and the pantomime of marital affection she put on for me and Steinhauer. She seemed to have few illusions about her husband.

"If he had gambling debts, sir? That would also make him vulnerable."

"Look into it."

IN NORMAL CIRCUMSTANCES, opening other people's letters carried draconian penalties, and deservedly so. However, in 1890 or thereabouts I had stumbled across a loophole: thanks to the ancient Liberties of that part of the City of London—quirks in the by-laws—letters routed through the Mount Pleasant sorting office were not protected. They could be intercepted and opened by anyone, quite legally. My first action back then had been to make damned sure no Special Branch letters ever went near the place, and my second was to arrange a secure room in Mount Pleasant office where we could if necessary open everyone else's letters. I was well aware of the irony, but were I not a hypocrite I could not do my job.

THAT SAME MORNING Kingsbury, Dubois and myself took up residence there, ignoring curious stares from the few members of Royal Mail staff who were unaware of the protocol—which was that we did not exist, and were not there.

The fourth member of our team that day was Malkovich, lugging his customary Gladstone bag clinking with equipment. Short, swarthy and taciturn, Malkovich was a chemist by training, but an artist in his chosen field. Quickly and precisely he laid the tools of his trade out on his workbench before turning to the letters, thirty-four in number, that had been intercepted at sorting offices all over London. As my colleagues and I watched, he set to work, with steam, solvents and exquisite delicacy, easing open each envelope in turn. Most were of heavy laid paper, like the letters within, which Malkovich withdrew with padded tongs and passed over to us. Following his example we wore cotton gloves to avoid leaving any marks on the paper and prised the leaves apart gently, taking care not to soften the creases.

It took some time to scan the letters; we were less interested in what they appeared to say than what they might conceal. In my most recent report to the King I had described an informant who had promised to deliver us Akushku for a colossal sum of money. It was an utter fiction, designed to trap the informant who tried to pass it on. I did not expect to see it plainly stated; rather we looked for those odd grammatical constructions and convoluted sentences that indicate a passage written in code or, failing that, some hint that any of the writers were under stress or in fear of discovery.

The stakes could not have been higher: the letters we were reading had been written by the King's personal friends, his senior ministers and his confidential advisers. If my actions were discovered, I could quote the ancient Liberties of the City and my special licence to open letters until I was blue in the face, but I'd be dismissed in disgrace all the same—unless we found solid evidence of conspiracy and treason.

Where affairs of state were discussed, I tried to forget those passages as soon as I had read them, and had instructed Kingsbury and Dubois to do the same. It was a mere fig-leaf of propriety that would not shorten the hangman's rope one inch. But for the most part the letters were utterly trivial stuff; one Lord's billet-doux to his catamite was vulgar and indiscreet in the extreme, but blackmail was unlikely, since the man's proclivities were pretty much an open secret at the time.

Lord Diamond, of course, was the correspondent in whom I took the keenest interest. There were no letters addressed to him, and he had sent out only two: one to an old school friend, brusquely refusing him a loan to pay a gambling debt, and the other to the editor of a provincial newspaper complaining about farmers who dared to ban steeplechasers from their fields. On the evidence of these letters Diamond was very much how he appeared on the surface: pompous, shallow, vain and obsessed with his own entertainment—another numbskull British aristocrat. Nothing suggested he was a traitor. And the behaviour my men had observed—drinking, gambling and fornicating the way he always had—was hardly that of a man engaged in a secret conspiracy to assassinate a head of state. If Diamond was concealing a connection to Akushku, he was a superb actor with nerves of steel, and from what I knew of Diamond, neither was true.

And what evidence had I anyway of Diamond's supposed connection to Akushku? An expensive fan that Lady Diamond had lost at the opera, when two score of the damn' things had been sold in the last few months. The case was so tenuous a jury would laugh it out of court.

By the time we had finished perusing the last letter my heart was in my boots. None of that was Malkovich's concern; he refolded the letters and replaced them in their respective envelopes with the same exquisite lightness of touch he had used to extract them. I watched him do it, enthralled as ever by his skill. Seeing him renew the seals, so they looked as fresh as when they had left the sender's hand, was like watching time running backwards—a conjuring trick that made the observer vanish.

And soon I might well wish I could vanish, I thought, as Kingsbury and Dubois took the letters away and Malkovich cleaned up his workbench. I was a poor conjuror; I had searched thirty-four aristocratic hats and produced no rabbit. The funeral was on Saturday, and it was now Wednesday afternoon, and I had still no clue who the informant was, or even if there was an informant. I had gambled most of a day—staked my job and my future and my reputation—and I had precisely nothing to show for it.

EVERY NEWSPAPER in the country, it seemed, and many from the Continent had reported the murders of William Lovegrove and Harry Bishop. Scotland Yard, like all of London, had ten mail deliveries a day, and what had started as a trickle of tip-offs in the morning had by the afternoon become an unquenchable flood. According to these informants, Akushku and Bozidar had been sighted all over London and the Home Counties, and as far away as Manchester and Edinburgh. Quinn had been forced to reassign officers to plough through the correspondence. One or two were feasible, most were hearsay, and some were downright nonsensical, but we still had to spend time sorting the wheat from the chaff. Where there was a credible lead, detectives had been sent to investigate; it was now nearly five, and half of those men had still not returned. To cap it all, on my return from Mount Pleasant I had encountered two scandal-mongering journalists in the very foyer of Scotland Yard, seeking more details on the brutal deaths of our "noble brothers in arms—so we can pay proper tribute to their work, Chief Superintendent." But I knew these hacks of old and the stories in which they specialized: lurid tales of true crime lovingly illustrated with every gory detail they could fit in.

"Throw these blackguards out," I told the officers on the front desk. They set to the job with gusto.

"I SEE YOUR EFFORTS TODAY have been as rewarding as mine." Steinhauer, clearly exhausted, dropped heavily into the chair facing my desk.

"Who told you that?"

"You are not usually an easy man to read, William, but I am afraid this time it shows on your face."

"By the look of you I take it you've made no progress either."

"If, as you fear, a highly placed informant is reporting our plans and progress to Akushku, all of our efforts to find these men will have been wasted," said Steinhauer. "He and Bozidar will have been ahead of us at every step. I wonder perhaps if the person who told you they were hiding in a club might have intended to set us searching in the wrong direction."

Of course it had been Angela Minetti who had told me that when I had visited her in the infirmary. I believed her then, and I believed her now. It would make no sense at all that the woman who had told us of Akushku's plot in the first place was secretly working for him. But Steinhauer was right about the clubs, at least; no point in continuing that search if Akushku had been tipped off.

I sighed and set aside the reports I'd been skimming, or rather trying to skim—the accumulated lack of sleep was starting to tell, and the words had started swimming about the page. I rubbed my eyes.

"Might I be so bold as to suggest that you take a short rest?" said Steinhauer gently. "All that can be done has been done, or is being done."

I snorted. "Short of cancelling the funeral."

"That I might find difficult to explain to His Imperial Majesty."

"What have you told the Kaiser?" I was too tired to waste my breath on honorifics.

"The truth. As you instructed me."

"Hm. It wasn't an instruction as such, Gustav. So what does His Imperial Majesty intend to do?"

"You mean, will he be returning to Germany? Of course not. Your King, if you will forgive me, has underestimated my Emperor. My master has a duty to his country, yes, but that duty does not require him to retreat at the first whiff of gunpowder. He tells me his soldiers face death every day on behalf of their Emperor, so he can demand no less of himself."

"I'm very glad to hear it," I said, wondering whether the Kaiser's noble sentiments were all his own, or whether Steinhauer had contrived to plant them in the royal head.

Steinhauer smiled, basking in his master's reflected chivalry. "An Emperor who will not appear in public for fear of a madman," he said, "does not deserve the title."

"Perhaps. The Tsar Alexander felt much the same, I believe."

My reply was in poor taste, but it found its mark—Steinhauer's smug grin vanished. He was not so young that he did not know the fate of Alexander II who, when a bomb was tossed at his carriage, insisted on stopping and getting out to confront the terrorists. They had thrown a second bomb, and the Tsar of All the Russias had bled to death in the snow with both his legs blown off.

"That was twenty years ago," said Steinhauer. "If you and I had been in charge that day, Alexander would still be alive."

Was he trying to reassure me, or flatter me? I wondered. I realised I was too bone-weary to work it out. There was no time to rest, but I could do the next best thing.

"Have you eaten, Gustav?"

"Not since this morning, as it happens."

"Let's go and see what delights await us in the canteen."

"I MUST SAY, I am impressed," said Steinhauer, blowing on a spoonful of watery Scotch broth, "at how you have managed to keep the facts of this matter out of the newspapers until now. Such censorship would not be possible, even in Germany. Word always gets out somehow."

"It's not censorship, it's common sense," I said. "Certain stories editors will agree not to publicise, knowing in time we'll return the favour."

"That sounds like a very cosy arrangement. In America they would call it corruption."

"That's rich," I said. "Considering any German newspaper editor who knocks His Imperial Majesty gets thrown in jail and his presses smashed." It was a welcome change of pace to be bantering with Steinhauer; teasing him was cheering me up.

"We are not so enlightened as the British or the Americans, this is true."

"There's no such thing as a free press anyway," I said. "Every newspaper is at the mercy of its owner, or editor, or its advertisers. Or, God forbid, its readers."

"Why 'God forbid'?"

"Because good news doesn't sell. Fear, outrage, disgust—that's what sells. Given half a chance, if there's nothing to be scared of, newspapers will invent something, and the public will believe it. And I don't intend to give the press that chance."

"Yet now, when there is something real that the public should be scared of, you are not telling them."

"I'll tell them when they need to know. The thing about terror—it's not merely the act, but its impact that makes the difference. The terrorists make the press their megaphone, use it to manipulate the public. The newspapers might claim to be shocked and outraged, but every time they report, they're feeding the fire. As far as terror is concerned, what the public doesn't know won't hurt them."

"Don't they have a right to know the truth?"

"Truth has nothing to do with it. Whatever truth is."

"You're saying there's no such thing as objective truth? I never took you for a cynic."

"Maybe there is, but you won't find it in the newspapers."

"You know"—Steinhauer waved his spoon—"print is not the only medium. You and I were at the kinema the other day. Maybe you can control what appears in the newspapers, but what about images projected on a public screen?"

I nearly spat out my soup. "Kinema? Sure that's just a novelty. Nobody's going to pay sixpence and sit in the dark to learn what's going on in the world."

"It is expensive, yes, but so were books at one time. And the kinema is more powerful than books."

"How so?"

"Because the audience does not need to know how to read. Or even speak a certain language." Gustav leaned forwards now, as animated as I'd ever seen him. "You and I live in Babel. We are a thousand nations separated by a thousand tongues. But images on the screen need no interpretation—the truth is there for the world to see."

"If you say so, Gustav." I pushed my half-empty plate aside. "But if you ask me, for a night's entertainment, nothing beats a good tune and a decent piano."

"Sir." It was Lawrence, in a rush, bearing a single small envelope. "This came just now, sir, addressed to you by name."

"They're all addressed to me by name," I said. That was another disadvantage of being a famous policeman. "Bring it to Chief Inspector Quinn."

"No, sir, the messenger who brought it—he said to tell you it's from your lodger." I confess I was mystified for a moment, before I realised the note must be from Angela, using an identity only I would know. I practically snatched the envelope from Lawrence and ripped it open.

"You take in tenants, William?" asked Steinhauer, clearly intrigued.

"The boy says she promised him threepence," said Lawrence as I scanned the note.

"Give him sixpence," I said, and kicked my chair back.

> William—I found Iosif—in old factory for furniture, Stone
> Street in Hackney—
> I keep watch—
>
> AM

18

HACKNEY WAS FORTY-FIVE MINUTES from the Embankment, but that day our charabancs made it in half an hour, the clatter of our bells scattering pedestrians before us. We were still a few streets away when I smelled smoke—not the comforting familiar fug of coal fires, but the harsh bitter stink of burning paint and horsehair plaster. Sure enough as we rattled into the broad cobbled road called Stone Street we saw a crowd gathered at one end, and beyond them two Fire Brigade engines, blinkered horses stamping uneasily between their shafts. The firemen had forced open the tall broad gates leading to the factory yard, and through the gap I could see the factory itself, a long, squat building disused for years, judging by the broken windows and the weeds that were sprouting from the gutters. The ground floor was ablaze within—the tall windows were glowing orange, and even as I jumped down from the charabanc another one shattered, sending down a cascade of glass fragments and releasing gouts of viscous black smoke.

I ordered Dubois and the other officers to stay back—our initial plan to surround the site and search it was redundant now—and forced my way through the crowd of gawkers to consult the senior fireman. He was easy enough to spot, sweating under his brass helmet, bawling at his men to gather their equipment and fall back.

"I need to get in there." I had to yell over the roar of the fire and the cracking of wood exploding from heat. I flashed my warrant card at him, but the fire chief barely glanced at it.

"Nobody's going in there," he shouted back. "In ten minutes the whole place will be ablaze—it's all we can do to stop it spreading." No need to ask if the fire had been set deliberately—even through the acrid smoke I could make out the tang of lamp-oil. Akushku must have doused the ground floor with it.

"Are the stairs intact?"

"At the south end, yes, but not for much longer—"

Steinhauer had fought his way to my side, and now he handed me a battery-lamp. It was as if he had read my mind.

"Akushku always burns his evidence," I shouted.

"So perhaps there is evidence in there," he shouted back.

We dashed through the open gate past the retreating firemen, ignoring the yells of their chief, damning us for fools and maniacs. At the southernmost end of the building the main doors had been hacked almost off their hinges by fire-axes. Beyond them was a broad hallway with stairs straight ahead and a roller door on the left giving onto a factory floor that was already an inferno, its heart a pile of wooden off-cuts and broken furniture that had been doused in oil and set ablaze. Smoke swirled around us, and as one Steinhauer and I pulled our scarves up over our mouths. He nodded towards the stairs and made to dash ahead of me until I grabbed his arm.

"Booby-traps!" I yelled, my voice—already muffled by the scarf—barely audible under the roaring and shattering and cracking. But Steinhauer heard me well enough; his eyes widened and he nodded. Turning back to the stairs he raised his lamp and moved upwards cautiously, checking every step for taut wires or triggers concealed under trash. The agonising seconds this caution cost us seemed to stretch into hours. My scarf was choking me, and the smoke stung my eyes; I could feel sweat coursing down my back in a torrent, whether from the heat of the air around us or from sheer funk I could not say. But both of us made it to the half landing and turned to the second flight—and Steinhauer, sensing movement, whipped out his pistol and held his lamp high. Following his look, I saw what had startled him—a rat, whiskers twitching, skittering along the topmost step, terrified of us below but terrified too of the approaching fire it could smell and taste. As it hesitated half a dozen more rats, filthy and panicking, ran past it and spilled down the stairs, round and between our legs and over our boots as Steinhauer stood transfixed, too revolted even to shudder. But only for a moment—Steinhauer ascended faster up this flight, and I hurried after him—hoping that if there had been any trap the rats would have set it off for us.

Now on the upper level we found ourselves outside another pair of doors, their cream-coloured paint flaking off in scabs and their frosted-glass panels cracked. Beyond them was only darkness—it looked as if the fire had not yet reached this floor. Gingerly Steinhauer pressed a hand against the door on the right, and looked at me. I nodded, and he shoved it back, turning sideways and bracing himself for a blast, as if that would make a difference. But no blast came. Had Akushku been in too much of a hurry? I wondered. I raised a hand, signalling Steinhauer to stay back while I went ahead—my turn to be vanguard. I stepped into the corridor beyond, scanning the rear of the left-hand door, but that too was bare of wires or triggers. On my right were two doorways, and a short distance ahead the corridor opened out into another workshop. As I stepped cautiously forwards, my own gun and lamp raised, I fancied I could feel the heat of the conflagration below through the soles of my boots. A quick glance into each office as I passed it revealed nothing except rubbish and rubble—apart from one angled desk still bearing a curling yellowed sketch, as if the draughts-man had wandered off in the middle of a job and never returned.

From below I heard and felt the rumble of collapsing masonry, and from somewhere beyond that angry shouting. Were the fire fighters yelling at us to get out? But we couldn't, not yet. I could feel Stein-hauer behind me, almost breathing down my neck, as I reached the end of the passage and turned the corner, and beheld a glimpse of hell.

The abandoned workshop was illuminated from without by burn-ing sparks flying up from the ground floor, and here and there even tongues of flame. The smoke that billowed and swirled around us refracted the light in lurid shades of orange, silhouetting in the middle of the room the figure of a man seated in a rickety wooden chair, his legs splayed out and head bowed. We crept closer.

It was Remington, the abortionist. His hands were tied behind the chair-back, holding him upright; his shirtfront was soaked in blood, some of it from his mouth, most from the gaping gash in his throat. Steinhauer stooped, lifted the dead man's head by the hair and peered up into his face. Rising again quickly he caught my eye and made a sign—a pair of scissors closing in front of his mouth.

They'd cut Remington's tongue out.

There was nothing we could do for him now, and nothing he could do for us. I felt a rush of guilt and shame at having coerced Remington into this, at the risk of his life—but then I thought, Akushku would have murdered him even if we had not been on his tail, even after he had treated Bozidar's injury. Remington alive was a liability. But the brutality of it, the sadism, was still sickening.

Steinhauer turned to his right to explore, I to my left. The smoke was so thick now my lamp could barely cut through it, and I nearly collided with a long wooden workbench that seemed to run the length of the room, scored and scarred by years of workmen's tools. It was thick with old dust and fresh ash, but otherwise bare—except, I noticed, for one oddity: a single frond of fern. Picking it up I saw it was almost fresh, curling a little at the edges, and dotted with white ash, but not dust. How on earth had it got here? I nearly tossed it aside but on a whim slipped it into my pocket—I needed something, anything, to show for the lunatic risk Steinhauer and I were taking.

"William!"

Hearing Steinhauer yell, I turned, and my heart nearly stopped. In the last thirty seconds smoke had started gushing through the gaps in the floorboards, and now there were founts of flame licking up the outside of the building and blackening the remaining windows. Along with ash drifting in the air were burning cinders—one settled on the back of my hand, and I brushed it off cursing as I floundered across the room towards Steinhauer, half fearing that in the murk I might collide with Remington's bloody corpse and fall. But there was Steinhauer, red-rimmed eyes just visible between his scarf and his hat, beckoning me. The other side of the workshop was lined with another long workbench reflecting the first, but this one was not bare—Steinhauer was pointing out a dark red stain that spilled over the lip of the bench, speckled now with white ash. Clearly this had served as Remington's operating table: at the edge of the puddle of blood was a discarded scalpel, and beyond that a severed arm. Where it had been attached to the shoulder it had been cleanly and surgically separated, but farther down, before the elbow, it was a bloody mass of discoloured flesh. The forearm and hand were intact but blackened—not with soot or dirt, but from within, by infection.

Remington had amputated Bozidar's shattered arm, and his reward had been a cut throat and a severed tongue.

Steinhauer made to pick up the bloody limb, but I tapped his shoulder and shook my head. We needed no grisly souvenir to confirm that Akushku had been here, and that Bozidar was still alive, and a viable threat. Remington's body too we would leave behind, or we'd be joining him on his pyre.

Steinhauer went before me, back the way we had come, but a damn sight quicker. The short corridor was so dense with smoke by now we could not even see the double doors at the end, and when we reached them I had barely time to glimpse the red glow beyond the glazed panels before Steinhauer, glancing back to check on me, shoved the door open and stepped out, only to drop out of sight before he even had time to yell. I dashed through after him and found the floorboards had given way beneath his feet, and he was wedged halfway through the floor, scrabbling for a handhold while a shower of sparks danced around him. Grabbing his arms I heaved with all my strength, praying the floor under my boots would not give way too and tip us both into the white inferno below. The air itself seemed on fire, and even through my scarf the heat of it scorched my throat, but I managed to drag the young German up far enough for him to throw a leg over the lip of the hole—I swear the cloth of his trousers was smouldering—heave himself out and roll free. No time for thanks or expressions of relief—we scrambled to our feet and headed for the stairs, praying they and our luck would hold, staying as close as we could to the edges where the steps might still be strong enough to take our weight. Somehow we made it to the half landing, and by now the very walls of the stairwell were on fire and flames rippling along the ceiling. Steinhauer clattered down the stairs and raced for the door. I watched where he stepped, then raced after him.

"HAVE YOU HEARD from Angela?" asked Amelia.

I was seated at the kitchen table, my wife dabbing butter onto my burned hand with a folded muslin cloth. I was pretty sure butter would not make a blind bit of difference, but it seemed to make Amelia feel better, so I let her dab away.

I'd told her I'd had to enter a burning building to retrieve some evidence. She hardly needed telling: all my clothes stank of stale smoke, my eyes were red, and for the last two hours I'd been hawking up disgusting black phlegm that had destroyed my handkerchief. Now I chewed on my moustache as she tended my burn, and pondered what to say. I wanted to blurt out everything—how Akushku had escaped us once again, how our every move thus far had been betrayed by a turncoat I still had not identified, how the days to the funeral were hurtling by and disaster was nearly upon us and how every scrap of evidence I'd found had crumbled to ashes in my hands. How I had very nearly ended up as ashes myself.

"I have," I said. "It was Angela that led us to that place."

Amelia paused and looked up, concerned. "She's still mixed up with that . . . man?"

"I asked her not to get involved, but . . ."

"What happened?"

The informant, whoever it was, would not have had time to send word to Akushku before we arrived. But somehow the anarchist had learned of the danger, and torched his hideout, and fled with only moments to spare. The only person who'd known I was coming was Angela.

What if it was she who'd torched the place?

The thought bubbled up like fetid gas from the depths of my mind, by now a swamp of suspicion, despair and exhaustion. I examined the theory all the same, before dismissing it as absurd. Why tip us off about Akushku's hideout, only to burn it before we got there?

The alternative was far more likely, and even more grim. She would keep watch, her note had said. And she had, and Akushku had spotted her, and caught her, and wrung from her that we were on our way; and now it seemed a near certainty that her body had been beneath that pile of timber soaked in oil and set ablaze.

"I don't know," was all I said. Amelia sighed and shook her head. Perhaps she did not believe me, but she knew better than to press. She was still a moment; then she covered up the butter-dish and, rising up, put it away in the pantry and tucked the muslin cloth into the pocket of her apron.

"I'll run you a bath," she said quietly. She picked up my coat from the back of the chair where I'd thrown it—I'd come in too shattered and dazed even to hang it on its hook by the door. "Will this need mending?"

"I haven't looked," I said.

"Wear your blue gaberdine till I've cleaned it." She sniffed the fabric, and recoiled. "And aired it." She started going through the pockets, but at the very first one stopped, and drew out the frond of fern I'd found in the burning workshop. I'd forgotten all about it; it was crumpled now and crushed almost beyond recognition.

"I found that," I said, stupidly. Why had I picked it up at all—some vague sense of it being an anomaly, like that blasted fan on Angela's wall? Amelia smoothed out the foliage, and lifting it to her nose drew in its scent. I could smell nothing myself except scorched cloth and singed hair.

"Forbidden love," she said, almost absently.

"What's that?"

"When Mary and Theresa and I were girls," said Amelia, "we'd spend hours composing bouquets that told stories. The language of flowers, you know? Silly stuff, but . . ." She smiled, sadly and wistfully; was she thinking of some childhood beau? "Maidenhair fern means forbidden love. Where did you find this?"

I did not answer. I was staring at her. I might have blinked; because amid the darkness and chaos and confusion and choking smoke, a feeble beam of light had broken through, and at last I thought I could see.

"Damn me for a fool," I said.

19

THE MORNING SUNLIGHT through the windows of St. James's Palace lit up countless dust motes, swirling in the air above my head as I stood waiting in the long panelled anteroom under the medieval rafters. In this ancient place, I realised, I was looking at the dust of kings, dancing in the draught. How did that quote from Hamlet go?

> *Imperious Caesar, dead and turn'd to clay*
> *Might stop a hole to keep the wind away*

I shivered, and tried to push that thought to the back of my mind. At that moment the door clicked and swung open, and His still-living Majesty the King entered. Something about his posture had changed, I noticed; it was as if the title of Emperor obliged him to stand up more straight.

"Melville! Dashed early for a conference. I thought our briefing wasn't until this afternoon?"

On closer inspection I could see His Majesty had made haste to join me. Although his black mourning suit was beautifully cut, his tie was a little crooked and there were toast crumbs adhering to his trouser legs, remnants of his breakfast. Queen Alexandra was in Sandringham—

which was just as well, given the nature of the conversation I was about to have—and Ross now materialised at the King's elbow. By the way he was twitching he must have been aware that his master's appearance was less than immaculate, but at that moment I didn't give a fig for appearances. I had waited too long for this audience as it was. All the same I took a breath and composed my thoughts; this meeting would call for some delicacy.

"Your Majesty, I think it advisable that our conversation should take place in private." I looked at Ross and smiled broadly, hoping to draw the sting from my request. Ross showed not the slightest reaction, of course, but Edward seemed to take umbrage on his behalf.

"Don't be absurd, old man—this is Ross."

"Nevertheless, Your Majesty."

I said no more, but merely waited. One cannot command royalty, nor even the lowliest member of a king's retinue, but there are ways of encouraging compliance. Edward scowled, clearly puzzled and irritated, but turned and gave Ross a brusque nod. His man departed as inconspicuously as he'd arrived. When the latch of the massive oak door clicked behind him, the King turned to me with a glare that said, Well?

"Your Majesty knows that my men and I are currently trying to apprehend the anarchist known as Akushku, who intends to disrupt the funeral." "Disrupt" was quite the euphemism, but Edward knew that as well as I did.

"Well, of course. I've been reading your reports."

"Your Majesty may not be aware, however, that our operations have been compromised."

"Compromised? What d'you mean, compromised?" Without thinking he had pulled his cigarette case from an inside pocket, but realising only now that Ross was not there to offer him a light, he put it away again. The King was a slave to his urges; that's why I was there.

"The men we seek have somehow gained access to sensitive information about our work. Two of my detectives were keeping a house under surveillance, hoping to catch Akushku. Instead he ambushed and murdered them. He knew they were watching him."

"Yes, I read your report about that. Shocking business, horrible."

The King seemed momentarily lost for words. "I'm very sorry, Melville. I know how fond you are of your men."

"Thank you, sir. We've been trying to trace Akushku's source, but with no luck, thus far."

Now the King saw where this was going, and his sympathy turned to indignation. "You're coming to me with this? Damn it, Melville— you're not suggesting it's someone in my own household?"

"Not in your household, sir, no."

"Can't see how it could be. None of them have any access to my private papers. Not even Ross, and I trust him with all manner of . . ." He stopped, and finished feebly, "I mean, I trust him implicitly."

"Sir, I regret to say it, but I suspect an acquaintance of yours is responsible. Someone who encouraged you to discuss my reports."

"Hang it all, Melville, I'm not an utter cretin. I never discuss anything in your reports with anyone, not even the Privy Council. I wouldn't even if they asked. And if they did ask I'd damn' well want to know why."

"Nevertheless, Your Majesty—"

"It's simply out of the question." Agitated, the King drew out his cigarette case again, looked around for a light and seeing the massive fire roaring in the grate strode over to it. "I don't mean to tell you your job," he boomed, "but I do think you've got the wrong end of the stick. Ten to one the problem will be somewhere in Scotland Yard—some cleaning lady or clerk, I shouldn't wonder." He held his cigarette's tip over a tongue of flame. I paused, and took a deep breath. Interrogating emperors is a delicate business.

"Lord Diamond is a close friend of Your Majesty."

"Diamond? I don't discuss affairs of state with him. Not that he's ever been interested." Edward sucked on the lit cigarette and peered at the end to check it was drawing.

"And his wife, Lady Diamond? Has she ever been interested?"

In the pause that followed we could hear nothing but the cracking of the fire, the distant rattle of traffic and the cries of the street-vendors in nearby Pall Mall. I waited, saying nothing. His Majesty had understood.

"Lady Diamond?" he said at last, affecting nonchalance, badly. His voice was suddenly thin, lacking any of its earlier conviction. I waited some more; I had no intention of letting him off the hook. "I know the lady, of course, but . . . she wouldn't—that is, I wouldn't . . . She is a friend, yes, a close acquaintance, but . . . ."

Now at last I could see him thinking it through. He licked his lips, uncertain of how to proceed, and I might have felt a twinge of pity, had his misjudgement not cost me so much in blood. "We have talked," the King conceded. "That is . . . I may have confided in her, yes."

"Might I ask, sir, precisely what you confided in her?"

"Good God, Melville. It's absurd, it's out of the question. The lady is loyal, utterly devoted, she's proved that—often—"

I'm sure she has, I thought, and he could see me thinking that, and he blushed crimson. But he carried on justifying himself all the same. It was a song I'd often heard guilty men sing, every refrain another nail hammered into the scaffold. "Yes, I've discussed some of these details with Lady Diamond. She's a most intelligent woman, a good friend, as I said, and I value her advice, and I have complete confidence in her."

"Is Your Majesty currently in correspondence with her?" I wasn't talking about billets-doux.

"I have seen her quite recently, yes, but our conversations were purely—damn it all, Melville!"

He had stumbled at the word "conversations," and I wasn't surprised. "Criminal conversation" was the legal term for adultery, and Edward was a keen conversationalist. When he was a student at Cambridge, his dalliance with an actress had caused a public scandal, and his father had travelled up there to lay down the law. The Prince Consort caught a bad chill on that trip, and two weeks later contracted typhoid, and a week after that he was dead. Heartbroken, Victoria had blamed her son for his father's death, and never truly forgiven him, and it had made not a whit of difference to his behaviour.

His wife, Alexandra, to her credit, put up with Edward's countless affairs, and I as his bodyguard refrained from passing judgement; my priority was the King's safety. But second only to that was the safety of the men who worked under me, and now Edward's weakness had cost two of them their lives. For the first time, it seemed, King Edward saw that too: he drew his hand down his face as if sweeping away cobwebs, or pulling off a blindfold. He was mortified, and momentarily lost for words.

"We have reason to believe, sir, that she and this terrorist Akushku know each other. That they may even have been intimate, at some point. And that they might still be."

"Dear God. Are you absolutely certain about this, Melville?" If he was seeking forgiveness or reassurance, I was in the mood for neither.

"I would never voice such an accusation without good reason, sir. And if as you say you have discussed our operations with her, you have just confirmed my fears. Might I ask, have you arranged to see the lady again?"

"I—yes. Tonight, in fact. But I'll get Ross to make some excuse. I've done that often enough, she won't suspect . . ." He tossed his half-smoked cigarette into the fire and watched it flare and burn, shaking his head in disbelief. "If you are right—I've been the most pitiful ass. Two of your men dead? It never occurred to me that Valeriya . . . I am truly sorry, Melville. You know I actually felt—" He stopped before he could humiliate himself any further, and I didn't press him. It was pointless; when colleagues have died, apologies are worth little, even royal apologies. I felt neither pity for Edward in his embarrassment, nor anger. Too late for either.

"We must find how she's been passing on the information," I said. "I doubt she meets this man in person—that would be far too risky for both of them."

"Will this matter become public knowledge?"

"Absolutely not, sir, if I can help it."

He was worried about scandal, of course, but we'd deal with that when we had to. The absolute priority was to prevent Akushku learning we had identified his informant; for the first time in this endless nightmare we would have the advantage.

"Everything you and I have discussed will remain absolutely confidential. There are lives at stake." Including his own, I did not need to add. Edward nodded.

"Understood, Melville. And—thank you, I suppose."

I bowed, briefly. "At Your Majesty's service, as always. If I might be excused?"

Edward tried a smile. "Good luck, old man." He made it sound as if I was going out on a fox hunt. Which I suppose I was.

MY CAB WAS WAITING in the freezing palace courtyard, its horse stamping and shaking its mane, the driver seated above, blowing on his gloved hands. "Back to Scotland Yard," I barked at him. There was no time for niceties. I nearly fell over as the hansom lurched out of the courtyard into the teeming traffic of St. James's Street, heading south.

"Well?" Even inside the cab it was so cold Steinhauer's breath was condensing in clouds.

"It is as I feared," I said. It would be futile, I'd decided, to try and hide this development from Steinhauer—he was too shrewd to be long deceived, and I would need his help for what came next.

"Hm," grunted Steinhauer. "Ironic that your King sent you to save my Emperor, when he has been the one endangering him."

"The danger comes from Akushku," I said, trying not to sound defensive. "The King and the Kaiser will ride together at the funeral. If my master has endangered yours, he has also endangered himself."

Steinhauer nodded. "This is true," he said. "I suppose then we are even." He smiled at my grim demeanour. "Chin up, William. Now we have a chance. This insight of yours . . . it was inspired."

"If you say so, Gustav." But I felt grubby all the same.

"ONE OF THE MAIDS left the house at nine," said Johnson in his customary drone. "A girl of about twenty, slight build, mousy-coloured hair."

"Lady Diamond's maid," I said. There were four of us—myself, Steinhauer, Quinn and Connolly—gathered in my office listening to Johnson's report.

"We followed the young lady to the offices of the *Pall Mall Gazette*, where she visited the Classifieds desk and tried to place an advertisement in the Personal columns."

"Tried to? You didn't intercept her?" said Quinn.

"Of course not, sir," said Johnson, unruffled. "We watched her pay for the insertion, then Digby followed her back to Berkeley Square, while I made myself known to the newspaper's editor. I have the advertisement here, sir."

He produced a crisp, heavy-laid envelope already slit open. I took it from him—no call for cotton gloves this time—tugged the note out and unfolded it. *"Dearest Wilhelmina,"* I read. *"A very happy birthday, with fondest love from all the family."* The handwriting was an elegant copperplate.

"I did ask, sir," said Johnson, "if that particular young lady had placed any adverts there in the past few weeks."

"And?"

"Seven days ago she placed a similar message, sir. I tracked it down." He flicked to the next page of his notebook. *" 'Dear Uncle Quentin, happy birthday from your devoted niece Lily.' "*

"Seven days ago?" asked Quinn.

"From *Q* to *W* is seven letters," said Steinhauer. We all looked at him, and the young German looked vaguely apologetic, as if he'd laid down a piece in someone else's jigsaw puzzle. "It's possible Lady Diamond is sending messages through a different newspaper or magazine every day," he explained, "in a sequence previously agreed."

"Good God," said Quinn, voicing what we were all thinking. If Gustav was right, to start decoding this message we'd have to track down all the others, and that would mean searching every classified advertisement in every newspaper published in the last week—and there were scores of daily newspapers, from *The Army & Navy Gazette* to *The Sporting Life*. With only two days to the funeral, there was simply not enough time for such a search. The only alternative was to interrogate the maid herself—which would immediately alert Lady Diamond and, inevitably, Akushku.

"When does *The Pall Mall Gazette* go to press?" I asked Johnson. He peered at my wall-clock.

"In just under forty-five minutes, sir."

"We can't let this run, sir," said Quinn. "Not without knowing what it means."

"*A very happy birthday, with fondest love from all the family*'?" said Steinhauer. "It means that all is well. It is too vague to mean anything else, and there is nothing else for her to pass on. The Chief Superintendent's latest report contained nothing of value to him."

"But unless we crack the code, we can't be certain of that, Herr Steinhauer," insisted Quinn, with some irritation.

"And if the advertisement doesn't appear at all," I intervened, "Akushku will certainly know we have smoked her." The four of them fell silent and waited for me to make a decision. Whatever I did, I thought, it would probably be wrong. But I could not do nothing. I tucked the note back into the envelope and handed it over to Johnson.

"Tell the *Pall Mall Gazette* to print it," I said. "Is the team still watching the house?"

"Yes, sir, six men, as per your instructions."

"We don't have time to sit and wait," I said. "Let's grasp this nettle."

20

WHEN THE HANDSOME young footman opened Lord Diamond's front door, I skipped the formalities and barged past him and saw that pompous fart of a butler gliding up the hall, his face rigid with contempt and disapproval.

"I understand Lady Diamond is at home," I said, before he could fob me off. The team watching the house had told me as much.

"Her Ladyship is not receiving visitors," said the butler, "and Lord Diamond is at his club. If you would care to leave your card—"

"Lord Diamond," I said, "is currently enjoying the delights of a bawdy house in Bloomsbury. Fetch Lady Diamond down here now, or I'll go and find her myself." The old flunkey's jaw dropped open and his eyes bulged in his head. He looked close to a seizure.

"Musgrave? What on earth is going on?" A regal female voice echoed from the landing above—without real anger or indignation, I noted, but with the same icy hauteur Steinhauer and I had encountered on our last visit. "What is all this babbling about?" The lady herself turned the corner of the grand staircase and paused there, looking down on Steinhauer and me with a stare intended to turn us to stone. Musgrave twitched impotently.

"My Lady—" he called out apologetically.

"We'd like a word, Lady Diamond," I cut in. I saw emotions flicker across her square, plain face—amusement, triumph and hatred—before she composed her features once more into the genteel mask she had worn when we last met. How long had she been wearing that disguise?

"Chief Superintendent Melville. And Herr Steinhauer, isn't it?"

Steinhauer smiled, and said nothing. He clicked his heels together, and his customary half bow had an odd air of insolence.

"I presume you have a reason for barging into a private residence, Officer? Apart from your desire to be dismissed from the police."

"If Her Ladyship would join us in the morning-room, a full explanation will be forthcoming." I smiled. By the look on her face, she already knew the explanations would be coming from her, not me.

NO OTHER MEMBERS of the household saw us enter the morning-room, which was the way I had wanted it. The fewer staff aware of our visit, the fewer could gossip about it, which risked tipping off Akushku. Musgrave the butler, red-faced and clumsy with indignation, shut the door behind us, leaving us surrounded by Lady Diamond's displays of dried flowers, including one I'd noticed last time, composed entirely of ferns.

"I am impressed, Mr. Melville," she said, "that you are so determined to find out what became of the fan I lost."

"The fan was never lost, ma'am. We will come to that in due course."

Taking a seat in a high-backed chair, Lady Diamond calmly arranged her dress. She didn't invite us to sit, but merely waited for me to speak.

"Your Ladyship is well acquainted with His Majesty the King," I said.

"Many women are," she replied coolly. "The King is known for it."

"It has come to my attention that you and the King have been in an irregular relationship. A criminal correspondence." Lady Diamond pulled a puzzled face. "Please don't waste our time by denying it."

She sighed, and shrugged. "I take it the King himself told you this? What a weak, indiscreet man he is. You must know this, you are his bodyguard. Though not a very good one, if our relationship comes as such a surprise to you."

"We are here because certain information passed between you."

"We talked. What of it?"

"You obtained sensitive information from His Majesty that you subsequently passed on to a third party."

She smiled, sweetly and coldly. "Third party? I have no idea what you are talking about."

"My Lady, I shall warn you for the last time, do not insult us with lies and evasions. I will speak plainly to you, in the hope that you will show me the same courtesy. An anarchist agitator who calls himself Akushku is planning to attack the royal funeral. We have very nearly caught him several times, but he has always managed to escape, because somehow he was being made aware of our movements."

The smile hovered on her face, but it seemed warmer now, perhaps because she was genuinely amused.

"You have been intimate with His Majesty on several occasions," I went on. "You have encouraged him to divulge details of our operations. You have sent your housemaid out every day to place advertisements in certain London newspapers. These advertisements are coded messages to Akushku, passing on what you have learned."

Still Lady Diamond said nothing.

"I take it from your silence you don't deny any of these statements?"

"You can take from it what you wish." She reached out to a small wooden box sitting on a table beside her chair, but before she could open it, Steinhauer was there, placing his hand over hers. Ignoring her frosty glare, he flipped the lid open, looked inside and smiled. He picked up the box and offered it to her; it contained nothing more dangerous than cigarettes. Smoking was hardly a habit one expected of a noblewoman, but perhaps she'd picked it up from Edward. On the scale of things it seemed an insignificant vice. Steinhauer struck a match from the box and lit the cigarette for her.

"You sent him a message this morning," I continued.

"Is that a question?" She inhaled deeply.

"Yes or no?"

"Why are you asking me questions when you have already decided on the answers? If time is so short?"

"Very well—where is this man Akushku?"

"I have not the faintest idea who or what you are talking about."

"You have been conspiring with a terrorist, madam. A man who wants to assassinate the Kaiser, and quite possibly the King himself, your lover."

"You think I love him?" Now Lady Diamond almost laughed.

"No. But I think you acted out of love."

Improbable as it seemed, she was in love with Akushku, of that much I was certain. An irrational, impetuous sort of love, if she was sending him secret messages with flowers, like some infatuated adolescent. How long had she known Akushku, and how had they met?

But those answers were less important than what Akushku meant to do next. I had to tread delicately; such nobles did not take kindly to being bullied or shouted at by the lower orders—the boot was usually on the other foot—but I sensed in this woman a core of cold steel. If it suited her she would retreat into glacial silence, and I could not afford that. If I was right, the passion that had motivated this treason was a secret she had carried for years, unable to confess to anyone; she must have been longing for a chance to set this burden down, to speak the truth for once. I had to lend a sympathetic ear, and draw her out until it was too late for retreat.

"A woman has so few weapons in this world," said Her Ladyship at last. "Men have all the power, all the freedom. Oh yes, I have a title, and wealth, and a position in society." The last word was tinged with contempt. "Little people like you bow and scrape to me and touch their hats. But the man who sweeps my chimneys is freer than I am."

"You're saying you were coerced?" said Steinhauer. "Was this man Akushku blackmailing you?" He glanced at me and encountered a hard look—*Don't interrupt her!* His nod of apology was almost imperceptible. Fortunately Lady Diamond had not even troubled herself to look at him.

"Really, you two are distinguished policemen? No wonder the radicals outwit you so easily. It is almost amusing to watch you stumble about in the dark, tripping over each other. No, I was not coerced. Whatever I have done, or have not done, was of my own free will. It is gratifying to make even a small difference."

Now we were getting close to a confession. I decided she needed a nudge. "The fan your husband said you lost, you gave it to Akushku, didn't you? So he could present it to the young lady he was lodging with, to turn her head? To assure her of his affections?"

Lady Diamond hesitated a moment, as if considering whether to carry on denying everything or to enjoy teasing us with details. "My husband purchased it for one of his . . . paramours. I found it and used it to a more constructive purpose."

Constructive purpose? It was as I'd suspected; she'd convinced herself of the justice of the anarchist cause. Trapped in a loveless marriage, she wanted to lash out at the world, and Akushku had offered her the opportunity. "Where did you first meet Akushku?" I asked. She knew the terrorist's true name, I was sure; I was hoping that given the right provocation she might blurt it out. But Lady Diamond was gazing into the distance, as if recalling a distant memory. I felt a flare of irritation; it struck me as a mannerism filched from a stage play, some melodrama in which she had cast herself as the tragic heroine.

"Do you know what it is like to be bought and sold, like livestock?" she said. "I was traded, at the age of fifteen, to that reptile, that excuse for a man, Diamond. A dazzling name for a lump of dung. A man who despised and resented me from the moment he laid eyes on me. My family had no need of wealth; they had enough and plenty. They had land, and houses, and servants—but they wanted a title." She made it sound like a useless frippery, a tin medal. "I was sold like a broodmare to Lord and Lady Diamond, for their son to mount. So they would not go bankrupt, and my family could call itself noble."

I waited, and nodded. This time Steinhauer followed my lead.

"Noble! Has any term ever become so debased, so perverted?" she went on. "Noblemen like my husband squander thousands on horses and cards and whores and opium, and sneer at the working people who slave and starve to keep them in luxury. And noble ladies like me, their wives, they hold tea parties and balls and receptions. We play the piano and press flowers, and we simper and curtsy for these . . . *sutenery.*"

That Slavic word I was not familiar with, but I could guess her meaning. "Lady Diamond," I said, "your friend is planning an atrocity, one that will not just hurt the nobility, but countless working people too. We mean to stop him, and we will. Help us, and I will vouch for you in court."

"In court? Really, have you thought this through? You intend to put me on the stand in a public trial, so I can tell the world about how your King behaves in private? You know, he is a big man, and lazy—he does not care to exert himself. He prefers that things should be done for him—or to him. Of course your tame English newspapers might not print such details, but the French and the Americans? The Germans? How the nations of Europe will laugh. Your King, your whole Empire, would be utterly humiliated. But, whatever you like—by all means, let me face a judge."

"You will stand trial." I dispensed with her title, as she clearly despised it. "What evidence the court will allow to be heard remains to be seen. Either way you can be of no further use to this anarchist. But you can still be of use to the British people, for whom you profess to care so much."

"The British people! Akushku is doing this for the British people, and the Germans, for working people everywhere. Why would I help you? So that I might not hang? So that I might spend the rest of my life in prison? I am already in prison."

"You might hate your husband," I said. "You might hate the King as well. But if your friend Akushku succeeds, this country, and all of Europe, will likely be pitched headlong into war. And it'll be Englishmen and German men, working men who will fight and die by the thousands. It's the wives of those working men who will have to scrape and scrimp to feed and clothe their children. It'll be their children begging in the streets."

"As if you give a curse!" spat Lady Diamond, her nostrils flaring. I'd struck a nerve at last. "There are already families begging on the streets not two minutes' walk from my door, mothers selling themselves and their children to buy a loaf of bread. Let there be war. Let this vile, rotten society, rotten with parasites like you—let it burn, let it be purified on the pyre of war. That is the only way working people will ever be free, through blood and violence and revolution. Yes, it will be bloody. Childbirth is always painful and bloody."

It was clear she knew very well what Akushku was planning, and she was not apologising for it—she was already celebrating it.

"Where will you meet him?" said Gustav suddenly. Lady Diamond blinked at this new tack. I nearly blinked myself; he had clearly thought of something I had overlooked.

"What?"

"Your friend, Akushku. You meant to elope with him, did you not? In the chaos after the attack. He has planned an escape route, for both of you."

"No. I have made my choice," said Lady Diamond. "I am dispensable. It is a small sacrifice." But she wasn't so defiant now—she was looking at the floor.

"With respect, madam," said Steinhauer, "you are lying. After all you have done for this man, for his great cause, he would leave you in this prison? Married to that pig of a husband, that *sutener*? Or, should your role in this ever be uncovered—as it has been uncovered—you would hang, and your body would rot in a common grave. What sort of man would abandon you to such a fate? No, that was never the plan. Akushku is your forbidden love, and you are his. Herr Melville found the token of love you sent him, because he kept it. You planned to meet him after the assassination, and to flee with him abroad, and start a new life together. Do not try to deny it. Tell us where you planned to meet."

This theory Gustav had not shared with me beforehand—I suspected he had just thought of it—but now he had voiced it aloud it seemed obvious. His inspired guesswork seemed to find its mark; Lady Diamond hesitated. When she spoke she tried to remain haughty, but her voice trembled.

"It does not matter. As you say, I have been caught. Whatever I do or say now, I will hang."

"We will make it matter, Lady Diamond. If you hang as a traitor, your husband will be humiliated. He will look a fool. He may even be tried as an accomplice."

"I had not thought of that. All the better." She actually smiled.

But Steinhauer hadn't finished. "And his household? The servants who wait on you? Have you considered what will become of them?" Now Lady Diamond's smile faltered, and she seemed paler than before. "These men and women," Steinhauer went on, "who—how did you put it?—starve and slave to keep you in luxury?" He bent down so his face was close to hers, and his threats seemed all the more menacing for his roguish, handsome grin. "I am a mere visitor to these shores, I cannot make them pay for your crimes. My friend Melville, on the other hand . . ." He grinned at me. "He is the most feared policeman in Europe. And for good reason. He will do whatever is necessary to protect the realm."

He straightened up, and started eyeing the room around him with its luxurious trappings and its framed pressed bouquets, for all the world like an auctioneer surveying a houseful of goods he'd been appointed to sell off.

"Every member of your staff will be arrested. From that old red-faced fool of a butler to that plain little maid who delivered your messages. For that alone she will face a life of hard labour in prison. The rest of them—they will serve maybe one or two years, that is all. But it will be enough. They will never be employed in service again. Your cook, your dresser, your scullery maids—they will be the ones sleeping in the streets. They will be the ones selling their children—and themselves—for a crust of bread."

He turned back to her with a smile so cold even I shivered.

"Have you ever tried to sleep on the street, Lady Diamond? Among the dung and the vomit, with rats that run over your face? Believe me, your former servants—they will dream of going back to prison."

"You are lying," said Lady Diamond, but with a shade less assurance. "This is not Russia, or Germany. This is England. Such injustice cannot happen here."

She actually looked at me, as if appealing to my honour and decency. The nerve of her, I thought. I kept my face impassive, and let Steinhauer carry on. His familiarity, his insolence, added an edge to his threats; all I had to do was stand there and stare at her. And at that moment I felt fully prepared to do all the things he had threatened, and more. Lady Diamond seemed to see that in my face, because her reserve abruptly evaporated. Suddenly she was appalled and vulnerable, and very close to breaking. Steinhauer sensed that too, and closed in.

"Forgive me, but you seem rather naïve." He actually giggled. "What did you say of this society—that it was corrupt and hypocritical? You are right. Do you really think, with the life of his King at stake, Melville will concern himself with justice?" Plucking the cigarette from between her fingers he tossed it to the floor and crushed it into the carpet with his shoe. "Have you asked your household if they are willing to sacrifice their freedom for your cause? Or is that something for their noble mistress to decide on their behalf?"

Lady Diamond at last seemed lost for words.

"If you care about them, about any of the men and women who work for you," I said, "this is your last chance to show it."

The woman's pursed lips quivered, but no words came out.

"Where is your rendezvous?" I asked her.

She turned her head away and shut her eyes. Her voice, when at last she spoke, was so soft it was barely audible. "In Chelsea, a street by the river. Aleksandr has arranged for a boat, to take us down the Thames, and across to Belgium, by night, on Saturday, after the . . ."

"Aleksandr?" I tried not to appear too eager, though my heart was thumping in my chest. "Aleksandr what?"

She glared at me with a hint of her former hauteur. "You may ask him that yourself," she said. "If you ever catch him."

"Tell him you want to meet tomorrow," I said. "Send him a message, the usual way."

"He will not come."

"He will come if you ask him," I said. "What newspaper do you use on Fridays?"

"*The Mayfair Gazette.*" All her reticence had evaporated, it seemed.

I crossed to the bureau by the window, found a pen and paper and pulled the chair back.

"Sit. Write," I said.

"It will be in our code," she said. "Perhaps I shall tell him it is a trap."

"You will write what Herr Melville tells you to write," said Steinhauer. "Otherwise, it will not just be you who pays the price."

THE CHELSEA STREET Lady Diamond had named was not hard by the Thames, as she had implied, but ran west some distance from the riverbank, then turned north along Chelsea Creek—a shallow muddy channel about forty feet across, down which a slick of oily black water ran to the river. On the west side of that creek rose an embankment crowned with a railway line, and beyond the railway line lay the massive Chelsea Gasworks; on the east, facing the embankment across the creek, was a maze of shabby decaying terraces once inhabited by fishermen and glue-boilers and washerwomen. The fishermen had long since given up trying to catch anything in the rancid waters of the Thames, and the other trades had vanished with them.

From the window of the upper bedroom of one of those cottages I surveyed the wooden wharves where the fishermen had once tied their boats. Only a few of those craft remained now, all long disused. The nearest was little more than a rotting wooden skeleton, stranded by the receding tide. Beyond it a few more lay overturned, shining with mossy green slime like the carcasses of turtles. There were few passers-by; a pair of filthy street urchins had passed through twenty minutes ago, kicking ahead of them a ball made of rolled-up newspaper and string; in the other direction a one-legged man had hobbled by, swaying on his crutches. Not Akushku in disguise, I knew, because one of my men, clad in the rags of a tramp, had jostled him and got close enough to smell the curdled beer on the cripple's breath.

I had other men concealed at the farthest end of the lane, and more in the dung-dotted alleyways that ran between the slums. I even had six officers stationed on the Thames itself, in steam yachts and rowing boats, although the tide had sunk so low no boat would be able to enter the creek for at least another hour. I could have used more bodies, but tonight these were all I could muster. The state funeral was to take place the very next day, and every policeman in the Home Counties had been requisitioned for crowd control and security duties. We might not have enough men, but we did have the element of surprise. Or so I hoped.

The rendezvous had been arranged for 5:00 p.m., a few minutes after sunset. It was now twelve minutes to the hour, and the grey light was fading fast. I took a deep breath; all we had to do was wait, though that was hard enough, with all that was at stake, and so little time to spare. I pushed those thoughts aside and calmed myself, aware that the very urgency of our task called for the utmost patience. This was the calm before the storm, a precious chance to reflect; I focused on the street before me, and thought about what led us to this place.

With the tearful help of the mousy maidservant—Elsie by name—we had traced every advertisement she had placed for her mistress in the last two weeks and gained some insight into Akushku's code. This information had been kept from Lady Diamond, which allowed me some measure of certainty that the message she composed under my instruction said what I wanted it to say. The possibility remained that she had omitted some vital code word, and thus flagged the meeting as a trap, but that was a chance I would have to take. If tonight's operation failed—if Akushku did not show, or merely sent some stooge in his place—Lady Diamond would answer for it. Whether her household would answer too, as Steinhauer had threatened, I had not yet decided. Failure was not an outcome I cared to contemplate; still less the consequences of failure.

Another train rumbled south along the embankment on the far side of the creek, and shuddered, clanking, to a halt; even at this distance I could feel the house tremble under the massive weight of its trucks. Two trains passed in each direction every hour, delivering coal to the gasworks, where it was cooked to produce gas, and the leftover coke sold as fuel. Soon came the distant roar as the coal wagons disgorged their cargo, sending up a cloud of black dust that obscured still further the evening sky. I could just about see the coke-stacks from my window, and beyond them two enormous gasometers—huge hollow metal pistons filled with coal gas that slowly rose and fell within towering steel frames, stabilising the pressure of supply to all this part of London. As the wind shifted I caught an eye-watering whiff of sulphur. What a hellish place to live, I thought, pitying the family who rented this hovel. At that moment all seven of them were gathered around the meagre fire downstairs, silent and tense. Probably dreaming of what they would do with the five guineas I had offered the family matriarch—an ancient washerwoman with only three remaining teeth—for the use of their home for surveillance. The cobwebbed ceiling of this bedroom sagged so low my hat brushed against it, and the windows were grimy with coal dust, but I could see the intended meeting place well enough—a lamppost next to a flight of stone steps leading down into the creek.

Lady Diamond would not be attending tonight's rendezvous; her part would be played by Lawrence, whom I had relieved of his duties at our reception desk. Of all the men available he was nearest to Lady Diamond in build. Steinhauer had retrieved a suitable outfit from her wardrobe, and Lawrence had tried it on in the office. There had been laughter, of course, but none of that lasted long after they saw the look on my face. As for Lady Diamond herself, she was at home in her bedroom, under house arrest until this business was concluded; there was nothing to be gained, and much to be lost, by dragging her off to a prison cell right away. As few people as possible were to know she had been exposed. I had given orders she was not even permitted to see her husband, though I doubted she would find that any great burden. Diamond knew nothing of her illicit activities, I was sure, and when he found out he was bound to make a fuss.

And I'd been right. Lord Diamond had come home just as his wife had finished composing her letter to her lover and demanded an explanation for our presence. I was preparing to spin some yarn when I realised any explanation would have been wasted on him. His talk was addled, his pupils were wildly dilated, and his clothing stank of opium smoke. He took in nothing of what little we told him. Oh, he had cursed us roundly as common scum, but that was merely a reflex action, like breathing; contempt for the lower orders has been bred into the British aristocracy over centuries. I had had him escorted to his room, and a bottle of brandy sent up after him to ensure he slept. Four uniformed men would keep an eye on Diamond and his wife until we had time to deal with them.

A hansom cab turned the crook of the road and headed up towards my lookout. I tensed momentarily, then relaxed again; this was not the cab I had arranged to come from Scotland Yard. It was travelling at a brisk pace, too—clearly the driver was taking a shortcut and did not expect to pick up any fares in this shabby backwater. Horse and cab hurried north into the gathering gloom, passing a cart coming in the other direction—a rag-and-bone cart drawn at little more than a walking pace by a thin, tired nag, its head hanging low. The wizened old man clutching its bridle cried out for custom—"Rag and bo-oh-nah!"—in a harsh shriek that made the hairs rise on my neck; it seemed to have a ring of mortality to it, like the squawk of a crow.

As his croaking faded in the distance I checked my pocket watch by the light of my dark lantern. Six minutes past the appointed hour. I craned my neck to peer along the street in each direction in turn and saw none of my men; that at least was precisely how I wanted it.

And here, seven minutes late as arranged, came the hansom driven by my old friend Forte, heading south at a slow trot, as if Forte was unsure of his destination. Finally his cab drew to a halt under the streetlamp opposite the cottage that concealed me and stood rocking at the kerb while the horse stamped its hooves on the beaten earth and shook its mane impatiently. The hansom bounced on its springs as Lawrence alighted, his male form concealed beneath the long dark dress, his head and face obscured by a broad hat and a veil. Young he might have been, but Lawrence proved a good choice; knowing a manly gait would betray him, no matter what he wore, he kept his movements delicate and his steps small. Forte too was playing his role admirably, reaching down to accept a coin from Lawrence's gloved hand and touching the brim of his bowler in gratitude. Then he cracked his whip between his horse's ears, tugged on the reins to turn the cab around and set off again northwards.

The hiss of his cab wheels on the muddy street merged with the rumble of another train approaching along the embankment, and the hansom vanished into the murk of dusk and smoke and steam. Now Lawrence stood alone under the streetlight, his hands—and his pistol—concealed in a fur muffler. He held his head upright, almost defiantly, just as Lady Diamond herself might have done had she found herself alone on the street in such a lonely, threatening location.

The critical moment was nearly upon us. Akushku was too shrewd to rush into such an exposed position; far more likely, I thought, that he would turn up an hour early and observe the location before he approached, to gain an advantage. That was why I had set up my cordon three hours earlier and ensured my men kept themselves concealed or disguised. I would have liked two stationed on the channel shore, but what could they have done there to look inconspicuous? Mend fishing nets? Comb the mud for treasure? No one had used nets here for a decade or more, and there was little to dig for in the mud but broken bottles and the rotting carcasses of dogs.

Steinhauer I had sent to the cottage at the northernmost end of the street, along with Dubois and Johnson. If our quarry were to make a run for it, that would almost certainly be his direction of travel—through the tangled backstreets of Chelsea to the crowds and shops of King's Road. The southern route, hemmed in by the river, offered no such escape.

Now I found myself wondering if I should not have kept Steinhauer by my own side, in case he should, through too much enthusiasm, spring the trap early or otherwise forget my orders. No, I thought; Steinhauer was shrewd and sharp and fast, and our encounter in the park the night before had persuaded me that in this matter at least he would do what he was told; tonight I was content to let him off the leash.

Fifteen minutes past the hour. Now doubt was starting to seep into me, eating at my flesh like frostbite. Perhaps the note had tipped

Akushku off, and he had abandoned his mistress to her fate. God knew he was ruthless enough.

Lady Diamond was by no means the first noblewoman I'd known to become infatuated with a villain and throw her lot in with him. Yes, she and Akushku might seem an unlikely pair—but how could we be sure of that, when we knew next to nothing about him, or how they had met? Was Akushku originally a Russian noble, like her, who had turned his back on his own class?

Lady Diamond would tell us, eventually, I thought. Willingly or otherwise. And if tonight went to plan, we might even get Akushku's side of the story too.

Suddenly Lawrence turned his head, as if he had heard something. I tensed, but made no move; it was too soon, and I knew no one could approach across that inlet, where the rank mud was deep enough in places to drown a man. All the same I wished I could hear what Lawrence was hearing. He had turned his back to me, and was peering down into the creek, which by now was merely a pitch-black chasm.

Then he pulled his hands free of the fur muffler, letting it fall, revealing the revolver clutched in his fist. He shouted a challenge into the dark.

I turned and ran for the stairs.

21

THE STAIRWAY was narrower than my shoulders, and the planks creaked dangerously under my weight, but I had not a moment to waste. I heard shots, then distant shouts and running feet. Ignoring the ragged family huddled round their feeble stove, I ran to the front door, wrenched it open and dashed outside to find Lawrence, scarf and bonnet and veil discarded, pointing into the pitch-black creek and shouting instructions to his colleagues as they closed in. From north and south shapes of men loomed from the shadows as my trap sprang shut—but on whom or what?

"In the creek, sir," said Lawrence as I reached him. "Someone was there, concealed under a boat—I thought I winged him with my first shot, but he turned and ran—"

I joined him in scanning the gulley below. Even this close it was no easier to make out any detail—a faint silvery gleam snaked along its depths, but the oil-black clay of the banks seemed to absorb all light. We had to get down there, but that stinking mud would be nearly impossible to wade through. Had Lawrence really seen someone? If so, surely they must still be there? Then again, if the fugitive had been hiding under one of those upturned boats, he'd be coated in that black filth too and almost impossible to see in this gloom. How long had he been hiding out here—had he taken position before we had even arrived?

Now Steinhauer was by my side, panting from his race down the street. "Do we have him?" he gasped. The rest of my men were spreading out along the bank of the creek, calling instructions to one another, but found their shouts drowned out as yet another train ran along the embankment towards the river, shaking the ground underfoot and filling the air once again with a harsh metallic thunder. I cursed in frustration—a passenger train would at least have cast a flickering light on the scene, but the pall of smoke and steam from this goods train was now drifting down from the embankment, making the visibility even worse.

There—a shudder of movement halfway up the far slope.

I raised my gun before I even realised I'd drawn it, and fired into the murk, but the movement I thought I'd seen was immediately obscured by swirling grey clouds of gritty smoke. All the same I carried on firing in the same direction, and Steinhauer and other officers along the creek raised their guns and fired too, wildly, until the tang of cordite mingled with the stink of the engine's fumes, and we were all of us half-deafened by the shots. The steam locomotive pushing the hopper wagons along the embankment added its piercing whistle to the cacophony, as if in protest. The hammer of my gun clicked on an empty chamber, and hurriedly I reloaded, but even though there were no civilians at risk, I realised I was wasting bullets I might yet need. The same thought seemed to occur to my men, and the firing died away; and then, as the goods wagons rumbled south across the river and the noise receded in its wake, we saw it—a low, dark shape that rolled up over the lip of the embankment to be briefly silhouetted against the boiling grey sky before it disappeared again down the far side.

Our quarry had escaped into the gasworks.

"Pierre"—I pointed to Dubois on my right—"take three men, head north, and then west. Get to the gasworks gate, and seal it—no one is to enter and no one is to leave, until I give the word. Go! You there, Sergeant, pass me that lamp—"

A uniformed officer, recruited at the last minute and looking slightly dazed by the gunfire, held out his oil lantern. I holstered my pistol and snatched the lamp from him.

"Steinhauer, the rest of you, with me—"

I found the steps at the top of the creek bank, hurried down to the bottom and stepped out into the mud. It squelched under my boots, but I did not sink—it was not so deep, this high up the bank. I called over my shoulder, "Where did he appear from, Lawrence, and which way did he run when you first saw him? Quickly, man!"

"A—a little to the left, I think, sir."

I held the oil lamp low and set off down the slope towards the thin trickle of silver. The deepening slime started to suck at my boots, but I tried to keep my pace steady, praying under my breath I would not fall and go headlong. Our quarry had stolen a march on us and every second was precious.

"What are we looking for?" asked Steinhauer, right behind me.

"He had an escape route lined up before we even got here—he must have done. Stepping stones or a causeway—around here somewhere—damn and blast it—!" Now the clay was so thick and deep it had sucked my right boot in and was not letting go, and the harder I pulled at it the closer I came to losing my footing altogether.

"There, sir," shouted Lawrence from the bank behind us. "No, to your right—a plank, I think—"

As the lantern swung wildly in my fist I glimpsed what he had spotted—a long, hard edge gleaming silver. Even as I spied it the water lapped against it, growing deeper—the tide was coming in. Throwing caution aside, I heaved my right boot free of the clay and strode out for the plank, barely pausing to test its steadiness before I brought the left after it. A second step, a third—two more and I was across, and now, when I held the lamp low, I could see a trail of footprints, the closest already filling with water. The track veered farther to the right, then turned left, up the embankment.

"Damn me for a fool—!"

"What?" asked Steinhauer.

I pointed. "Steps, in the embankment. You can barely make them out." Yet Akushku had known they were there. All of this had been planned, but there was no time to reflect on what that signified. I felt the ground shudder.

"Another train's coming," I called to Steinhauer, and raced up the embankment, feeling the legs of my trousers, soaked in filth, slap against my calves. "Quickly!" The steps up the bank were as steep as a ladder and at one point I nearly fell backwards, but steadied myself. I felt Steinhauer close behind me, but I could not turn to see how many of the others had followed—I knew I had to cross that railway line before the next goods train arrived. Now I could hear it, rumbling in from the south across the river bridge, and as I staggered to the top of the embankment I glanced left and saw it—a massive black shape trailing a plume of grey smoke that glowed orange with sparks, wreathing the metal struts of the bridge. For a moment I thought the train was standing still—but that was only because Steinhauer and I were directly in its path, and in seconds it would pulverise us.

"*Scheisse!*" Steinhauer yelled. "*Schnell*, Wilhelm!" Seizing my elbow the German hauled me forwards, and we danced across the first set of tracks—I could hear them ringing with vibration—then a second, and a third, and suddenly we were scrambling and sliding down into the gasworks yard, steadying ourselves with outstretched hands. I felt filthy grit gathering under my fingernails and heard a rattle of stones following me down.

At last the ground levelled out, and it was no longer mud and earth under our boots but cinders that crunched and cracked with every step. Enveloped by clouds of choking smoke, Steinhauer and I staggered upright, then I glanced back; Connolly and one uniformed officer, the one who had given me his lamp, had made it over the embankment behind us. The rest of my men were trapped for now on the other side.

As the smoke and steam thinned I looked around to find my bearings and work out which way our prey might have fled. To the south by the river were the fuel stacks that the railway wagons fed—massive heaps of glistening black coal, at their foot a score of workmen shovelling the stuff onto conveyor belts that rattled and clanked towards a broad, low brick building to the west. Dead ahead was the gasworks itself, judging by its tall chimneys and the tangle of pipework that ran from it. North of that, along the western side of the site, were the vending sheds. The pipework ran towards the gasometers I had seen earlier, and now close up the two of them loomed over us like plate-iron mountains, their cylinders filled to capacity. The whole site was wreathed in acrid smoke and steam and the racket from the engines that powered the belts and machinery.

"Take Connolly and this constable with you," I yelled to Steinhauer, "and head north to the main gate. No one is to leave or enter—workers, merchants, nobody—go!" The three of them raced off.

"And you—!" I shouted to a passing workman, his clothes and face as black as a miner's with coal dust. The man stopped dead in confusion, probably wondering where the devil all these men had come from, but there was no time for explanations.

"The site manager's office—where is it?"

"Over there," the workman pointed. "But—"

"Take me there, now."

I didn't wait for him to lead, but grabbed his arm and dragged him along in the direction he'd shown me. I had thought at first our fugitive, caked in stinking river mud, would be easy to spot—but since every man I could see was black with coal dust and running with sweat it would have been all too easy for our quarry to have blended in. That said, he was a stranger all the same, and his best chance of slipping out unnoticed was via the vending sheds, where sacks of coke and coal were loaded onto merchants' carts. There he could mingle with the coalmen, maybe pass himself off as a helper, and hitch a lift off the site to safety; that was why it was imperative we close the gates. I needed to contact the site manager and get him to shut down the machinery, then assemble the workforce and round up any strangers. If that did not flush out our fugitive, we would comb the site inch by inch until we had him.

"Dead ahead, guv'nor," the workman shouted, pointing upwards. "Big office, top of the stairs—"

I was distracted by shouting to my right, from inside a grey cloud that swirled around the nearest gasometer. Not the shouts of men at work—these were shouts of panic, shrill enough to pierce the thunder of the coal conveyors and the passing train. Abandoning my guide, I raced towards the commotion. Perhaps there had been an accident and someone had been injured, but that would have been a damned odd coincidence.

Hurrying into the murk I nearly collided with three figures rushing in the opposite direction—two labourers propping up a third between them, a man whose face was a mask of blood and whose legs were unsteady.

"What happened here?" I demanded.

"Eric's been shot in the head, that's what's bleeding happened," said the worker on the left, trying to push past me. He was filthy, wiry and a head taller than the other two. "Let us by—"

"Stop—let me look at him—"

As gently as I could, I lifted the injured man's sagging head. He blinked at me, in pain and semi-conscious, and I saw the livid gash under his grimy hair.

"It's a scalp wound, that's all, he'll live. Who did this?"

"A bloody madman, covered in mud, waving a gun about—chased us out of the valve-house."

"Get this man some first aid," I said, drawing my own gun again.

"That's what we were bloody doing, begging your pardon—"

The three of them hobbled on in the direction of the manager's office, vanishing into the grey murk. I headed in the direction from which they had come and found myself on the other side of the cloud, in a yard that was deserted and oddly quiet, as if the fug in the air muffled the sounds of the site. Before me stood the valve-house—a shed of corrugated iron sixty feet long and two stories high, connecting the two gasometers. Its tall iron windows were yellow with gaslight, and in the centre of the shed, straight ahead of me, its metal entrance door hung ajar.

A dozen steps and I was on the threshold, gun raised and ready.

Reaching out I hauled the door wide open, quickly stepped inside and immediately moved to my right, keeping my back to the wall and my gun levelled, covering the floor in front of me. Ahead was a gloomy labyrinth of pipes and junctions and gauges and valve wheels, a vast bank of machinery thirty feet high. Halfway up was a maintenance walkway of metal mesh, accessed by an iron staircase. I swept the room for movement, but saw none, nor any sign of a fugitive. Neither could I see any second door by which he might have escaped. Gun at the ready I stepped cautiously forwards, towards the foot of the staircase—then paused. Dead ahead of me, in the shadow of the walkway, I could see on the concrete floor a small dark puddle of what looked very much like blood. As I stood there another drop fell into it from the platform above.

"Closer, policeman. I won't kill you just yet."

Now I could make out a shape through the mesh of the platform—a tall, thin, mud-smeared man folded up against the machinery, seated on the walkway with his knees pulled up, bracing his back against a broad vertical pipe. One arm clutched his belly from where blood was dripping. The other, if he had one, I could not see. I pointed my pistol at him.

"Put down your weapon and place your hands on your head," I said.

"I do not think so."

"Surrender, and we will get you medical help."

"So I will be well when you hang me? I die here."

His accent was more Serbian than Russian, and though I could only make out his profile I recognised it.

"You'd give your life for Aleksandr?"

"I am Aleksandr."

"No, you're not. I saw you, last week, after I shot you in the arm. Bozidar, also known as Ljubo Gubec, from Belgrade. Born 1874, I believe."

"Died in London, 1901."

"It doesn't have to end here, Ljubo."

"Here, now, is good time." He chuckled; he was a tough customer, all right—a bullet to the belly would have brought down most men, never mind a man who'd had his left arm amputated less than two days ago.

"Lady Diamond thought she could escape," I said. "She and Aleksandr both. They planned to run off together."

"Valeriya . . . Valeriya needed to believe."

"It's over. We know what Aleksandr has planned for tomorrow. He's going to fail."

"He has not failed yet."

"He failed tonight. We have you." No answer, but another chuckle, this time ending in a ragged gasp of pain. A stomach wound meant he would die in an hour or two, and painfully. Though he would probably pass out before then. So what was he waiting for? Did he expect me to run up the stairs and get shot in the face before I'd even reached the platform? Come to that, why hadn't he fired on me as I came in, when I'd been silhouetted in the doorway?

Taking a tiny step forwards I looked more closely at Bozidar's folded form. He was pressing his right arm across his belly to staunch the flow of blood, but his right hand was resting on a crate of some sort—a small wooden crate that did not seem to be part of the plant. I heard a scuffle in the doorway behind me, and a breathless voice—

"William—"

"Stay back, Gustav." I did not turn around.

"And here is Steinhauer." The anarchist laughed. "The butcher and his dog. But which is which?"

Keeping my eye and my gun on Ljubo, I stepped slowly back towards the doorway and crooked a finger for Steinhauer to come closer. The German, his own gun raised, came to stand by my side. "Gustav," I murmured, as softly as I could, "you must not react to what I say next." Steinhauer responded with an almost imperceptible nod of his head.

"I am going to order you to fetch more men," I said. "But you must not. You must leave the building immediately and evacuate the site. Get everyone clear, including yourself."

"But what about you?"

"That device, the one he's shielding with his body, it's a detonator. They planted a bomb in this place long before we got here."

"Under the gas holder?" Steinhauer muttered a curse in German.

"He means to take as many of us with him as he can." I raised my voice so the anarchist could hear. "All of them, Gustav. Here, now."

Steinhauer replied loudly enough for Bozidar to hear, "Yes, Chief Superintendent. Right away."

He backed out of my field of vision, and I heard him scramble through the doorway.

"In a few moments I will have the building surrounded, Ljubo," I called out. "Put down your weapon and I promise you will come to no harm. You won't hang, and you'll serve your time in a British prison, not a foreign one."

"Even though I killed two of your men?"

"I've made deals with the devil before."

"Ah, yes. The spider spins his web of lies and waits for the fly. In all of Europe there is no policeman more despised than you, Melville."

"You can bleed to death up there if you like. It's all one to me."

"I will not bleed to death."

Another attempt at a laugh, more ragged and painful than the last. He was weakening; time was running out.

"Answer me one question all the same," I called. "Why do you even trust Aleksandr, when he used to be an agent provocateur for the Okhrana?"

Bozidar snorted. *"Svinjska sranja."*

"On the contrary, I have it on good authority. From a Latvian I know."

"Your informer is lying."

"I'd sooner believe him than you."

"You think Aleksandr is Russian?"

"If he's not, what is he?"

No reply at first, just harsh, painful breathing. Then an angry groan. "Where is your friend? Steinhauer? Why don't you ask him?"

What did he mean by that? But I had no time to wonder.

"He'll be here momentarily." I took a small step backwards, then another, until I could feel the draught from the open door on my back. There was a lip at the bottom of the doorway, I remembered, two inches high, which would trip me up if I was not careful. If Bozidar saw me moving, he would know I'd guessed his plan: to keep talking as long as possible, while reinforcements arrived—so as many Special Branch officers as possible would be within range of his bomb. But I too had been playing for time, while the yard was evacuated.

Now all I had to do was to get myself well out of there.

"Steinhauer," I said, as if greeting Gustav behind me. At the same time, forcing myself not to hurry, I turned and stepped through the door. Then I took to my heels, barely hearing the Serbian cry out a curse of despair.

"Prokletstvo doðavola!"

I raced for my life, blindly into the fog.

I heard no explosion, but I felt heat blossoming behind me, scorching my exposed neck—I fancied I could smell the hairs there singe and shrivel. Then a giant's hand caught me in the small of my back—no, not the small of it, all of it—and pushed me, harder and harder, till the breath left my body and I was lifted off my feet and sent flying, spinning head over heels with the night whirling around me, and only now was I aware of the whistling roar in my ears blocking out every sound. I wanted to yell but had no wind, then I felt something brush the top of my head, and I slammed into a pile of loose rocks, sinking down into them, the shock of the impact resonating through my body till it ripped out from my mouth in a bellow of pain. There was a fire close to my face, and I screwed my eyes tightly shut, trying and failing to work out which way was up. For a moment I felt as if I was hanging in space, my arms and legs splayed out anyhow like the limbs of a discarded doll kicked into the gutter.

Had I been maimed? The thought appalled me. Eyes screwed shut against the heat I forced each of those limbs to move, in turn, but it was as if I was swimming in clay—all my movements were sluggish, and my arms and legs were slow to respond. When I lifted my right arm and let it drop, the ground beneath it seemed to shift. Now I realised the stuff under my back was not solid at all, but shifting and sliding, its teeth digging into my flesh. Hundreds of jagged teeth that seemed loose somehow, just as my own teeth felt loose in my head.

I opened my eyes.

Steinhauer was looking down at me, his expression grim, his face bright with fire. The night sky beyond him was not dark—it was a boiling pillar of sparks rushing away from us. When he saw I was conscious, the young German's anxious expression dissolved into a smile of relief. His face was lit by flames; his hat was gone and his hair was singed on the right side of his head. "Can you move, William?" His voice was faint and almost drowned out by the ringing in my ears. I was lying on my back, I realised, with my feet higher than my head. When I tried to right myself, the loose rocks underneath me gave way, rattling about me so I wallowed like a drunken walrus. Steinhauer actually laughed as he reached down to help, staggering as his own feet sank into the heaps of coal.

Coal. I had been thrown into the air by the explosion and I had landed on one of the supply mounds, head downwards—the teeth chewing on my back had been lumps of coal. My limbs were all in working order, thank God; I was just dizzy. With Steinhauer's help I turned and twisted my body until my head was higher than my feet, then shuffled and slid down to the foot of the stack, a dozen feet below.

The ringing in my ears was starting to recede along with the dizziness, but for a moment I still wondered groggily how long ago the explosion had occurred—it had been night when I had raced from the shed, but now it was bright as day. And then I felt anew the heat on my face and squinted up at where the right-hand gasometer had stood. Now it was a giant crucible of fire.

"The men," I said to Steinhauer. The word came out as a croak, but Steinhauer knew what I meant.

"To the best of my knowledge they are all safe. The workers too. But I imagine there are broken windows for miles around." He peered at me. "What of our man? Akushku?"

"That was not Akushku," I said. "It was Bozidar."

"Did you learn anything from him?"

I shook my head, then wished I hadn't. It set my brain swirling about in my skull like a badly set blancmange.

"I am sorry, William," said Steinhauer. I frowned; what was he apologising for? The German merely grinned and nodded at the enormous conflagration.

"Not even you will be able to keep this out of the newspapers," he said.

22

OUR GROWLER JOLTED through the night-time streets north towards Berkeley Square, the driver rattling the bell for all he was worth to clear a path through the evening traffic. Every clang was like a nail driven into my skull, and every jolt fired bolts of pain through my limbs. But there was not a moment to lose. The poky windowless compartment reeked of scorched cloth and singed hair—a stench that came from myself and Steinhauer.

We'd remained at the scene of the bombing long enough to rally my men and check for casualties: there were none, thank God, save a few scrapes and cuts from flying glass and metal. As Steinhauer had predicted, windows and doors had been blown in for half a mile in every direction; local people had dashed out into the street, shaken and fearful, but they were in more danger from their own panic than from the explosion or the fire. The supply to the ruptured gasometer had been quickly shut off and the secondary gasometer brought into service, and apart from a brief drop in pressure, the gas supply to West London had been unaffected. Thank God for German engineering, Steinhauer had remarked with a smirk; Chelsea Gasworks had been built by his compatriots—there was even a square named after them nearby.

Uniformed officers had quickly arrived on the scene, and I had told them what they needed to know, which naturally included nothing about bombs or terrorists. An accidental fire in the coking plant had led to an explosion, I said—and despite the evidence of their own eyes, Special Branch was not there, had never been there, and was in no way involved. As I'd said to Steinhauer, what the public did not know would not hurt them, or hurt the reputation of Special Branch.

Akushku had planned his trap days before—weeks, possibly. Once again he had been three steps ahead of me and once again I'd nearly paid for it with my life. But then my men and I were at a disadvantage—death in service was not something we aspired to. For fanatics like Akushku it was the ultimate glory, especially if he could take twenty coppers with him.

Now we had one fewer of Akushku's friends to worry about, but that was small consolation. For a conspirator as thorough as Akushku one assassin would be enough. Was the man really Russian? I wondered. Rachkovskii had denied it, and perhaps for once he had been telling the truth. What had Bozidar said, in those moments before the explosion? That I should ask Steinhauer.

Was Steinhauer still hiding something, after all we'd been through together?

I glanced across at the young German, who was half-asleep, his head lolling on his chest. At that moment he looked less like an elite policeman than a tramp who'd slept in a ditch. I must look much the same, I realised. I was not going to dance to Akushku's tune, I decided. He had tried to kill us, and failed, and though we were both exhausted and at the end of our strength, we had to persevere—the man we sought was still on the loose, and now only Lady Diamond could lead us to him.

I felt a surge of anger when I thought of Lady Diamond, with her melodramatics and her fake tears of pity for her servants. She had been prepared all along to sacrifice them and herself for her lover, her hero—whatever Akushku was to her. She had led me and my men a merry dance, straight to the slaughterhouse. I made an effort to remain calm and dispassionate; she would not fool us again. In fact, I had to give her credit—she had proved herself a consummate actress.

Yet another talent her social position forbade her to indulge. I smiled bitterly to myself, and felt my skin crack—my face was scorched, and stiff with dirt.

Our growler slowed and clattered to a halt; Steinhauer shook himself awake and climbed down after me, and we found ourselves in Berkeley Square, directly outside Lord Diamond's residence. No need for discretion now. Steinhauer and I brushed ourselves down—a hopeless endeavour—and ascended the broad granite steps. But when I lifted the knocker, the door drifted open on its hinges.

For the briefest moment I was baffled, then I understood. Something was badly wrong.

Heaving the door back, I stepped into the hall, Steinhauer at my heels. There were voices coming from upstairs—hushed, urgent, confused and alarmed. The two of us headed up there two steps at a time and found the servants clustered on the landing like frightened geese, the old butler Musgrave hissing at them to return to their stations and Elsie the mousy maid weeping in the arms of a buxom older servant whom I took for the cook. Musgrave glared at us, but made no protest—this avalanche of events was far beyond his control. And now, farther down the landing, I could hear raised voices: the indignant, patrician tones of Lord Diamond, and what sounded like a working man reasoning with him, urging him to calm down, all coming from Lady Diamond's bedroom.

Steinhauer and I entered to find Diamond, still in his waistcoat, but with his shirt-collar removed and cuffs flapping, standing swaying by a concealed door in the corner that gave into the dressing room. He was red in the face, still drugged, clearly furious and waving a pistol in his right hand, its muzzle pointing now here, now there. Calmly pleading with him to put it down was Sergeant Anderson, one of the uniformed officers I had stationed outside the room earlier to guard Diamond's wife.

Lady Diamond herself lay sprawled across the four-poster bed, a crumpled form in a long black dress. Blood was staining scarlet the cream-coloured bedspread beneath her, while the other constable who had been on duty—PC Jacobs—was trying to staunch her wounds with a towel.

"I have exercised my rights as a husband!" Diamond was bawling to anyone who would listen. "I am not standing idly by while my good name is dragged through the mud by this, this Slavic whore—"

Ignoring his babbling I hurried to help, but it was too late; Lady Diamond's eyes were staring upwards, glassy and lifeless. Her face wore an odd expression—a grimace of pain, or a smile of triumph? No way of telling now. At rest her face had a sharp angular beauty; I glimpsed in it the passion and spirit that had turned the King's head. She was the only reason, I saw now, that Edward had tolerated that chinless popinjay Diamond.

"I'm sorry, sir," said Jacobs. His hands were red with blood and he could not think where to wipe them, afraid of making the bloody mess worse. "He must have come in through her dressing room—we didn't know there was a back door—"

"It's all right," I told him, though it wasn't.

"She betrayed our country, and our King. And she disgraced my name," cut in Lord Diamond. There was spittle on his chin.

"Leave," I said to Anderson. "You too, Jacobs. Send the staff downstairs, and get yourselves cleaned up."

"How dare you point a gun at me in my own house!" Diamond was looking at Steinhauer, who I saw had levelled his weapon at Lord Diamond's head. The German did not waver.

"Put down the gun you are holding, my Lord, and I will lower mine," said Steinhauer.

"Gustav," I said, "holster your weapon." Steinhauer instantly obeyed, keeping his eyes fixed on Diamond. "My Lord," I said, "what happened here?"

"What happened?" Diamond snorted. "What does it look like? I confronted the bitch, and she confessed—she laughed about it, damn her." He was flapping the pistol around as if it were a flannel. I stepped around the bed, closing on him; if his wife had said anything to him about Akushku, we had to know what it was.

"She confessed to a relationship with the King?" I asked.

"I knew about that, damn it. That, that, that—that was a mere dalliance—"

"The gun, please." I held out my hand. Diamond frowned, as if he had forgotten he was holding a pistol, then passed it to me without protest. I checked the cylinder; three bullets remained.

"And the other man?" I said. "I presume she told you of the other man."

"She practically threw it in my face. Some blackguard she called Aleksandr. Another damned foreigner like her, I shouldn't wonder. Once a peasant, always a peasant. They prefer farmyard animals."

"And what did she say about Aleksandr, exactly?"

"Some nonsense about trying to kill the King. Stuff."

"What else?"

"Damn it, wasn't that enough?"

"Did she mention Aleksandr's surname? Where he is hiding? Anything about his plans?"

"Who gives a damn about her nonsense? Hang it all, I've had enough of this—"

He skirted round me and headed for the bedroom door.

"One moment, please, my Lord."

"I don't have to explain myself to a blasted Paddy peasant—"

But Steinhauer had shifted to block his path, and now looked him coldly in the eye. Diamond had several inches on the German, and a stone in weight; but I knew it would be no contest if the drunkard was stupid enough to try fisticuffs. Diamond must have thought the same, for he turned back to me.

"What do you intend to do, arrest me?"

"I could. This was murder, plain and simple."

"Don't be such a cretin!" Diamond yelled, and he was perfectly serious. "She was an adulteress! No jury in the land would convict a man for defending his reputation—his family's ancient name—"

"Adultery is not a capital offence, my Lord," I said, "and a title is no warrant."

Diamond rolled his eyes, clearly running out of patience.

"You bloody fool," he sneered. "It's not just about me. Do you really think that slut was the only entertainment I arranged for Bertie?" Lowering his voice, he leered at me. "Your job, Melville, is to protect the good name of the Crown. To draw a veil over His Majesty's . . . indiscretions. So do your damned job."

He was right, of course. It was my sworn duty to protect the royal family, even from its own mistakes. Especially from those. I sighed, and surveyed the broken body. "Yes . . . , we could record it as a suicide," I conceded. I examined Lady Diamond's corpse more closely. "But three bullets in the stomach might stretch the credulity of the coroner. And there are none of the powder burns on her clothing you would expect if she had held the gun in her own hand. See for yourself, my Lord."

There was nothing to see, of course, but Diamond did as I asked without thinking about it, and paused to look down at his wife's corpse. In that moment, in one swift movement, I raised the revolver's muzzle to his right temple and pulled the trigger.

The shot was deafening in the confined space. Diamond's brains and blood blew over the rear wall, and a deal of it back over me, but then I was filthy already. Diamond's legs folded awkwardly under him and he was dead before his body hit the floor. There was a short scream from downstairs—another housemaid, I guessed, already hysterical at the carnage—and a thunder of constables' boots approaching, but I ignored all that. Stooping down I placed the gun in Diamond's lifeless hand and wrapped his still-warm fingers around the handle and trigger.

"Dear God in Heaven," said Steinhauer faintly.

"Ruthless enough for you, Gustav?" I said.

The door burst open and the constables reappeared. I rose to my feet, wincing as my knee joints protested.

"Sir?" said Anderson, his eyes wide with horror. I looked to Steinhauer.

"Lord Diamond has shot himself," said Steinhauer. "Confronted with his wife's infidelities, he murdered her, then took his own life."

"Before either of us could stop him," I agreed.

"Sir," grunted Anderson, and I saw him catch Jacobs's eye. But I did not care what they believed.

"Take charge, Sergeant. I'll send officers from Special Branch to clear this up. Gustav?"

Without a backwards glance either at Steinhauer or at Diamond's twitching corpse still bleeding into the rich wool rug, I headed for the door. We had some answers, but nothing like enough; our mission had failed. Akushku was still out there, closing in for the attack, and every lead to him was gone. There was naught to be done but pray, and hope, and brace ourselves for whatever would befall us tomorrow.

Steinhauer and I parted at midnight with barely a nod. He headed to his hotel, but it was pointless for me to go home—in five hours I was to brief the officials in charge of the funeral about security arrangements. I returned to Scotland Yard, sent men to clear up the mess at Lord Diamond's home, cast aside my ruined suit and shirt and hat—there was a change of clothing in my locker—took a hot bath and collapsed onto the couch in my office.

And for a few precious hours I slept like a corpse.

23

A BOUT THIRTY YEARS OF AGE, of muscular build, about six feet tall, missing the ring finger of his left hand. Do not concern yourself with his superficial appearance—he is adept at disguise and at blending into his surroundings. Rather, your men should look for behaviour that provokes suspicion."

The audience in that room, made pale already by the harsh yellow gaslight, watched me in solemn silence and barely disguised dismay. These were the foremost dignitaries of the Government and the City and the Court—including the Earl Marshal the Duke of Norfolk, the Lord Chamberlain the Earl of Clarendon and Sir Frederick Ponsonby, Victoria's erstwhile private secretary. The Earl Marshal and the Lord Chamberlain had nearly come to blows a week earlier over which of them was in overall charge of the funeral; Ponsonby had been forced to take charge, and he'd done an admirable job. Everyone present knew their roles and responsibilities, and this meeting had been planned as a mere formality, to iron out last-minute details of logistics and protocol.

Instead these appalled dignitaries were learning for the first time that their precious ceremonies might quite possibly end in bloody catastrophe.

My public reputation, I knew, had always been one of competence and unflappable calm. The calm I could still manage, but my reputation for competence was disintegrating with every word I spoke. Anderson, my boss, was conspicuous by his absence; insisting that his presence was needed "on the ground" to supervise arrangements, he'd secured for himself a place in the procession among the mourners walking behind the catafalque, some distance behind the kings and emperors. No doubt he felt less exposed there than standing in this briefing room with me.

I made no mention of the explosion at Chelsea Gasworks; why would I? It had no bearing on the matter in hand. And despite Gustav's crack, there had been next to no coverage about it in the morning papers—the royal funeral dominated, to the exclusion of all else. I had expected as much: the papers' editors would have already composed their memorial editions and would never scrap those layouts and start again just because of what appeared to be an industrial accident. And there had been zero casualties, officially at least, which made it less newsworthy still.

"The mourners today," I went on, "will be interested in the royal catafalque; that is what they have come to see. The man we are after will be far more interested in the dignitaries that follow it—His Majesty King Edward, His Imperial Majesty the Kaiser and His Majesty King Leopold of Belgium. All police officers and personnel helping with security are to face the crowd. Any man carrying a parcel or bag who looks tense or apprehensive, they must take aside and question immediately."

"Face the crowd?" The speaker was an old acquaintance, the Chief Constable of the Metropolitan Police. I had long considered him an idiot, and his next question confirmed it. "Are you suggesting my officers turn their backs on Her Late Majesty?"

"It is not a suggestion," I said. "Your officers are not on parade. They are there to guard the late Queen's dignity and the safety of her subjects. They can best honour Her Majesty by performing their duty." I nodded towards Steinhauer, seated on my left. "With the help of Herr Steinhauer here, of His Imperial Majesty the Kaiser's household, we have eliminated this man's two accomplices. He is now working alone.

A single gunman, even at the front of the crowd, has little chance of success. If our man dares to make an attempt, he will almost certainly use a dynamite bomb. Your officers must be ready to challenge anyone, male or female, with any sort of package. With all shops and businesses closed along the funeral route, no one will have any good reason to carry a parcel."

"Might I ask," Steinhauer interjected, "if the sewers and drains have been secured?"

"All of them. Checked and checked again." The speaker was Bastion, a burly, red-faced engineer from the Office of Works, and he looked almost offended that his beloved underground labyrinth was being impugned. "I've had men down there two days now, sweeping the lines twice a day."

Steinhauer nodded, satisfied.

No one thought his concern far-fetched. Twenty years ago the Kaiser, Chancellor Bismarck and the entire German Imperial Court had very nearly been blown to shreds by a massive bomb planted in a drain under their feet. The device failed only because rain had washed out the fuse; it was not even discovered until weeks later, after an anarchist arrested for an unrelated offence had confessed to planting it.

"I take it, Chief Superintendent, you will be at the operations centre in Marble Arch?" This time the speaker was the Deputy Mayor of London, a slight, prematurely balding man whose name I could never remember. I had the impression that he was less interested in my answer than making himself look important.

"Inspector Patrick Quinn will be there," I said, "co-ordinating our forces. I will be out and about with Herr Steinhauer, on foot among the crowd."

How casual that sounded, how assured, as if I had planned it all along, when in truth it was one last desperate throw of the dice. I had to be doing something, anything, not just sitting on my arse in an office waiting for the worst to happen. At one point I had even considered riding in the cortege, so that if it came to it, I might be able to place myself between the King's party and the assassin. But the order of procession—who would lead, who would follow, who would ride and who would walk—had only been agreed, I'd been told, after torturous negotiations over precedence and protocol. And anyway I was no horseman, especially compared with aristocrats who had spent half their lives in the saddle. I'd learned to ride on Sean Casey's carthorse, a vicious beast better at biting and kicking than dressage, forty years ago in Kerry, and I'd got no better since.

Steinhauer was probably a better horseman than me—anyone was—but he had declared earlier that he too would rather be on foot. "For most of the route His Imperial Majesty will be surrounded by an escort hand-picked from Queen Victoria's German regiment. Half a dozen officers."

"Big men, I presume?"

"Not one less than two metres tall."

It was the first I'd heard of such an arrangement, and I wondered what those noble panjandrums who fancied themselves in charge had made of it. "And the Palace has consented to this?"

Steinhauer shrugged. "My master does not need anyone's permission. He is determined to attend his grandmother's funeral, but that does not mean he intends to make himself a sitting duck."

"Forgive me, Gustav, but six huge men in a ring around His Imperial Majesty might look slightly conspicuous."

"They will fall back in the course of the procession through London, where the public expects to see him."

"Then they'll be as much use as the feathers on his helmet."

THE CITY OFFICIALS I dismissed at 6:30 a.m. to brief their people while I went to brief mine. Every Special Branch officer available was on duty that day, the lame and the halt included, and they already knew very well where they were to be stationed and what was expected of them. But I went over everything again anyway.

It came as something of a shock when at 7:22 a.m. Steinhauer and I finally stepped outside the doors of Scotland Yard; I was not as fortunate as my men: no one had told me where to go or where I needed to be. Steinhauer seemed to have had the same thought.

"Where now?" he said.

I hesitated. The route was two and a half miles long and certain to be packed with bodies—our task would be like sifting the sands of the Sahara. Steinhauer saw me fretting.

"William, in the end, this Akushku is just another terrorist. And no one knows such people better than you. You know how they think. So what is he thinking?"

Perhaps it was mere flattery, but it was reassuring all the same. I looked east towards St. James's. "Those huge men on horseback," I said. "How far will they escort His Imperial Majesty?"

"As far as Buckingham Palace. Then they will fall back."

"Akushku won't strike while the Emperor is surrounded. He can't—he'll only have one chance."

"So he is more likely to try after the procession passes the Palace."

"He knows we are looking for him. He knows the route has been swept and the sewers are guarded."

"He'll want to get close."

"And he'll want maximum freedom of movement. To keep his options open, and escape afterwards, if he can."

"And where would he find that?"

"Along Park Lane," I said. "The west side. Hyde Park will have all the open space he needs to manoeuvre. He could run the entire length of the cortege without any crowds to slow him down."

The night was dying, but its pall still lay over the city; the new day was breaking slowly, bitterly cold and damp. As the gaslights grew pale, every street beneath them became thronged with figures swathed in heavy coats and scarves, swarming up from Waterloo and Charing Cross Stations and west towards Pall Mall and Park Lane. Emerging from Green Park onto Piccadilly we were faced with an unbridgeable ocean of humanity; thousands and thousands of mourners, of every age and trade and class—men, women, children, pensioners, cripples on crutches—flowing inexorably westward, flooding the pavements and spilling into the roadway, slowing to a crawl the handful of cabs and vans still working that morning. The faces of the crowd, pinched with cold, were for the most part solemn, but underneath that solemnity was a suppressed shiver of excitement at this historic moment, as if it were a festival. Here and there over the silent masses and mingled tramp of countless feet there were even hoots of laughter from the younger and more boisterous attendees, which drew tutting and glares of disapproval from their elders.

No one could stand their ground in such a current, so Steinhauer and I let ourselves be carried along. I felt my freshly blossomed hope shrivelling in the face of the sheer enormity of our challenge—did we seriously expect to stumble across one lone assassin in such a vast crowd? But I pushed the thought aside. We had made our choice and had to stick with it.

I checked my watch; if all was proceeding to plan, the coffin would at that moment be on its way from Gosport aboard the funeral train, scheduled to arrive at Victoria Station at eleven. That gave us just under four hours to apprehend a man whose face we had never seen, but who almost certainly would recognise me on sight. Both of us were armed, but in this crush we would have to be within inches of the assassin before drawing our weapons—and even that risked setting off a stampede. Quite apart from the injuries and deaths that would cause, it would offer Akushku the perfect opportunity to strike, and then flee in the panic.

Towards the junction of Park Lane and Piccadilly the human current started to slow, and the crowd thickened until the press of bodies was almost impossible to penetrate. There was no weaving through this multitude to reach the cordon. Late arrivals were pushing forwards from the rear, squeezing more and more spectators into the available space, all craning their necks to see over those at the front. Even now, hours before the cortege was due to pass, the crowd was thirty or forty deep. Steinhauer and I exchanged a look, turned back while we still could and started to jostle our way out, fighting against the human tide. Eventually we reached a point along the cordon to the south where the pack was not so dense—where the view of the procession was obscured by a kiosk—and flashed our papers at the officers on duty there. Ducking under the cordon we hurried over to the west side of Park Lane.

By now there was a brighter glow to the east, but the sun's rays failed to pierce the low misty cloud. The rooftops and buildings of the West End and the City to our right were nothing but black looming shapes, and ahead of us the avenue of trees faded into grey. Our breaths mingled with those of the crowd and the thousands of uniformed men on duty along the route, rising in white fumes and adding to the pall.

Already every window and balcony along the far side of Park Lane was heaving with black-clad spectators, who'd paid handsomely for the privilege; to our left, in the trees along the eastern edge of Hyde Park, younger and more agile mourners had scrambled up to perch on branches, like outsized crows. But even with these hundreds of thousands of spectators, the whole length of Park Lane was oddly hushed; those who spoke kept their voices lowered, and there was none of the everyday racket from hawkers and bootblacks and traffic. At one point, as Steinhauer and I ploughed our way through the fringes of the crowd, I heard a blackbird sing out, so pure and sweet I was for an instant transported to a morning in the bogs above Sneem, where I used to cut turf for our family's fire.

I shook my head, cursing myself for daydreaming. The crowd was still closing in from the west across the grass of Hyde Park and piling up against the western cordon as thick as leaves in an autumn storm. Like me Steinhauer was looking hard at every face, hoping against hope to glimpse that vital clue—a furtive sidelong glance and turn away, a shock of recognition suddenly masked—but all we got were puzzled or neutral looks in return. We should split up, I thought briefly, only to realise how equally hopeless that would be. Our task was infinite, and dividing infinity by two would be futile. And if, by the slimmest of chances, we did encounter Akushku—and recognise him—two of us combined would have a better chance of bringing him down than one. As I elbowed my way through the press of mourners, my right hand rested on the butt of the pistol in my pocket. If I had to use it, there would be multiple casualties—in this heaving mass that was inevitable.

"For shame! For shame! And at the Queen's funeral—I shall call the police—"

"Madam, as God's my witness, it was an accident, tha'sall, look—no harm done, I'll be on me way—"

The voices were ten or so feet and about twenty people away, ahead of us to the right—an angry older woman and a younger man with a reedy voice, and around the two of them more voices were joining in, indignant and self-righteous. Immediately I closed in on the fuss, barging my way through the crowd like a swimmer ploughing through debris. I could sense amusement in the crowd as well as anger; this was the finest diversion the onlookers could have wished for—some rascal about to take a beating at the hands of the mob.

"You're not going nowhere! Who else you robbed?"

Now the man's protests were growing higher pitched and less coherent, as if he too could sense the fury of the crowd and feared what they might do to him. All the same, about six feet away I stopped and raised my hand to signal Steinhauer to hold back. Ahead of me two older men had seized a younger, wiry man in a shabby shiny suit of dark blue too small for him, and his victim was clutching her bag to her bosom as if afraid someone else might try to snatch it.

"Check his pockets, go on, see what else is in there," she was saying. In her forties, she was stout and florid and loudly respectable; her other hand wielded a black umbrella like a weapon.

"Hands off me! You got no right!" the wiry young man protested, struggling. One of the men holding him punched him hard in the kidneys. He yelped and winced and sagged, and some bystanders laughed and urged that he be hit again. And still I stood back.

"He's a dip, that's all," I murmured to Steinhauer. It was not my concern—we weren't there to protect the crowd from pickpockets, or vice versa. If the mob turned nastier still, and decided to beat that young man to a pulp, I resolved to let them. I had no intention of making myself conspicuous by intervening; instead I swept the crowd for any passer-by who seemed uninterested in the disturbance, or who wanted to avoid the two uniformed policemen with truncheons drawn I could now see barging through the crowd towards the disturbance. But I noticed no one like that, and once on the scene the officers were brisk, efficient and merciless.

"Thank you! Thank you, ladies and gents, we'll deal with this, make a way there, please!" one officer shouted as the other seized the suspect by the collar. The skinny man in blue looked relieved to be rescued, and he had good reason.

"Picking pockets at Her Majesty's funeral, you want to string him up!" scolded the woman with the purse.

"Don't you worry, ma'am, he won't be trying it again."

The two uniforms dragged the pickpocket away, but not in the direction of the nearest station—on a morning like this there was no time for paperwork. They'd most likely find a secluded alley to impose a non-custodial sentence with fists and truncheons, then get back on duty. The sideshow having concluded the crowd closed in again as if nothing had happened, and I beckoned Steinhauer onwards, heading north.

Soon we were roughly a third of the way up Park Lane; the light was at last growing stronger, and the fog seemed to be thinning. We could see more clearly on the far side the purple drapes hanging from the town-house balconies, rippling in the occasional breeze. It was Victoria who'd specified purple and white decor for her funeral— black was too gloomy, she had said. An odd decision for a woman who'd spent most of her adult life in widow's weeds.

I paused to check my pocket watch—no easy matter amid that press of bodies.

Nine-thirty.

Ninety minutes from now the cortege should start out from Victoria, and half an hour after that—God willing—it would reach Hyde Park Corner, then proceed up Park Lane to Marble Arch, and onwards to Paddington Station. Steinhauer and I barged on through the crowd.

Now I fancied I could hear murmuring—but this time it was a voice in my head, telling me that from start to finish this entire operation had been a farce, a disaster. I and Steinhauer and all of Special Branch were still running round in circles, like a herd of cows panicked by a wasp. It was a fool's errand, and I was the fool who'd ordered it. Why had I not pursued more leads, raided every anarchist club and radical household in the country, cracked heads till someone talked? Why had I wasted so much time going cap in hand to those lying gombeens from Russia and France, begging like a dog for scraps of intelligence? After all this time and effort and danger and death, I knew nothing about Akushku, or even his target. What if the man was working for the Turks or the Boers? What if the so-called plot against Wilhelm was a decoy—what if he really meant to attack King Edward or Leopold of Belgium or some European duke? If the worst came to the worst, could I even rely on Steinhauer to stand by me?

About us the crowd milled and jostled and craned their necks even though there was nothing to see, and wouldn't be for another—I checked my watch again—fifty-six minutes. Dear Christ! It had gone ten.

"There," said Steinhauer, his voice soft yet sharp in my ear. "To your right. In the bowler hat."

When I saw the man I knew immediately why he had caught Steinhauer's eye. He was standing about twelve feet back from the cordon—a twitchy, well-built man in his late twenties in a heavy black coat, with pale pockmarked cheeks, wispy eyebrows and long unwashed fair hair tucked behind his ears. He seemed to radiate tension and resentment, his eyes flicking uneasily over the crowd, and his right hand constantly reaching into his coat as if to touch something. But it was not just his demeanour that caught my eye—it was the package under his left arm. Bound in cloth and fastened with a leather belt, it was the size of a large shoebox, but much heavier, judging by the tension of the suspect's arm and shoulder. His left hand was tucked into his pocket; I could not check for a missing ring finger, but the hairs had risen on the back of my neck.

I moved to my right, and from the corner of my eye saw Steinhauer take the opposite tack, weaving almost unnoticed through the press of bodies. For my part I had to shove the mourners aside, and I did it brusquely and without apology, ignoring their protests, keeping my eyes locked on the target. I was less than ten feet away when the pockmarked man became aware of me closing in. His eyes widened in alarm and he tried to slip sideways into the crowd, closer to the cordon, barging with his left shoulder while his right hand slipped once more inside his black overcoat. I ploughed after him, but I was slowed down by my own bulk and was still two arms' lengths away when I saw the pockmarked man tug something black and metallic from inside his coat—a gun. I snatched my own pistol free of my pocket, roaring:

"Clear a way, there! Make way!"

The scrawny man turned back towards me, raising his right hand, and I raised my own, and my finger tightened on the trigger—but before I could fire, the man's arm was flung skywards. His shot went wild, but the crowd around us heard it and surged back, screaming and shouting. Steinhauer, who had knocked the gunman's hand upwards, now kicked his legs away from under him. I barged through the last few mourners blocking my path and brought my boot down hard on the wrist that held the pistol. The gunman screamed and clutched at his parcel as I bent down and wrenched the gun from his grasp and stuck it in my coat pocket.

"You cannot stop me! You cannot stop me!" he screeched. He went on protesting in a thick Slavic accent as Steinhauer rolled him over and wrenched his arms up behind his back. Around us the crowd yelled in confusion and anger and milled and shifted, threatening to trample us all underfoot, but I shoved back and snatched up the cloth-bound bundle. It was as heavy and solid as it looked. Steinhauer had hauled the suspect to his feet.

"Som anjel poslaný bohom," he spat at us, his long greasy hair tangling in his mouth. "I have been sent to free the people—"

"Move," I grunted, and hauled him by the collar away from the procession route, aware all the time of the parcel under my arm. We were just opposite Grosvenor Gate, from where more mourners were flooding by the minute, staring at us uneasily as we dragged our prisoner past them through the gates to the trampled grass of Hyde Park itself. I saw two more constables hurrying towards us and, consigning the prisoner to Steinhauer's tender mercies, turned my attentions to the bundle and its leather strap. I shook it, gently, and listened: but it did not rattle, nor did it smell of chemicals, and its weight was distributed evenly throughout its bulk. I fumbled at the buckle and unfastened the belt, ignoring Steinhauer's alarm and the incoherent protests, in various languages, of the scrawny gunman, because on some level I knew what I was going to uncover, and when I did, I stifled a curse.

It was a Bible, a huge household Bible bound in leather. I opened it, almost hoping to find the pages carved to create a compartment for a bomb, but they held nothing except sacred verses in Cyrillic script.

"You are fools, you are puppets, you will burn!" The pockmarked man's eyes grew wide, and spittle flecked his lips. As the first constable arrived, I shoved the book at him.

"DCS Melville, Special Branch. Hold this."

"I am Lucifer, the bringer of light!" The young lunatic wrenched at the cuffs locked behind his back and struggled in Steinhauer's grip. "I will free this world from darkness!"

I glanced at his left hand and saw there four intact fingers and a thumb. When I pulled the gunman's pistol from my pocket for a closer look, the barrel was plugged with lead, and the cylinder had only one chamber. The blasted thing was a starting pistol. This idiot could not have fired a shot at me, or anyone—and I'd nearly blown his head off.

"*Scheisse,*" said Steinhauer in disgust, and he shoved his prisoner towards the second constable.

"Victoria was the whore of Babylon, and her children are the spawn of the Antichrist!" the fanatic babbled. "The dragon has seven heads and ten horns and seven diadems on his heads—"

"He's a lunatic," I told the uniforms. "Stick him in a Black Maria, and get back on duty."

And at that very moment came a thunderous crash of artillery from the heart of Hyde Park. The salute had begun—the cortege was on its way. I turned and headed back the way we had come, shouldering through the throng with Steinhauer on my heels. I kept my head up and kept looking, but in my head I could hear the Fates cackling at me.

Damn the Fates, I thought. This jig's not done. Akushku hadn't struck yet, and with every moment that passed, his window of opportunity was closing. Our task was not impossible. I had to focus, to think like Akushku—and if that had not led us to him yet, I had to think harder.

24

AND STILL the crowd grew denser—fifty deep, sixty. It felt as if every man, woman and child in the Home Counties had crammed themselves into that one long avenue, and behind them every other resident of Great Britain was arriving. Their voices murmuring together sounded like a restless sea, interrupted every few seconds by the crash of the artillery salute and accompanied by the mourning bells that had begun to chime from all of London's churches. Underneath the solemnity and decorum I could sense too the crowd's growing excitement. Yes, it was a sombre occasion, but it was also a spectacle the like of which might never be seen again—kings and princes and nobles from every corner of Europe and the Empire, marching together in all their magnificent pomp and finery.

Steinhauer and I had no appetite for the spectacle but hurried north, approaching Marble Arch. To the right I could make out one of the platforms erected for the press and noticed two photographers jockeying for the best vantage point, fencing with the legs of their tripods. The artillery salutes pounded steadily on, and I felt a shiver run through the crowd, and the hushed eager chatter faded. Around me spectators were craning their necks to look south, listening intently—and now I could hear it too: the beat of muffled drums. The cortege was coming up on Hyde Park Corner. I glanced again at my pocket watch: eleven thirty-five, perfectly on schedule. The fatal moment was upon us, and Steinhauer and I were adrift on a black ocean of people, as helpless as shipwrecked sailors.

As the crowd surged forwards towards the barrier, the two of us pulled back. Already packed impossibly tight, the onlookers wanted to pack themselves tighter still. Even if we'd been able to, there would have been no point in fighting our way to the front of the crowd—we'd have been wedged fast there, unable to move.

"Whatever he's planning, he'll be in position by now," I said to Steinhauer. "Our best hope is to get to the other side of the cordon, into the road itself, and scan the crowd from there."

"Then let's get to a crossing," said Steinhauer.

As we set off towards Marble Arch, where there was an official access point to the funeral route, I was swept by a fresh wave of frustration. At the start of this affair, a lifetime ago, Gustav had had a high opinion of me; after today, he would not. He was about to see firsthand my disgrace, and it was all too likely I'd drag him down with me. And to fail so publicly, with the whole world as witness! I glared up at the platforms where the photographers had stopped jostling and were poised with fresh plates at the ready.

I stopped so abruptly that Steinhauer nearly ran into me.

"What does he want?" I asked aloud. "Akushku."

The German looked puzzled, but only for an instant. "To change the world," he said. "To make history, by killing my Emperor."

And now, through the melee of bobbing heads and hats, I could see the head of the procession approaching from the south: Villiers the Lord Chamberlain and the rest of the royal household on foot, staffs of office in their hands, and beyond them, emerging from the mist, came eight white ponies drawing a catafalque draped in white and purple.

"In public, for all the world to see," I said. The final crash of the artillery echoed off the buildings opposite us; now the only other sounds were tramping hooves, jingling harnesses, marching feet and the muffled drums. We were nearly shouting, but there was no danger of being overheard.

"Public or private, what difference?" said Steinhauer.

"Remember what we talked about, Gustav: it's not just the act, it's the impact—on the people. Akushku wants not only to kill Wilhelm, but for everyone to see him do it. That is why it must be here, today, now."

At those words something flickered in the back of my mind—pastel-coloured fragments, edged with ash. Blackened and singed paper rustling in the draught, in a grate piled with ashes.

"The tickets."

"Tickets?" Steinhauer looked baffled.

"In Angela's fireplace, after the raid. He'd burned the music-hall tickets. Angela said Akushku always burns his evidence . . ."

"You have lost me."

And now I saw it. "They weren't music-hall tickets—Christ preserve us!" I gasped. "With me. Quickly!"

I ploughed through the crowd towards the cordon, and it was like running through a herd of cattle, as more and more spectators pushed forwards at right angles to our path. As I tried to shove my way through I could see the vanguard of the procession almost abreast of us and feel the pounding of the muffled drums hammering on my chest—just as my own heart was hammering, so hard I thought it might burst. Let me not be too late, I prayed, let me not be too late—

"Where are we going?" said Steinhauer. He had to yell to be heard over the hooves and boots and jingling harnesses.

"The Arch," I said. "The platforms—"

Ahead of us was Marble Arch, the massive monument that had once served as the entrance to Buckingham Palace, before being moved up here to the western end of Oxford Street. Around it the crowd was solid, packed perhaps two hundred deep, bodies wedged in between barriers lined by two rows of troops, in the bright red tunics and white pith helmets of a colonial regiment. I moved to the left, skirting round the back of the crowd, like a man trying to edge around a quagmire.

"They weren't for the music-hall," I was babbling to Steinhauer. "The tickets in the grate. A man like Akushku has no time for music-halls."

"Then what were they?"

"Tickets for the kinema! Over there, look—" I pointed to the second wooden platform that had been erected in the shadow of the Arch, offering a commanding view of Marble Arch and the road around it. "The kinematograph cameras on the platform—"

"*Gott in der Hölle*—you think he will strike here, in front of them?"

"Yes, so all the world can see it—"

At last we had reached the knot of officers guarding the crossing point. The sergeant in charge, a good head taller than me, scowled as I fumbled for my warrant card, clearly taking us for troublemakers.

"We need to get through the cordon now, and you need to come with us," I said.

"You'll just have to wait till the procession's gone past—"

"Now," I said. I found the document and stuck it under his nose, and he stiffened to attention—even saluted, the bloody fool. His younger colleague was quicker-witted. "This way, sir," he said, leading us briskly towards the cordon, where two wooden barriers at right angles to the main barrier formed a long passageway designed to allow the free movement of military personnel. By now the crowd had grown so dense the two barriers had nearly been clamped shut by the pressure, and the four of us—Steinhauer and I and the two policemen—had to squeeze down the narrowing path in single file, elbowing away the spectators on either side.

At last we were on the road itself, free of the crowd, only to find the cortege less than a hundred feet away, bearing down upon us like a juggernaut. The drums were thundering and the burnished breastplates and helmets of the Household Cavalry gleamed as a solitary ray of sunshine pierced the pall of cloud. Steinhauer surveyed the crowd, scanning the faces, but such was the mass of humanity surrounding us it was like trying to spot one leaf in a forest. The huge sergeant and the willing constable who had come with us hovered at our shoulders, waiting for orders, as the tramping and the jingling and the drumming grew so loud they nearly deafened us. We had a perfect view now down the whole length of the procession—a dazzling array of gilded uniforms and cloaks, and in their midst the gun carriage, moving silently and smoothly on rubber tyres, bearing a pitifully small coffin draped in purple silk and topped with the sceptre and crown.

And directly behind it, three abreast, rode King Edward, his brother the Duke of Connaught and Kaiser Wilhelm in his billowing grey cloak, their horses trotting steadily three abreast—a perfect, slowly moving target. We were too late. In God's name—why had I not thought of this earlier? Steinhauer was staring at the platform where the photographers were lined up. He was trying to calculate the sight-lines, I realised, to identify the place where his Emperor would be directly before the cameras, just as Akushku would have done . . . But among the pack of photographers there were three moving-picture cameras. The operators were cranking furiously; each of them had a grandstand view, and now the catafalque was almost at the arch, Edward and Wilhelm and the Duke in its wake. Any moment now those three cameras would capture moving images of a massacre, preserving them in hideous detail for all time.

Three moving-picture cameras. I shook my head and tried to remember—it had been late at night, I'd been so tired I could barely think, and I'd skimmed Quinn's memorandum about the platforms for the world's press. At Marble Arch, eight photographers, and two moving-picture cameras, one from Pathé, the other from a firm called Hepworth—

Two cameras. Christ in Heaven. Not three.

I pulled my hat off as if about to pay my respects and held it in front of my face. Steinhauer beside me did the same, though he still did not grasp quite why. With no time to explain—the procession was nearly upon us—I turned and strode across the road only yards from the head of the advancing cortege, willing myself not to break into a panicked run and praying that the assassin would not recognise us and launch his attack prematurely.

We had less than sixty seconds before the Kaiser and the King reached this spot.

At the foot of the steps leading up to the platform a uniformed constable of barely nineteen was on duty, already standing to rigid attention for the passage of the cortege. When I flashed my warrant card in his face he looked panicked and indignant.

"The moving-picture men, you checked their papers?" I barked.

"Yes, sir, well, my sergeant did, he's over the other side—"

"Did they all have permits?"

"Yes, sir. Well, most of them, one had so much equipment he couldn't find his—"

"Which?"

"Er—the one at the far end, in the dark green suit—"

I didn't wait for the lad to finish but pounded up the steps to the platform, pulling my pistol clear of my pocket. The photographers were hiding under their black-cloths; two of the kinema operators, cranking away, did not even notice my ascent onto the platform, while the third—the one in the green suit—lifted his head from his eyepiece, straightened up and looked directly at me.

He was a striking young man, Akushku: athletic in build, with fine, even features, wavy fair hair and piercing blue eyes that now betrayed the merest glint of recognition—and not a trace of panic. With calm, swift movements he stepped back from his moving-picture camera and stooped to grasp the handle of a polished oak equipment box behind him.

The wooden lid of the box shattered with my first shot, blowing off the handle and sending vicious splinters flying in all directions. Akushku fell back, clutching at his face, while I cursed—I'd been aiming for his head. Blinking away the shrapnel the young man threw himself down among the tripods and equipment of the cameramen crowding the platform, so absorbed in their task they were bizarrely oblivious to the lethal drama unfolding at their feet. They were blinkered by their black-cloths and had not even heard the shot—the cacophony of thumping drums, jangling horse-brasses and clattering hooves was drowning out every other sound.

I wove among them, trying to get a clear second shot, closing in on Akushku, determined at all costs to stop him from grasping that polished wooden box and hurling it at the cortege. The box was the bomb, I was now sure; my wayward bullet had very nearly blown me and him and every man on that platform to kingdom come.

As the anarchist scrambled for cover I saw Steinhauer haul himself up onto the scaffold at the far side to outflank Akushku. The terrorist saw him too and reaching round behind his back wrenched a pistol from his waistband. For one dreadful moment I thought Gustav would get shot point-blank in the face—but seeming to realise in that instant he could either fight or flee, Akushku chose the latter. Rolling towards the rear edge of the platform, he tumbled backwards off it and simply dropped out of sight.

25

G USTAV," I CALLED OUT. "Check that crate of his—but carefully, for God's sake—"
        I rushed towards the far edge of the platform—even now Akushku could be fighting his way back towards the procession— stashed my pistol, gripped the edge, swung over and dropped down, half expecting to catch a bullet before I'd hit the ground. But when I staggered to my feet, there was no sign of the anarchist anywhere.

The platform stood on a tangle of wooden struts; to each side and the front the crowd was packed more tightly than sardines. Akushku could never have fought his way into that tight mass of onlookers—he must have escaped north-east. At that very moment he might be struggling through the rear of the crowd, tracking the procession up the Edgware Road, hoping for another chance to strike. In the second it took me to work that out, the huge sergeant and his young colleague dropped heavily from the platform above me, landing with an almighty thump of hobnailed boots; and over the thunder of the drums, the tolling of church bells and the pounding of a thousand horses' hooves, I had to bawl to make my voice heard.

"Don't use your whistles. Find more officers, spread the word, we're looking for a fair-haired man of thirty, missing his left ring finger, in a dark green suit—no hat." That detail alone would mark him out—

only a lunatic would walk the streets bareheaded. "He's armed and dangerous and he must be stopped at any cost—go!"

They dashed away to either side, grabbing nearby officers and shouting instructions. I left them to it and raced away north towards the Edgware Road. Off to the right was Oxford Street; all of its shops and offices were closed. There was only a handful of pedestrians that I could see, and they were heading towards me, not away, and none of them was the fugitive. I ran on to the corner of Great Cumberland Place, the narrow road heading north parallel to the Edgware Road, thinking that perhaps Akushku had sought a back route, but the street was blocked with horses and military wagons; the army had set up a temporary base here, the last barrier an armed anarchist would try to penetrate.

Among all this mourning black, Akushku in that green suit should have been easy to spot, so where was he? The man had vanished. No, that was impossible—he'd had only moments. He must have found a hiding place, and not just on the spur of the moment, but reconnoitred in advance. He might have forced a window or a door so he could get off the street until the hue and cry died down. Entering a building would mean allowing himself to be cornered and run to earth—he would want to keep moving. But short of flying, or escaping along a sewer tunnel, there was no other means to escape unseen—and the sewers had been secured.

Then again sewers weren't the only tunnels.

I spun on the spot. There, a hundred yards north of the camera platforms, was the new Marble Arch Underground Station, opened only a few months previously. I raced towards it. Every Underground line had been shut down for the duration of the funeral, and the entrance to this station was blocked by a metal trellis stretched across the entrance to the ticket hall and secured with a heavy padlock and chain. I tugged at the lock—it had not been tampered with. To the right of the public entrance was a staff door, painted red to blend in with the shining tiles of the station's outer wall, and that too was shut firmly. But there, still glistening on the paving-stone immediately before it, was a single speck of blood.

Akushku's? Had he been cut by a flying splinter when I fired at him? Seizing the handle, I gave the staff door a hard shove, and felt it move, half an inch. The lock had been picked.

Bracing my shoulder against the door I shoved again, harder. It yielded slowly—something heavy had been wedged up against the far side. Either that, or Akushku was behind it pushing back. I retrieved my pistol from its holster and slammed my shoulder into the door again, once, twice, forcing it back, until the gap was wide enough for me to pass. And now I hesitated. I knew very well I should be calling for assistance—but I also knew that if Akushku got as far as the lines below, nothing would stop him running along the tunnel to the next station. He might yet have an opportunity to strike.

Squeezing through the gap, I stumbled into a dim, unlit ticket office. The weight against the door was indeed a filing cabinet; Akushku had heaved it over onto its side. At the far end of the office the door to the main concourse lay open. Cocking the hammer of my revolver I moved quietly towards it, aware that he could be watching me, concealed in an alcove or behind a pillar, and aware too that I was doing everything I always told my men not to do: pursuing a suspect without calling for assistance or telling anyone where I had gone. But I was so close, and every second was critical.

Bracing my pistol with two hands I swept the concourse, my finger sweating on the trigger. The station was empty. Three lifts carried passengers down to the platforms, but they had all been switched off, and their doors lay wide open. Beyond them yawned a dim green-tiled passageway under a sign that read EMERGENCY STAIRS. I headed towards it, straining my ears, and caught far below a clatter of shoes on metal-edged steps. Nothing for it—I had to follow. The distant footsteps were drowned out by the sound of my own boots clomping down. If Akushku paused, or turned back, I hoped I would hear him before I ran into him.

The spiral staircase seemed to drill downwards forever. It descended anticlockwise; with my gun in my right hand I would have a clear shot. Was Akushku left-handed? It would make little difference in a space such as this, I realised; bullets and ricochets and broken tiles would fly all over the place like shrapnel.

All at once the staircase ended, and I found myself facing another narrow green-tiled hallway, this one bending off to the right. I moved along it briskly, trying to soften my footsteps, hugging the wall to my left and keeping my gun raised and ready.

I emerged from that passage onto the deserted Underground platform, at each end a brick-lined tunnel that curved off into darkness, only the first thirty feet or so lined with electric lights. I stopped, and held my breath, and listened, trying to block out the sound of my heart thumping in my chest. There, from the eastbound platform, behind me—a scrabble, a skitter of ballast. I ran through the connecting passage and scanned the platform on the far side; it too was empty—but now I could hear a noise from the tunnel to my left: footsteps, as faint as rats' claws on rock.

Akushku was fleeing eastward, as I'd feared, along the tunnel to the next station.

Quickly I clambered down over the edge of the platform, stepped out onto the tracks and headed after him. The electric lights, intended for cleaners and maintenance men, were so caked in grease and soot their illumination was as feeble as starlight.

No, I thought, ten steps down the tunnel—this is idiocy. I had taken enough headstrong risks without pursuing an armed terrorist alone along a railway track. It was time to return to the surface, raise the alarm and send a team of men to each and every station along the line. With my gun raised I started to walk backwards, slowly, towards the safety of the eastbound platform.

"Stop there, Mr. Melville."

The voice that rang out was firm and calm—melodious, even—and the accent unplaceable; it sounded like Oxford English, slightly tinged with Russian, or perhaps German. I stood still, too angry to even curse my own folly.

"Stay very still. And kindly drop your weapon."

His exquisite politeness, and that patronising tone, were making my blood boil, but he had me at an utter disadvantage. I stretched out my arm, carefully uncocked the hammer of my pistol and let the weapon fall. It struck a rail with a clang and tumbled into shadow. Now, too late, my eyes were adjusting to the dimness, and I could see, at intervals along the tunnel, the arched recesses where workmen could store equipment or shelter from passing trains. Akushku had concealed himself in one and waited, and I had walked right past him, into his trap.

"Can I turn around, at least?" I said.

"This might go easier for you if you did not."

"Easier for you, you mean." Keeping my hands out clear of my sides, I turned slowly around to face my fate. It came to me briefly that I should have gone home last night—said goodnight to Amelia, kissed my children one last time—but I shoved those thoughts aside. Wishes were no good to me now.

Akushku had emerged from his alcove and now stood silhouetted in the light spilling from the platform ten feet beyond him. I could just make out his sharp cheekbones and his slight smile—neither smug nor gloating, but wry, as if to him this victory was just a minor skirmish in a long war. I could make out very well his raised pistol and the rock-steady hand that held it.

"So will you tell me your surname, Aleksandr?"

"Why do you need to know my name?"

"For my own satisfaction. I presume I won't live to pass it on."

He tilted his head. "I have many names. The one I was born with . . . I don't particularly care for."

Why had he not pulled the trigger? He could have shot me and been on his way by now. Behind him the empty platform curved away, bright and bare and empty. I thought I glimpsed a flicker of movement at the very far end, but only for an instant; it was wishful thinking, I scolded myself, born of desperation. I shifted my weight very slightly towards Akushku. How quickly could I cover the distance between us?

"Don't," he said quietly. He stretched his arm a mite farther, and the muzzle of his gun stared at me, a little black abyss.

"You know, Aleksandr," I said, "you might kill me, but a hundred officers will take my place."

"Perhaps, but none of them will be as dangerous as you. Europe's most infamous policeman. You very nearly stopped me."

"Nearly stopped you? I think you'll find I *have* stopped you."

"Today, yes. But I will get another chance. And killing the great Melville will be some consolation."

"Well, then, don't let me delay you." I spoke with more coolness than I felt. I didn't want to plead with this dog for my life, but I didn't want to provoke him either, with bluster or threats. It seemed he wanted to talk, and I was happy to let him, in the hope that . . . well, I didn't know what I hoped might happen, but I wanted to be alive when it did.

"I just need to understand . . ." Akushku hesitated.

"What?"

"Why you do this. You are a man of some intelligence. You do not despise working people—you were a peasant once yourself. For centuries the Irish have been persecuted and starved by the English bourgeoisie, and yet you work for them. How do you sleep at night? What lies do you tell yourself?"

A political debate was the last thing I'd expected. Indeed, it might be the last thing I did.

"I believe in democracy," I said. "It's slow and it's inefficient, but it's our best hope. Mankind can better itself without violence. Men like you demand Utopia and don't care who you kill to get it. You shoot and bomb because your arguments have failed. Maybe you mean well, but you're deluded."

"*I'm* deluded?" Akushku laughed. "You really think democracy makes a difference? That the bourgeoisie would ever agree to give up one ounce of their wealth and privilege? They grow fat on the work of the poor, and when the poor rise up, the rich hire men like you to beat them down. And you tell yourself you are doing it for the good of the people. Which of us is really deluded?"

I was poised on edge, tensing myself to lunge at him. He might shoot me, but that was his plan anyway, and I didn't see why I had to go along with it. However his concentration never seemed to waver for an instant, and the muzzle of his gun barely drifted.

"Look where your delusions have led you," he went on. "You are going to die alone, here in this tunnel. You will sacrifice yourself for the bourgeoisie. Yes, they will miss you, like they miss a good hunting dog, or a fine horse. But tomorrow they will buy another."

"I don't do this for the nobs. I do it for ordinary men and women. The ones who just want work and bread and a roof over their heads and to raise their children in peace."

"All this talk of peace, from the man who came down here to kill me."

"I came down here to prevent a war."

The young man shook his head, as if in regret. "Then you are a fool."

"You meant to kill the Kaiser, and start a war. But I stopped you. I've done my job, and you've failed, so . . . here we are."

"You are mistaken. Yes, I want to kill the Kaiser. But I am not trying to start a war. I am trying to prevent one."

"Away and shite," I snapped. His pious sermon had started to irritate me.

"The perfect royal servant," snorted Akushku. "You stand at the shoulder of the King, you hear everything and understand nothing. Wilhelm despises your King Edward. He means to take his—"

The crash of the gunshot in that confined space stabbed into my head like a knife, and instinctively I clapped my hands to my ears and crouched. For a moment I even thought that I had been shot, and braced myself for a wave of pain—but there was nothing. Ears still ringing, I opened my eyes and stood up straight and saw the man once called Akushku sprawled across the rails, one side of his face pressed into the grimy gravel, his eyes wide, blood spurting from his nose and from the massive wound to the back of his head.

Thirty feet away Steinhauer leapt down from the station platform and raced towards me. He was in his socks, I noticed—he must have taken his boots off to creep unheard along the parallel platform. Akushku's mouth was working, as if he was trying to speak.

"William!" called Steinhauer. "Are you hurt?"

"I'm fine, I think, Gustav, thank you—" My own voice echoed in my head; hearing it I realised I was still alive and felt a rush of gratitude and relief. "He was about to tell me something."

There was a faint groan from Akushku. He blinked, and the fingers still loosely curled around his pistol's butt and trigger twitched slightly.

"*Scheisse,*" said Steinhauer. He pointed his revolver downwards and fired twice, at close range, into the anarchist's skull, blowing it into a misshapen mess of hair and bone and brains.

26

THE LITTLE CHURCH in Stepney was empty but for myself, the organist and the pallbearers I'd hired. I stared at the plain deal coffin resting on two trestles before the altar and listened to the organ music reverberating softly round the chapel and realised this was the first moment of quiet contemplation I'd had in weeks. I wasn't sure I wanted it.

After Steinhauer had administered that hasty coup de grâce we had not lingered by Akushku's corpse. We left the body where it lay on the tracks, clambered back onto the platform, retrieved Gustav's boots and headed back up that endless winding staircase, only to collide with four uniformed officers hurrying down. The big sergeant I'd met at Marble Arch had spotted the open door of the Underground station and summoned reinforcements. I'd misjudged him earlier—once he was properly briefed he acted decisively; with his assistance I had the station secured and the body spirited off to the mortuary, all unnoticed by the public. By the time the place reopened, there was nothing to mark Akushku's passing but some glistening stains on the ballast between the tracks.

Steinhauer had hurried off to rejoin his Kaiser, relaxed and almost jovial now he had fulfilled his mission. For my part, even now we had dealt with Akushku, I could not drop my guard—there were plenty of other malcontents out there, though few of them so lethal. I passed the word around that the suspect with the missing finger had been apprehended. Those who needed more details would get them in due course.

Victoria's funeral had carried on, though not without further incident. When the cortege arrived safely at Paddington, where the funeral train waited to carry coffin and mourners to Windsor for the late Queen's lying-in-state, Wilhelm's last-minute escort of giant Germans demanded seats on the train, causing some ruffled feathers. There were more shenanigans still when the coffin finally arrived at Windsor: the honour guard of the Household Cavalry had been waiting for hours at the station in the bitter cold to draw the catafalque to the royal chapel, and their horses had grown fractious; when the procession started they set off so briskly the traces connecting them to the hearse broke. While the cavalry officers squabbled sotto voce and blamed one another, the party of common sailors who made up the Royal Navy's escort ripped the emergency cord from the train, lashed it to the hearse and towed the coffin to Windsor chapel themselves. The military brass and the civilian dignitaries quickly fell into line behind them, as if this arrangement had been intended all along.

All this I had witnessed without trying to intervene; there were already enough cooks involved to ruin the finest broth. Of course the press had loved the sailors' gesture, hailing it as a spontaneous demonstration of affection for the late Queen, and a fine example of British military initiative. Next time there was a royal funeral, I had no doubt, British sailors would draw the hearse again, and the nobility would claim that part of the ceremony had been their invention.

What a circus, I thought now, as I sat in that Stepney chapel watching a shaft of sunlight warm a saint's stained-glass halo. True, I had been part of the troupe, but it amused me when real life, in the shape of crying children or flatulent horses, disrupted pompous ceremony. It was always the most shallow and precious courtiers who got into a flap. Victoria herself, when I knew her, had never been thrown by such interruptions; she'd been in the job so long she'd grown a sense of proportion.

But Victoria had been dead for weeks, and now she lay at rest in the royal mausoleum at Frogmore beside her beloved Albert. Kaiser Wilhelm and his enormous Imperial retinue had gone home; Steinhauer and I had embraced at the station, fellow veterans, the battle won.

"You must visit Berlin as my guest, William."

"I will, Gustav. Very soon."

The other European nobles had dispersed to their own kingdoms, and their security was no longer my concern.

As for the Akushku business, that was quickly becoming a mere anecdote between myself and Steinhauer. No one else—not even my Special Branch officers—knew the whole story, and I was sure I would never tell it. Posterity could go hang, and historians too. They were little better than journalists anyhow, in my opinion, trying to pass off speculation, gossip and invention as fact. Already the everyday details—the mishap with the cold horses, the squabbles over seating— were being polished out of the record, and all official accounts of the funeral were full of breathless, sentimental reverence.

Even the kinematographic records of the funeral were misleading, I realised now. The footage had been duplicated hundreds of times and distributed to every corner of the British Empire. I'd first seen it in the company of the King himself, all of us sitting in flickering darkness, listening to the rattling of the projector. We both saw that moment when Edward and the Kaiser had ridden past that platform by Marble Arch, and Edward's steed had bucked and reared. It had been spooked by my gunshot, but I had already put about the rumour that it was the racket of the camera itself that had scared the horse. The King for his part had made no remarks and asked no questions; and I for my part had volunteered no answers. So much for Gustav's contention that kinema showed the whole unvarnished truth.

Now the door to the vestry rattled open, rousing me from my reverie, and the young priest I had engaged for this service emerged clutching his missal, followed by two altar boys. The body of the deceased had been dragged from the Grand Union Canal near King's Cross two days earlier. She had been so long in the water her features were unrecognisable, apart from the fair hair that fell in tangles round her face and shoulders. Around her neck I'd hung a crucifix on a chain; she'd been a Catholic, after all, like myself. Under the chain's links dark purple marks were still just visible on her grey skin.

"Strangled," the mortician had said. "Perhaps because of the baby she was carrying?" I'd made no comment, but let him wonder.

The priest caught my eye, and I nodded and rose to my feet. Turning to the altar he raised his hands, and the tootling of the organ faded into silence.

"In nomine Patris, et Filii, et Spiritus Sancti . . ."

Perhaps I had saved the German Emperor, and saved Europe from war, but it had been a damned close thing, and now I thanked God for guiding me to that platform where Akushku had lain in wait. And I asked him to look kindly on those colleagues of mine who had given their lives assisting me, and to have mercy on the souls of those who died less nobly—Lady Diamond, her husband and the unfortunate young girl lying in a plain deal coffin before me.

"Incline Thy ear, O Lord, to the prayers with which we humbly entreat Thy mercy, and in a place of peace and rest establish the soul of Thy servant Angela Minetti, whom Thou hast called out of this world . . ."

27

WITH THE HELP of Herr Steinhauer, bodyguard to His Imperial Majesty the Kaiser, my officers identified the terrorists, hunted them down and dispatched them in short order. And now, six weeks later, the press and the public are none the wiser. The operation can be accounted a complete success." Anderson had delivered his summary with an offhand modesty. The Prime Minster, Lord Salisbury, nodded thoughtfully. A giant of a man both in height and girth, with a massive beard of a style that had been fashionable twenty years earlier, his physical stature made the King look slim and dapper, and he seemed permanently short of breath.

"I believe some credit is due," suggested the King, "to Chief Superintendent Melville." Edward leaned back in his winged armchair—we were meeting in a drawing room at Buckingham Palace—and tapped his cigarette into a gilded ashtray on a stand to his left. Victoria would have been disgusted at her son's smoking in an official audience, but Victoria was gone now, and etiquette followed the Crown, not vice versa.

"Of course, sir," agreed Anderson. "The Chief Superintendent demonstrated outstanding initiative and courage from first to last."

Salisbury and Anderson were seated on sofas facing Edward; I was standing, not quite to attention, to the right of the King and two steps back, keeping my face impassive and disinterested, as if the three men were discussing the weather. But I was paying careful attention. Twenty Prime Ministers had served Queen Victoria, four while I had been her bodyguard, and I had never been asked to attend an official audience until today. It was Salisbury who had specifically requested my presence; that was not a good sign. This Prime Minister disliked commoners who did not conform to their station, and he considered me little more than a hired thug. I doubted he was going to recommend me for a medal.

"So Chief Superintendent Melville was working under your direct supervision?" asked Salisbury. It was such an innocuous question I was immediately on my guard, but the Assistant Commissioner seemed happy to go on blowing his own trumpet.

"Indeed. William reported to me throughout and kept me fully informed of all developments. We work as a team. Following my advice and guidance, of course."

"And you, Chief Superintendent. Did you follow the advice and guidance of the Assistant Commissioner?"

"His leadership was invaluable, sir," I replied. Anderson gave me a sharp look, as if he'd expected a more fulsome tribute, and still didn't sense where this was headed. The Prime Minster addressed his next words to the King.

"While His Majesty's Government is relieved and grateful that these nihilists were successfully dealt with, I am sorry to say I have serious concerns regarding the Chief Superintendent's methods." Hang it, I thought. He knows. "In fact, I am appalled by certain of his actions."

Gone was the anodyne exchange of compliments; Lord Salisbury's wheezing voice was hard-edged, barely concealing his disgust. Anderson looked to me, then the King, for a lifeline. Finding none, he prevaricated. "William is something of a rough diamond, inclined to cut corners. But his methods are effective—"

"I am referring," cut in the PM, "to the interception of privileged correspondence. Specifically, private letters written by His Majesty's Privy Counsellors which last February Chief Superintendent Melville opened and read. It is an appalling breach of protocol which can on no grounds be justified." I wondered how Salisbury had learned of our operation at Mount Pleasant, but it was hardly a question I could ask him.

"This—this is the first I have heard of the matter—" stammered Anderson. But Salisbury had now turned to me.

"Do you deny it, Chief Superintendent?"

I didn't feel inclined to oblige him with a confession or an explanation. Anything I said would have sounded like an excuse, and it looked like I was for the high jump anyway. "I have no comment to make, Prime Minister."

I saw the PM bridle at my impertinence, but in the presence of the King he had to rein in his temper. "I believe I am entitled to an answer, sir!"

"I assure you, my Lord," cut in Anderson, "I shall get to the bottom of this." If he meant to pivot to the Prime Minister's side, it was an ill-judged move. Now Salisbury turned on him.

"Get to the bottom of it? You said this man acted under your direct supervision. Did you know about this?"

"Extreme cases call for extreme measures—"

"A simple yes or no will suffice, Mr. Anderson."

"I knew about it," said Edward.

Salisbury wheezed to a halt, mid-charge. The King peered at the lit end of his cigarette as if it were a rare jewel. "Melville had my express permission."

I maintained my poker face, but I was secretly impressed; I had once declared Edward was no actor, but now he exuded sincerity. "It was a matter of national security," the King continued. Salisbury's eyes narrowed until they almost disappeared into that fleshy face behind its enormous hedge of beard. "Sensitive information about Melville's search was being conveyed to the terrorists themselves by certain . . . disloyal parties. To catch them in the act, it was vital that no one knew about the operation beforehand. And afterwards, well . . . least said, soonest mended."

Salisbury grunted. He had not risen to the peak of his profession without knowing when he was being sold a spavined horse. "Might I ask if this . . . collaborator . . . was ever identified?"

The King did not look at me but merely raised a finger. I took my cue.

"His Lordship will recall," I said, "the unfortunate incident involving Lord and Lady Diamond on the eve of Her Late Majesty's funeral."

"Lord Diamond?" spluttered Salisbury. He seemed lost for words as he tried to absorb the revelation. I did not blame him for discounting the involvement of Lady Diamond—I had made the same mistake myself, after all—but I didn't set him straight either.

"I was as shocked as you, Prime Minister," said Edward. "But the matter has been resolved, without scandal. Let that be the end of it."

But Salisbury, it seemed, had a pound of flesh on his shopping list.

"Would that we could, Your Majesty. This offence against the privilege of the Crown's Privy Counsellors cannot go unaddressed. Their advice must remain sacrosanct and confidential, or all trust is lost." An old-fashioned Tory landowner, Lord Salisbury despised anything that smacked of progressiveness and considered terrorism to be a direct result of educating workers. It was not hard to imagine how he felt about a jumped-up Paddy peasant reading his correspondence; the man must have nearly burst a blood vessel.

"I rather think," said Edward, "that the Crown should define the privileges of its Privy Counsellors, don't you?" But his former assurance had slipped; he sounded defensive, even petulant.

"Indeed, sir," the PM pretended to agree. "And the Crown has defined those privileges over a thousand years of custom and practice—traditions that must not be lightly set aside. This affair cannot be allowed to set a precedent. It is a grievous breach of protocol and those responsible must answer for it."

Damn, there goes my pension, was my first thought. Someone's head was going to roll. Salisbury's appeal to custom and tradition was aimed squarely at the King's Achilles' heel—his mother, the Empress Victoria, had made clear over decades how unworthy she considered him to defend the Crown and the Realm, and how inadequate.

"Melville has answered for it," said Edward. "He has answered to the King, and the King is satisfied." And now it occurred to me that after decades of being browbeaten by Victoria, even the towering figure of Salisbury held little dread for Edward. "I will not see the man who saved my life, and the life of the Kaiser, punished for his efforts." There was a pause; Salisbury did not blink, or lower his gaze, and neither did the King, and I did not dare to breathe. The pause grew painfully long; the tick-tock of the mantel clock filled the room, and a log spat sparks from the fire. It seemed to me the first man to utter a sound would lose this battle.

Assistant Commissioner Anderson cleared his throat, nervously, and thus sealed his fate. Edward turned to him.

"Assistant Commissioner, you say you supervised this operation. That you were kept fully informed, and that your officers acted under your guidance."

"Yes, but—I—that is . . ." Anderson rowed back furiously, but the tide had turned. "Yes, Your Majesty."

"Your actions were commendable. The operation was, as you say, a complete success. When you retire, you can do so knowing you have distinguished yourself in the fulfilment of your duties." Anderson's shoulders sagged perceptibly at the King's unspoken order. He needed no translation: he knew all too well the ceremony of the scapegoat, and its accoutrements: the confession inscribed on the finest vellum, the razor whetted and the hot bath drawn.

"Indeed," the King went on, "given the right circumstances, We should not be surprised to see a knighthood on Our next Honours List."

These words had a miraculous effect on Anderson; he straightened up like a parched flower in the rain. The King, and Salisbury, and indeed the entire Metropolitan Police force knew how much the Assistant Commissioner had longed to rise one day as Sir Robert Anderson. "I am Your Majesty's humble servant." Anderson stood, straightened his frock coat, and bowed. "You shall have my resignation before the end of the day." He smiled, but I could see the words nearly choked him. Edward turned to Salisbury.

"I believe that resolves the matter?"

Salisbury nodded, appeased by the sacrifice.

And not for the first time it struck me that politics is a stately dance with poisoned daggers, and that I would rather take my chances with terrorists than count such men as friends.

"Thank you both," said the King to Anderson and me. "Melville, if you wouldn't mind waiting outside, I'd like a word with you presently."

IN THE PALACE LOBBY a valet helped Anderson on with his overcoat. It seemed too big for him now, as if he had shrunk in the course of that audience.

"I'm sorry it came to this, sir," I said.

"A little forewarning would have helped, William."

"I had no idea the PM knew."

"I mean, before you opened those letters."

"If I had asked your permission, would you have given it?"

The valet handed Anderson his hat.

"This collaborator who passed on your reports," said Anderson. "You must at some point have suspected it might be me."

"I never doubted your loyalty for a moment, sir. I've worked with you for seven years."

Sir Robert Anderson, former Assistant Commissioner of the Met, snorted and tapped his hat-brim in a token salute.

"Good day, Chief Superintendent." He turned and walked down the staircase, carefully. An old man scared of falling.

And for seven years I've been reading all your correspondence, I could have called after him. But I decided to spare him the dignity he had left.

"ABOUT LORD AND LADY DIAMOND . . ."

The King and I were walking through a long gallery lined with paintings of his royal ancestors, towards a massive portrait of Victoria as Empress of India. I noticed Edward did not look up at them, or at me either, and although he had sent out all the servants he was keeping his voice low.

"Yes, Your Majesty?"

"Your report said he shot her, then turned the gun on himself."

"A very sad business, indeed."

"You didn't say why he shot her, though. Was it from jealousy, or . . . ?" Was the King blaming himself? It hardly seemed fair to let him.

"Lord Diamond had never been under any illusions about his wife," I said. "And there was little love lost between them. Perhaps she provoked him. I doubt we'll ever know the whole truth."

Edward nodded, reassured. "I'd never have dreamed Geoffrey was capable of such a thing." Did he mean the murder or the suicide?

"It was a crime of passion, sir," I said. "It could not have been anticipated, or prevented." We paused before the portrait of Her Late Majesty, decked out in all her Imperial finery. The King looked up at last. Neither of us had to wonder what she would have said about the whole sorry business.

"Did Lady Diamond ever tell you why?" the King asked, after a moment.

"Forgive me, sir. Why what?"

"Why she took up with . . . that Russian madman."

"She took that secret to her grave, sir. But I am making enquiries."

28

I T WAS AN UNSEASONABLY warm day for late March, and I could feel sweat beading under my collar as Rachkovskii and I strolled alongside Rotten Row. The Russian spymaster seemed merry, loudly appraising the horses and riders—especially the attractive female riders—trotting along the bridle path, and engaging me in empty banter whenever we were within earshot of passers-by. I was sure this sunny mood of his had nothing to do with the approaching spring; he knew something I didn't, and he wanted me to be aware of that. He wanted to watch me squirm and perhaps even beg. And after I had done all that, he might choose to tell me nothing at all.

But then, why suggest this meeting? It would have been going to a lot of trouble just to gloat.

"Oh, yes—you asked me some time ago about that Countess who was murdered by her husband," said Rachkovskii at last. By now we were approaching the Albert Memorial, and there were no passers-by close enough to eavesdrop.

"Lady Diamond?" I feigned uninterest. "What of her?"

"I have heard from my people in Odessa."

He said no more, forcing me to ask. "And have your people learned anything useful?"

Rachkovskii shrugged, as if he was unsure if what he had gleaned was useful or not. "The lady's father, Piotr Mikhailovich Volosenko, was a horse-breeder. A very successful one. He still supplies excellent mounts to His Imperial Highness the Tsar."

"Not the sort of family one would associate with anarchy," I said.

"You are quite right. Volosenko is a commoner made wealthy by his own efforts. He would be the last to throw in his lot with social agitators and egalitarians. If they ever came to power, he would lose everything he had achieved through honest toil."

"What about Lady Diamond's mother?"

"Also tediously respectable. From a long line of kulaks."

"Farmers, you mean?"

"Forgive me, yes, farmers. Again, not the stuff of which revolutionaries are made."

"So how was it their daughter got mixed up with a man such as Akushku?"

We were at the nub of it, finally, and Rachkovskii was beaming now, almost chuckling to himself. I let him relish his moment of fun. Whatever enlightenment he had to offer me, I was sure, would carry a sting in the tail.

"Lady Diamond—or, as she was then, Valeriya Alekseyevna Volosenkova—was raised as a respectable young woman with all the advantages of wealth. Her parents hoped that with a suitable dowry she would marry well, hopefully into nobility."

"As indeed she did. She said herself, they sold her off like a brood mare."

"Of course the daughter of a mere horse-dealer, even a wealthy one, would hardly be an acceptable bride for a nobleman. So the girl had to be taught all the genteel virtues: deportment and manners, how to play the piano, an appreciation of culture and literature—not so much, of course, that she would become a . . . a . . ." He clicked his fingers.

"A bluestocking?" I suggested.

"Precisely, a bluestocking. And to this end the family hired a governess, herself from a noble family, but widowed, and living in reduced circumstances. Eager to support her only son."

He paused, presumably to let that sink in. I did not respond; my mind was racing ahead. "And this governess's son was taught alongside young Miss Volosenkova?"

"That was the young lady's one request. And seeing no disadvantage to the arrangement, and keen to secure her services, Piotr Mikhailovich agreed."

"So this boy, the son of the governess, grew up to be Akushku?"

"From the description you gave me," he said, "of the man you and Herr Steinhauer encountered, it does seem likely that they were one and the same. For six years—from the age of nine—the man we now call Akushku, he and Valeriya Alekseyevna Volosenkova spent every day together. They became firm friends."

"More than friends, I take it."

"Indeed, if the household servants are to be believed. Much more than friends. And in time this . . . inconvenient relationship came to the attention of Volosenko himself. He claims now the governess left because his daughter needed no more education. But it's rather more likely he fired her. I imagine he was worried about having to sell— how do you put it—shop-soiled goods?"

"So what became of this governess?"

"She returned with her son to her own country and died, in poverty, only two months later."

"Forgive me, Colonel—her own country?"

Rachkovskii grinned. Now we come to it, I thought.

"Her married name was Maria Adelheide Lippe-Detmold, of Bavaria. Her husband had been a distant cousin of the late Count Lippe-Detmold before he died. Of typhus, very sad."

"This governess—and her son—they were German?"

"Akushku's real name, I am reliably informed, was Aleksandr Ruprecht Lippe-Detmold. After his mother passed away, the boy was penniless, without prospects. So he joined the army. The German army. Presumably it was they who discovered and developed his remarkable talents. After that, I am afraid, we have no further information—what a magnificent filly!"

Rachkovskii pretended to admire a grey horse cantering by, but his eyes were fixed on the slim outline of its young female rider. Very young; I made a mental note of the Russian's taste. Rachkovskii turned back to me as if he had just been struck by an amusing idea.

"Perhaps your young friend Herr Steinhauer might be able to help." He offered the suggestion with the merest hint of a smirk. "He is, after all, German."

"I WAS SORRY TO HEAR about Miss Minetti. She was a woman of great spirit."

"She was," I said. "But it was the death of her, in the end. I should have looked after her better."

"You did what you could, William," said Steinhauer. "I shall light a candle in her memory. Were it not for her courage, who knows what horrors might have come about."

He leaned back and drew on his Cuban cigar. It had been his suggestion that we meet in Paris, where I was laying the groundwork for a state visit by His Majesty in a few months' time. King Edward wanted closer relations with France; the German government had made approving noises from the sidelines about the joys of peace and the friendship of nations, but few believed them, and I thought it interesting that Steinhauer had turned up in Paris just now. This visit had offered me the chance to catch up with certain old acquaintances, some more openly than others. No doubt the same applied to Steinhauer.

At this time of the afternoon the Café de Flore was relatively quiet, and we could talk without fear of being overheard. All the same, in the ten minutes since we had embraced like old warriors, neither of us had uttered anything worth overhearing; our conversation had been banal observations about European politics of the sort one might read in any decent newspaper. Of course, men who have faced death together and saved each other's lives don't need to retell their war stories; such an experience forms an unbreakable bond. Steinhauer and I would always be friends; but that did not preclude the possibility that someday we might be enemies too. How likely that was, I was intrigued to find out.

"I picked up some interesting gossip about our old friend Akushku," I said.

"Indeed?" said Steinhauer, with an air of polite detachment.

"Or I should say, Aleksandr Ruprecht Lippe-Detmold?" Steinhauer raised an eyebrow but said nothing.

"You might have told me he was one of yours, Gustav."

The young man sighed. "He was by no means one of ours."

"He was German. Your people recruited him. Trained him to infiltrate anarchist groups. Deployed him. He was indeed an agent provocateur, but for the Kaiser's secret police, not the Russians'." I waited. Steinhauer had the grace to feign embarrassment; he nodded.

"Yes," said Steinhauer, "my people, as you put it, did train him. Long before I joined His Imperial Highness's service. I like to think that if I had come across Herr Detmold before he was deployed, I would have prevented it. You said yourself, William, that an agent provocateur is an unreliable weapon, one that can blow up in your face. Detmold proves your point. I am sorry I did not tell you sooner."

"You did not tell me at all, Gustav. In fact, you confidently informed me he was Latvian."

"How could I admit that one of our own agents had set out to kill the Emperor? If it had ever come out, someone would have had to answer for it, and you know the politics of the Court—that someone would almost certainly have been me. I am sorry I lied to you, but I had to cover for myself. And what good would the truth have done, in any case? He was beyond our control. He had renounced his country, betrayed his oath to the Emperor. He might have been Japanese, for all the difference it would have made to our quest."

That last remark was so disingenuous as to be laughable. The smallest scrap of genuine information on Akushku would have helped us track him down; we might have connected him to Lady Diamond that much sooner. At the very least it might have stopped me making a fool of myself pestering the Russians and the French. Steinhauer had kept vital information to himself, risking my life and those of my men.

But he had risked his own life too. Why?

Though I was inwardly seething with indignation, I kept my tone as affable and casual as I could manage. "Akushku's mother, after she was widowed, was disowned by her late husband's family. With no income, and no home, and an infant to feed, she was forced to seek work as a governess, and found a place in Russia," I said. "Then she lost that job too and was thrown out on the street. She and her son returned to Germany, where young Detmold, who'd just been parted forever from the girl he loved, had to watch his own mother die in poverty." I flicked the ash from my cigar with more vigour than I'd intended. "So who, in God's holy name, thought a lad with such a history could be relied upon to serve his country?"

Steinhauer shrugged. "What can I say? You are completely right. But it was before my time. And the men I serve are—how can I put this—not always as shrewd as one would hope."

"But you still follow their orders."

"Of course. I am an officer in His Imperial Majesty's service."

"Were you ordered to keep Detmold's history a secret from me?"

"William, I swear I would have told you had I thought it would help."

"Were you ordered to kill him before he could tell me what he was trying to do?"

Steinhauer frowned, as if I was not making sense.

"We know what he was trying to do. He was trying to assassinate the Emperor."

"But you shot him before he could tell me why."

"I shot him before he could shoot you."

"Just before you arrived, Detmold told me the Kaiser despised my King."

Steinhauer smiled. "This is hardly a state secret." His own cigar had nearly gone out; he screwed it into the ashtray between us.

"And that the Kaiser intended to take something from Edward."

Now Steinhauer looked amused as well as baffled. "A mistress, perhaps? Your king can certainly spare one."

"Detmold's last words were, 'The Kaiser despises your King. He means to take his . . .' What do you think he was referring to, Gustav?"

Steinhauer shrugged. "Alas, we shall never know."

"Edward's crown, perhaps? His kingdom?"

Steinhauer chuckled, as if he thought I was joking. I watched him, and waited. Finally he seemed to decide to humour me.

"William, Detmold was mad. A nihilist, a terrorist—a brilliant one, yes, and at one time he had been our agent—but he was insane. And insane people invent absurd conspiracies. You know this."

"He did not strike me as mad."

"Such lunatics are the most dangerous kind."

Steinhauer clicked his fingers to catch the eye of a waiter and mimed with his thumb a bottle topping up our brandy glasses. Then he turned back to me. "And even supposing he had been in his right mind," he went on, "how would a renegade agent, who for years had been living among anarchists and agitators and criminals—how would such a man have any idea what the Kaiser was planning or not planning? The two of them did not spend evenings together drinking beer and playing billiards. I have no idea what His Imperial Majesty is thinking, and I am at his side constantly."

I know you are, I thought.

Steinhauer leaned forwards and lowered his voice. "William—the very notion, that my Emperor wants to take your King's throne, is ridiculous. War with the British, with the greatest Empire in the world? Between two nations bound together by history, by family, by friendship, by trade? We have no navy worth speaking of, while Britain rules the seas. The whole idea is so absurd, only an anarchist would credit it. They want to believe that our civilisation will destroy itself, and save them the effort. And I think you are forgetting . . ." He trailed off, as if he was ashamed to point out my mistake.

I took the bait. "What have I forgotten?"

"More than my Emperor, more than your King," said Steinhauer, "Akushku—Lippe-Detmold—hated you. You are Europe's most feared policeman, anarchy's greatest enemy. You had foiled his attempt on the Emperor's life. He wanted you to die in despair, thinking your mission had been a failure. So he lied to you."

Any one of those excuses might have convinced me, Gustav, I thought.

But all of them? You protest too much. I sighed inwardly; Steinhauer and I had for a while been as close as brothers. And now I wondered if we would ever again be honest with each other. Or indeed if we ever had.

"You're right, I'm sure," I said with my best rueful grin.

"His Imperial Majesty wants no war with England, or any nation," declared Steinhauer.

"I'm sure he doesn't. But then, what was it you said, back then? Sometimes the Emperor's servants think they know better."

"Sometimes the Emperor's servants are fools," said Steinhauer with a snort. "That does not mean anyone listens to them."

So they are talking about it? I thought. I smiled. The waiter arrived with the brandy decanter.

"Just a large one, for me," I said. As the waiter topped me up, I had another thought: What if Gustav had arrived a moment later, after Akushku had finished telling me the Kaiser's true intentions? Would he have shot Akushku, then turned his gun on me, and tearfully told everyone afterwards he'd been too late to save my life?

Steinhauer raised his glass, smiling.

"To brothers in arms."

"Brothers in arms," I echoed.

Yes, I decided, he damned well would have.

"HOW WAS THE SERVICE?"

"Simple. Surprisingly touching."

It was a lovely mild spring day and I was walking with a young woman round the pond at Barnes, watching a heron on the bank motionlessly poised to snap up a fish.

"It was good of you to arrange a funeral for this girl no one knew," she said.

"She deserved a decent sendoff. More than some I could mention."

"I should have liked to be there."

"Your presence would have defeated the whole object, Theresa. Angela's dead; may she rest in peace."

The heron made its lunge, rose from the water and flapped languidly away, a silver fish twitching in its beak.

"I am not sure I like the name Theresa," said my companion.

"It's the name on your passport. Theresa Foy, from Guernsey. You'd best get used to it."

The girl I had once known as Angela Minetti pouted, but slipped her arm through mine. Her hair, now dyed raven black, was straying rebelliously from under her hat. It was just as well we were so far out of London and strangers here, or salacious gossip might have found its way back to my wife. Had she known, Amelia might well have asked some awkward questions; Foy was her family name from Guernsey, and Theresa Foy was her little sister, dead of consumption at the age of twelve. Angela had needed a new identity; all it had taken was two guineas and Theresa's birth certificate.

"I bought my ticket for Berlin today."

"Good," I said. "The hotel I've chosen for you is not the Ritz, but you'll be safe. And I've arranged for a small allowance."

"I shall be your kept woman after all."

"You'll be your own woman," I said.

"But what shall I do there, William?"

"Do you know what a type-writer is?"

"A man who uses one of those typing machines."

"Or a woman. I think you should train as a type-writer."

"So I can become a clerk?"

"So you can pass for one. While you work for me."

"Good." Theresa smiled. "I want to be useful."

"You will. Just don't go attacking any more policemen. I won't be able to spring you so easily over there."

She laughed.

Akushku had caught her, just as I'd feared, when she'd been watching the derelict furniture factory. He'd been trying to drag her off the street when by chance a passing constable intervened. Thinking on his feet, Akushku had claimed to be the long-suffering husband of this wayward wife, and it nearly worked. The policeman was about to leave them to it, until Angela—also thinking on her feet—launched herself at the constable and raked her nails down his face. Akushku had fled. It was a mad, impetuous act that saved Angela's life, and got her arrested—and very nearly committed—until a message from her had finally reached me, a few days after the royal funeral.

I'd told no one she'd survived, not my colleagues, not Amelia and certainly not Steinhauer. At first this was merely out of habit; no one needed to know, I'd reasoned, and if the world thought Angela Minetti was dead, she'd be safe from any hothead who wanted to avenge Akushku and punish an informer. I'd arranged accommodation for her, and a new identity, and told myself I was being chivalrous—what better way to rescue the girl from the sordid pit she'd fallen into?

But I soon admitted to myself that my intentions had never been so selfless. Theresa Foy, née Angela Minetti, was a woman of courage, initiative, intelligence and beauty—qualities I would have been a fool to overlook. Between her, Lady Diamond and my own Amelia, I'd underestimated the talents of women. That mistake I was determined never to repeat.

"I'll send word soon," I told her, "and let you know what I need you to do."

I WAITED, standing not quite to attention, as the Prime Minister's private secretary passed him letters to sign. The man was short and slight, and the way he bent around the huge form of Lord Salisbury put me in mind of those Egyptian birds that pick the teeth of Nile crocodiles.

The Prime Minister already looked irritated by my presence: *This briefing is not going to go well*, I thought. My memorandum had requested a private audience to discuss "certain matters best not put in writing." Did Salisbury think I was merely referring to another of the King's unfortunate liaisons? As his private secretary slipped out of the room, the PM settled back in his chair, already wheezing, and waved at me to get on with it.

"You remember, Prime Minister, the matter of the anarchist who called himself Akushku, and his attempt to bomb Her Late Majesty's funeral." Salisbury nodded, coughing noisily into a massive and not-very-clean handkerchief. "We have since established that Akushku's real name was Aleksandr Ruprecht Lippe-Detmold, and that he was a former agent of the German secret police."

Salisbury seemed to think he'd misheard. "German, you say? But I thought his intention was to assassinate the Kaiser?"

"It was, sir. It seems he'd gone rogue. Thrown in his lot with the anarchists he was meant to infiltrate."

The Prime Minister harrumphed and started to make some remark, possibly about damned treacherous foreigners, before another fit of wheezing coughs overtook him, stifled eventually by that grubby handkerchief. He was so overweight I wondered that he could breathe at all. I waited for the paroxysms to subside before I continued.

"Before he was brought down by the Kaiser's bodyguard, Herr Steinhauer, Lippe-Detmold said something to me that in hindsight seems significant."

"Hmm?" Salisbury peered into his handkerchief, already losing interest. I came straight to the point.

"He told me the Kaiser planned to declare war on Britain and take His Majesty's crown." That got the old man's attention; for a moment he forgot to wheeze.

"War? You did not mention this before. This Detmold character actually said that?"

"He was about to, sir, when Herr Steinhauer shot him."

"Wait a moment. Did he say it, or didn't he?"

"He meant to, sir. I have no doubt of it."

"Hm. Do you indeed? And this man was a renegade? A nihilist?"

"Yes, sir."

"Well, then, why on earth should we credit anything he said? Or even intended to say?"

I confess I hesitated. At the moment Detmold had spoken, I had not believed him. But everything I had learned since then, and every instinct I had, convinced me that he had not been lying after all. Only ten days earlier Walther, my young friend from the German embassy, had fallen under a train at Clapham Junction. The coroner had pronounced it misadventure rather than suicide—the deceased was happily married, with two infant children and another on the way—but I was sure it had been neither. Instinct told me Walther had been murdered because he had been leaking secrets to me; the Germans were cleaning house.

But citing my instinct as evidence would probably impress Salisbury no more than it had impressed Robert Anderson. Indeed, the way this meeting was going, Salisbury might well use it as an excuse to ignore everything I was telling him.

"Experience, sir. And, certain other, indications."

"Oh, poppycock. These people are masters of lies and malicious invention. They know a well-placed rumour can do more damage than bombs or bullets, with less effort and far less risk. Have you any concrete evidence for what you're claiming?"

"None that I can share at this point, sir."

"Well, if you wish me to take this matter to the Cabinet, you'd better find some evidence that you *can* share."

"I wasn't suggesting you take it to the Cabinet, sir."

But Salisbury no longer cared what I was suggesting. "It's those blasted Boers you should be worrying about. They're the ones we're at war with, they're the ones with sympathisers and spies over here—might I suggest that you focus your efforts on them? Rather than on a friend and ally, whose help we might very well need in the near future, now the French are back in bed with the Russians. The Kaiser may not love our King, and he is certainly headstrong, but I refuse to believe—"

He ran out of breath, and the rest of his sentence was lost in wheezes delivered to his handkerchief. I did not need to hear the rest of it, but I had resolved not to leave until I had made my case.

"Nevertheless, Prime Minister, I think it would be wise to take some elementary precautions. We should assign officers to monitor German activities in Britain, and to identify and keep track of Germany's agents. I've already—"

"Please, Melville!" spluttered Salisbury. "If this is a request for more funds, or for an open warrant to spy on private correspondence, I will not countenance anything of the sort."

There it was. *Private correspondence.* He would discount all my warnings because King Edward had once taken my side against his, and this was his chance to repay me for the slight to his vanity. I'd hoped for better from this wheezing, corpulent old duffer, but politicians rarely failed to disappoint me. Some sort of subtle threat would be next, I thought.

"You do very well as it is for money and men," Salisbury was saying. "And I cannot tell you how to run your department. You are not directly accountable to me, and doubtless that is as it should be. But should Parliament ever learn that Special Branch has wasted time and resources investigating such transparently ridiculous rumours, you should not expect my Government to defend you."

Should Parliament ever learn. As a threat it was not even particularly subtle.

"I understand, Prime Minister. Thank you."

Salisbury inspected his handkerchief briefly before stuffing it back into his waistcoat pocket.

"And in future if you have such concerns I would be obliged if you take them to your new Assistant Commissioner, rather than waste my time. Now send my private secretary back in, would you?"

I did not bother hailing a cab. Scotland Yard was only a few minutes from Downing Street, and it was a fine May morning, and I needed some time to think. Salisbury himself had conceded there was nothing to stop me setting up a section within Special Branch to detect and monitor German agents. The new Assistant Commissioner, Edward Henry, was at least an experienced policeman—he had made his name in India—and I thought it unlikely he would dismiss my concerns out of hand. But such operations cost money, and my budget was overstretched as it was. Without support from the government—if the Kaiser was indeed planning for war with Great Britain, and mobilising his intelligence services against us—we'd be a peasant rabble facing a cavalry charge with pikes and pitchforks.

"Chief Superintendent Melville?"

A chap had fallen into step beside me, almost without my noticing—mid-forties and slim, with probing brown eyes and the gait of a military man. A senior officer, judging by his suit. It was of a non-descript navy blue, the sort that would vanish in a crowd, but close up I could see it was exquisitely tailored.

"You have me at a disadvantage, sir," I said.

"Trotter's the name. Colonel James Trotter. I wonder if you might spare a few moments to join me at my club. It's not far, just up Piccadilly."

"Might I ask why, Colonel Trotter?"

Trotter smiled. "You've just had a meeting with Lord Salisbury," he said, "and I gather it was not entirely satisfactory."

"And who, pray, told you that?"

Trotter smiled again. He was a popular man with the ladies, I suspected—and some of the gentlemen too. "Let's just say, I work with certain people who share your concerns about developments on the Continent, and mean to do something about it. We could use a man of your experience, and you come highly recommended."

I'm a bit long in the tooth for all this flattery, I thought. But I was intrigued all the same.

Trotter nodded in the direction of Piccadilly.

"It shouldn't take more than an hour."

AFTERWORD

It's hard to imagine how this novel could have been written were it not for Andrew Cook's exhaustive and painstakingly researched biography of William Melville, *M: MI5's First Spymaster*. Cook's masterly work led me in turn to Gustav Steinhauer's autobiography, *Steinhauer, the Kaiser's Master Spy*, and his first-hand account of the late-night raid which became the inspiration for *M, King's Bodyguard*. From the moment Melville and Steinhauer board the London train to the moment Melville takes the fan down from the wall of Minetti's lodgings, this book follows Steinhauer's account in every detail—although it does stretch credulity that Steinhauer could have remembered those details so vividly when writing about them almost thirty years later. Nevertheless it's Steinhauer to whom I owe the greatest debt.

I must thank Anne Messitte, a dear friend and an amazing editor, for her enthusiasm and encouragement from the very beginning. Thanks are also due to Val Hoskins, my agent, whose patience and support kept me on track over a decade of rewrites. And to my wife, Erika, I offer my deepest love and gratitude for putting up with me and my "artistic temperament" for more years than either of us cares to admit.

I would also like to thank Edward Kastenmeier, my editor at Pantheon, for his advice and guidance, and particularly Sue Betz, my copy editor, whose superb eye for detail saved me from many excruciating errors and anachronisms, some of which had persisted from the earliest drafts.

Any that remain are wholly and exclusively my own.

NIALL LEONARD
London, August 2020